Man with a Plan

Love her Tender

Book one of the Besties Series

J. Ellen Daniels

J. Ellen Daniels
Published by TomJo Media, LLC

Cover design by Andrea Cardella.
Cover photo by Bridget Barrett
Cover model Michael Konczak
Author photo by Bridget Barrett

Book signings and appearances can be arranged by contacting the author at www.JEllenStories.com
Printed in the United States of America.
ISBN: 978-1-946653-26-0

Playlist & Contents

Note from the author:

When you read each chapter in this book, you'll notice the chapter title is the title of a song. Find the playlist at my website JEllenStories.com, and listen along while you read.

Table of Contents continued

DEDICATION

To my Asman sisters-in-law. The late Sandy Nuckles, you packed a lot of love into your sixty years, and I'm not the only one who will always wish you were here. Debbie Kwiecinski has the brightest smile and incredible passion for living. I love you both; thank you for not losing my number after the divorce.

Additional Notes – Italian to English words and phrases

Sedersi - Sit
Poletto - Meatball
Maleducato - rude
Vergogna - shame
Pigro - lazy
Patatina (female) - potato
Tesoro - treasure
Semplice - Simple
Finito - all done
Fare il bravo - be good
ti amo - I love you
il mio cuore e solo tuo - My heart is only yours
Ti amo cosi tanto - I love you so much
Non-vedo l'ora di sentire le tue mani su di me –
I can't wait to feel your hands on me
Prepotente - badass
Tenera - Tender

Prolog

Grenade

Bruno Mars

The Past – Ten years ago

Rocco

"I wonder?" Roberta asked her brother as they watched their cousin Rocco Gagliardi drive off.

The two Scalese daughters had married Gagliardi men. Theresa married Antonio Gagliardi, and Stella married Antonio's Canadian cousin Joe, another Gagliardi. And despite living in different cities and other countries, the families remained close.

Michael now cocked his head and said to his sister, "Don't you think it's pretty obvious?"

"*Ah*, no. If it were, would I be asking?"

"It's his way of saying I'm over it, and I don't give a shit," Michael said, eyeing the taillights of Rocco's car.

"Do you think he's really forgiven Francie and me? Really, not just a for-show thing?" Roberta looked at her big brother.

"Why don't you ask him? If you really care, ask him."

"I will ask one day. If he said, he hasn't... I don't want to face him and hear it from him. I don't want to think about it, I guess. For now, I just want to be sure Francine's dad is okay, the baby's okay, and Robert is okay."

Michael chuckled and shook his head. "Mr. Slaughter is none the wiser about you and Francine. He may not be happy about the marriage to Rocco; he's never liked Rocco. I don't know why the old man swallowed down why suddenly Francine had to live in Windsor, but he did. The main thing is, he's not having a stroke about Francine being an unwed mother either. Even if I think Francine holds the title of drama queen, she wasn't wrong about her dad's reaction to an illegitimate grandchild. He absolutely *would* be on some life support device. But, there was a wedding, so Mr. Slaughter is okay. The baby is going to be fine. Robert isn't weirded out about any of this; he's fine. Which I think is totally nuts and a little disturbing, but hey, I never did get the twin thing with you two, so, whatever, he's fine being the donor. You're just feeling guilty about Rocco, is all."

"A fair assessment," Roberta said, now staring hard at her shoes.

"Just be sure to live up to the agreement. I can see Francine getting a little too full of herself and pulling some bogus crap."

Roberta looked irked, but Michael wasn't wrong about Francine; Roberta knew. Francine could get a wild hair and go off the rails. She had done it before. Usually, it was over something that was really best left alone, but Francine would get stubborn about it. Most recently, it was to be gonzo lesbian.

Roberta thought it was the new acquaintances Francine met from university. They were great girls, and Roberta liked that there was a wonderful sense of community with them. It would be important with Francine's pregnancy, but there was a ton of man-bashing. Those sentiments were what Francine gravitated to lately. It would be no big deal if she kept it where the others did: within the group. However, Francine was being Francine, and Rocco was currently catching its brunt. It was cruel, especially when Rocco was doing them such a favor. “I get that. I hear you. I don’t appreciate you saying that about her, but yes. The big test will be the family 4th of July party. The baby will be old enough to have along by that time.”

Michael just looked at her. “I don’t think you understand the agreement.”

“Why? What do you mean?” Roberta turned to face her brother.

“When Rocco said no family interaction, he didn’t mean just for now. He meant going forward and for all time,” Michael said sternly.

“I... I don’t think he...” Then she thought about it. The initial meeting was when he agreed to the marriage. The final meeting was today at the courthouse when everything was signed, including the codicil about any future connection. “That’s harsh,” she said.

“It may be, but that is the agreement, Roberta. No interaction means you and Francine do not show up at family events where the Grosse Pointe Gagliardis are present. There is really only one, July 4th, and possibly a wedding or two, but this isn’t that much of a hardship, so don’t ignore that stipulation. It isn’t like he’s asking for anything outrageous. I can understand he doesn't want Francine's big mouth and the betrayal in his face."

Roberta ignored the negative *Francine* comment and honed in on the rest. 'That's how everyone sees this, isn't it? A betrayal." Roberta sniffed, annoyed at the thought.

"Well, yes. What would you call it?" Michael looked hard at her.

"It wasn't exactly like that."

Michael let out a mirthless laugh, "It was exactly like that. Rocco's girlfriend, practically his fiancée, cheated on him. And she did it with you, his cousin.'"

Prolog - continued

Love Hurts

Nazareth

The Past – Ten years ago
Christina

Christina held her breath as Keith pulled her panties down her legs. This wasn't the way she had imagined it. She felt like yanking her panties up and running out of Keith's mother's house. But then... she played the internal discussion she had had with herself over the past year. The internal discussion about having a boyfriend and being a couple and what was expected.

Keith, for his part, seemed to be as inexperienced as she was. However, he did let it slip that he wasn't a virgin. She had seen a picture of his last girlfriend. Keith never said that that girl was his lover, but probably. That girl and maybe others.

Keith was a good-looking guy. He was the subject of conversations with many of the girls Christina went to high school with since he moved into the district. That was after his parents divorced, and Keith had to relocate in his senior year. She had heard months' worth of speculation about Keith and his love life. He always flirted with her, but Christina never felt like she could hang with Keith. He was too smooth, too good-looking, too popular, too much. Besides, the flirting seemed more incidental than serious. Then a month before the end of the fall semester, Keith started being far more intentional, aggressively pursuing Christina.

She didn't know if she liked him, but he was good-looking and had a measure of popularity for a newcomer. There were worse reasons to date a boy.

The one boy she sort of liked had been her boyfriend until the summer between their junior and senior year. That July 4th, he gave her an ultimatum; he was not going into their senior year with a girlfriend that refused to even jack him off.

This was the first time he had expressed concern over sex or the lack of it, and Christina was so stunned she couldn't put her thoughts together enough to answer his question. Instead, she silently got out of his Jeep with him yelling at her. She heard the words *immature, frigid, lesbian, cock tease,* and none of it made any sense to her. It was never before a subject of discussion. He came around the next day to apologize, but she couldn't get the hateful words out of her head. He left but not before a dose of more angry words.

The week after, her neighbor and sometimes friend let Christina in on a not-so-secret rumor that Christina's boyfriend had been talking to his friends about the lack of intimacy between himself and Christina, and they told him he was a fool; no girl was worth putting up with that. The neighbor said it got pretty intense. It still didn't justify the anger and the angry words. A week after that, he was dating a girl from Warren. Christina had seen them around; his public displays of affection were over the top. Christina had seen it, and it was clear he wanted Christina to notice.

She wondered what his end game was. He couldn't expect Christina to offer herself and beg him to come back. She supposed it was a middle finger to her and all her *uptight, frigid, lesbian, immature, cock teasing* ways. He would never again claim her time or emotions, but it did make her think. She was the only one in her circle of friends and acquaintances who had a V card.

So when Keith began pursuing her, she decided that if it got even a bit serious, she would cash in her virtue.

When Keith stripped her of her panties that night, she decided – she was all in. She unbuttoned her blouse and unclasped her bra, which seemed to be all she needed to do. Keith had their clothes off in a hot second. He was busy getting the condom on, and without any ceremony, a stiff dick stabbed at her until it found its mark. There was no easing into anything. He grunted his satisfaction that she was tight, which was the end of any intelligible words. It was grunts and groans. He grunted in his pleasure. She groaned in her pain. The best that might be said was how jackrabbit fast Keith completed.

The one thing he did that made it somewhat bearable was cuddling afterward. They spent the next hour or so in each other's arms, with Keith falling asleep.

If there was an upside to any of this, it was that there weren't many opportunities, and Keith wasn't so demanding or uncaring as he was obtuse. It was over in under ten minutes when it did happen. That was under ten minutes from the first kiss to when Keith pulled off the condom.

Christina listened to other girls talk about sex. The other girls liked it and looked forward to it. *God, why?* She'd think.

As far as Christina and Keith as a couple, it was fine, good even. The final semester passed, and Keith took her to the Snowball dance and the prom; he was always respectful and attentive. He always sent her texts and never missed a chance to take her out on the weekends. She felt like an ingrate considering her former boyfriend and his treatment of her during those final days of their relationship. Keith even defended her to some of the crowd that goaded her former boyfriend into breaking up with her. Keith was the perfect boyfriend except for the sex part. She was ashamed to admit it, but she hated the sex part.

As the school year came to a close, Keith confessed that he would be returning to Burlington, Vermont, where his dad lived, to attend the University of Vermont. But he would be back on any major holidays and maybe even the entire summer.

She liked him, but she had to admit that not having his jabbing penis to endure was a huge plus.

Christina held his hand and told him *to turn the corner and move on.* He needed his freedom; if it was meant to be, they would find a way back to one another. She meant this sincerely, and the look of relief on Keith's face confirmed the wisdom of her declaration. Keith left with his father the day after their graduation ceremony; if he had returned for any holiday or summer break, Christina was unaware of it.

That day after high school graduation was also a place to move on for Christina. But it wasn't to find another Keith. No, she knew what she was. Nope not a lesbian, not a tease or immature, and she wasn't frigid. She was asexual, a nonsexual being who needed to only date men as asexual as she.

Chapter 1

Under My Thumb

The Rolling Stones

“That’s... small,” Nigel commented and handed the ring in its plastic case back to his brother, Neville.

“I’ve never liked jewelry that looks like some Detroit Rapper bought it.” Neville took the case back and pocketed it.

Nigel looked up, snickered, shook his head. and said, “God, you are so.... “

“Practical,” Neville finished.

“Not even close to what I was going to call you. Did you ask Christina what kind of ring she liked?”

Neville smirked, “It’s supposed to be a statement. It’s supposed to be the proposal. I’m not ruining the moment like that.”

“Did you confer with her friends? A close friend of hers would give you some direction.”

“Her friends,” he said dismissively, “I will be doing all I can to help Christina rethink her choice of friends. Neither one of those women is worth a damn. The one is a foreigner, Indian, I think. The only ring she’d know about is the one they stick in their noses. The other one is white, and she does have a solid background and family, but she grates on my nerves. I’ve never liked her. Why would I want an opinion from either?”

“Wow,” Nigel said disgustedly, “you didn’t ask my opinion, so I won't bother you with it.”

“I would have thought you would be supportive. You were very positive about Christina when I’ve had her along.”

“Oh, she’s a great girl. No question. Beautiful girl, smart, sweet, poised, and polite. And I think it says volumes about her that she’s got a career and has managed to move herself up the ladder as young as she is. She checks all the boxes.”

Neville rolled his eyes dramatically. "Career? It's Holtzbergs she works for. That's hardly a Fortune 250 company. I'm not saying she isn't bright or that her little job isn't a good place for her, but it's disposable. And that's all to the good because when we start a family, I want her home," Neville said, snapping his fingers at a busboy. "Get our waitress," he said dismissively.

Nigel cringed at his brother's attitude and behavior and said to the busboy, "Please ask our waitperson to come back when she has a moment. Thank you."

Neville rolled his eyes and smirked. "These people are $10.00 an hour high schoolers. You won't impress anyone."

"Not the point. And back to the actual point I want to make. Holtzbergs may not be a large international company, but it is a very solid mid-sized local firm with a stellar reputation for being a great workplace. As the HR Director, Christina is a good part of that well-deserved distinction."

Neville just blinked at his brother.

And Nigel shook his head; it was a waste of breath. Neville had his head so far up his own ass that he'd never get the picture. Nigel reached into his wallet, "Well, I need to be out the door." Nigel pulled out five twenties and stood up. "I hope it works out with Christina. I'll let you tell the family about it when you're ready." He patted Neville on the back and walked away.

The waitperson placed the folio with the check inside in front of Neville. "When you are ready, sir," she said, moving to the next table.

Neville looked at the bill, which totaled $78.50. He took out his wallet, put one of the twenties his brother left in it, and scurried off.

■■■

Where is he taking you?" Marisol asked Christina as they put away their yoga mats.

"That steak house in Windsor Casino. I think he had a gift card from a vendor he wanted to use. I've never been there before, but I know it's nice," Christina said.

Holly stood, her beautiful silky black hair falling from the pony she put together just before the class started. She took it down and pulled her hair in a ponytail that started coming down as fast as she got it up.

"Holly, honey, let me," Christina offered, "I've got a better band. It will stay better." Christina pulled a hair tie out of her pocket and deftly worked Holly's hair back into the high pony Holly was trying for. "There."

"Thank you. It drives me crazy, falling into my eyes. It's bad enough here. When I'm at the gym, it's a problem because it takes me out of my zone."

"You need to put it in a braid with a better tie and use hair spray," Christina explained.

Holly knitted her brows together as if Christina suggested donning a jockstrap.

"Have you ever been to that restaurant?" Marisol asked Holly.

Holly smirked, "The steak house? Wait, let me say that again." Holly rolled her big brown eyes at her friend. "The non-vegetarian restaurant where they serve the flesh of animals." She pointed to herself, "Desi, Hindu. Getting the picture?"

"Right, right. Sorry," Marisol said, "I think that's where Garrett took me to meet a client of his. I remember that they had a really wonderful black truffle butter."

Christina smiled, "As long as I'm there, I think I'd like to try that butter."

"*Yeah*, well, be careful you don't spend too much of Neville's gift card. We might be called upon to rescue you and pay the bill," Holly said.

"Not that we would have a problem doing that," Marisol added.

"That's right. *We* will always be there when you need us," Holly said, "like that time when Neville dropped you off at a Target because he didn't want to have to drive all the way from his condo to your mom's place on a work night."

"I know he can be odd, but he has many good qualities," Christina countered.

"What? Like a double-jointed tongue and a penis with the girth of a coke can?" Marisol laughed.

"That actually sounds painful," Christina said, "not the tongue, the really thick penis. And maybe tongue too."

The yoga instructor, a woman in her forties who sported a boys' regular crew cut, walked past, giving the three women a withering look.

"Anyway, Neville is polite to my mother, and he's not pushy about... you know," Christina said.

"Okay, you just described my Uncle Bob's Golden Retriever after they had him neutered," Marisol said.

Holly was standing off to the side, considering, and finally added, "It's your life. I've appreciated that you two have been as nonjudgmental of my dating choices as you have. But, have to say, you, Christina, you deserve more."

Christina was quiet for a moment as they headed for the locker area. She finally said, "I think I need to ask for a girls' night after my evening with Neville."

"How about Pinky's and that cooking demonstration at the Royal Oak Theater on Thursday?" Holly suggested, getting back the affirmative nods from Marisol and Christina.

Chapter 2

(Could You Be)
The Most Beautiful Girl in the World
Prince

Rocco was already seated when his cousin Michael entered the restaurant. They greeted in that same old-school way their fathers might, a kiss on each cheek.

"God, how long has it been since we got together? Too long. It's really good to see you." Michael clapped Rocco on the arm.

The restaurant's host was ushering a couple to the table near where Michael and Rocco were seated. The man was tall, with a pinched face and too much hair product.

Rocco's seat faced the couple's little alcove. The man took his seat without helping the woman into hers, which caught Rocco's attention. The woman was on the tall side. She had that classic hourglass figure his male relatives reverenced. For probably the first time in his life, Rocco understood why. Her dress wasn't revealing, but it didn't hide her generous hips, slender waist, and very right-sized chest. Rocco registered all this as she gracefully seated herself. At that moment, her face was turned so that Rocco had time to look at her. She stole his breath. Dark lustrous hair, luminous skin, full lips, and big brown eyes. There was a freshness about her: not scrubbed, but clean and not overly made up. "Beautiful," Rocco murmured.

This drew Michael's attention to the newly arrived diners. "Wow," Michael said before each man got ahold of himself.

Rocco softly cleared his throat and looked at Michael as Michael turned his attention back to their own table as the sommelier approached.

"I took the liberty of ordering the wine," Rocco said.

"That's *ah,*" Michael looked back at the woman diner for a moment. "That's appreciated."

At the next table, loud enough for anyone close to hear, the man cautioned the woman, "You can order a cocktail. As in one and only one." He gave that a beat and then continued, "But that means no wine with dinner if you do. It would probably be best if you had a soft drink. The gift card is generous, but it has a limit."

"I'd prefer wine with dinner, if that's okay?" she said softly.

"Of course, you would. You Italians. It's amazing to me that anything gets done with the amount of alcohol consumed." The man shook his head, "The house red is under $10.00."

"You should order for me if you would please. I don't want to get it wrong," the woman said demurely.

The server next appeared table side and took the food order for Michael and Rocco. As soon as they were alone again, Michael said, "Why is she with him?"

"I had the same thought," Rocco gave his head a little shake and noticed the couple again.

The man was now telling the woman what she could order. "No lobster, but you can have the smaller cut prime rib."

"That sounds great. May I have the Black Truffle butter with it?" she asked.

The man put the menu down and looked at her disgustedly. "That's an extra. Why do you need that?"

"I don't have to have it. The fillet will be wonderful," she said.

The server approached, and the man began rattling off the food order. "I'll have Cesar Salad, the mashed potatoes, and the ribeye - well done. She'll have the house salad, the baked potato, and the small fillet - well done."

"Oh, sorry, may I have the fillet rare, please?" the woman said.

The man let out a breath, "I can't eat at a table with meat served like that. The blood makes me sick."

"Sorry, can I have that almost well done?" she said, then whispered, "no blood, please."

The server smiled at the woman and said, "Of course, madam."

Rocco looked over at Michael. "I need to take care of something," he said and left the table, returning after a moment.

"What did you do?" Michael asked.

In a low voice, Rocco said, "I paid for the Black Truffle butter and got her the Nero d'Avola instead of the house red. They will give her a second glass too. We worked it out like *oops*, here's a second glass for free – end of the bottle."

Michael laughed, "God, thank you. I wanted to yank her away from him and give her a better dining experience.

Rocco tried to get back into engaging with Michael, but it was near impossible with his attention on the brunette.

The sommelier poured the wine for the woman to swirl. She did and brought the glass to her nose. Her face lit up, she sipped, and her face lit up again as she placed the glass for the sommelier to pour. "This is wonderful," she said, smiling at the sommelier.

"Madam has excellent taste," the sommelier said and gave Rocco a glance as an acknowledgment.

The server appeared at the couple's table and apologized for the mistake with the Black Truffle butter. "Madam, we are sorry an error was made, and Black Truffle Butter is included with your dinner. If madam is okay with it. And of course, this would not be charged to the check."

The smile on the woman's face was brilliant. "What a lovely mistake," she said, "thank you."

The woman excitedly turned to her companion, who had pulled out his phone and looked away from her.

Rocco and Michael returned to their respective dinners. Rocco had been so consumed in the little drama at the next table that he almost forgot the purpose of the evening.

At the next table, the sommelier brought the woman the second glass of wine Rocco had paid for. “Don’t add that to the bill,” the man said.

“Absolutely not, sir. This is the end of the bottle if madam wishes.” The sommelier offered.

The woman’s smile made Rocco’s heart seize. She was stunning.

She beamed at the sommelier. “This is a wonderful red; many thanks.”

As the sommelier left, the man sniffed, “You don’t have to gush. It’s a little unseemly.”

“It is a very good wine, house wine or not, and I’m enjoying the heck out of it,” the woman said.

This made both Michael and Rocco offer each other a knowing look.

The woman did enjoy the wine and, from what Rocco could tell, loved the hell out of the Black Truffle butter too. It pleased him.

The man then reached into the breast pocket of his coat and produced a little box. He opened the box and pulled out a ring. Without ceremony or another word, he roughly took the woman's left hand and put the ring on her finger. She held it up and turned the small stone to an appropriate position as the man silently looked on. "No," he said.

"No?" she asked.

"It doesn't fit. Too big." And with this, he took the ring off her finger and put it back in the box. "I'll have it resized. Drink up. I've got an early day tomorrow." With that, he stood. "I'll settle the bill; go use the restroom; I'm not stopping anywhere between here and your house. Meet me outside when you're done."

The woman looked at her hand, now missing the ring, and frowned but then took the last sip of the wine and smiled.

The man looked at her as if she was a difficult child and said, "Chop, chop."

She rose, carefully straightening her dress, and walked toward the restrooms. She encountered the server and warmly thanked her.

The man noticed this pleasantry and shook his head as he answered his phone. "Hello... I'm at the restaurant now... yeah, done with that chore. No. It's too big on her. I might have known. Nothing with that woman ever goes smoothly. I don't know.

She didn't say, but why wouldn't she like it? Women love jewelry. Yes, you can tell mom. Listen, I've got to go. I have to pay the bill. *Yeah*, you too." He ended the call, placed the gift card on the table, and left.

"What a dick," Michael said.

"No argument from me," Rocco said as his eyes trailed the woman's retreating figure. She was the stuff of myth, all soft curves, and long legs. His cock jumped. It had been a while since that happened. He thought he should chide himself, but what the hell? She was spectacular, and he was the only one who knew the extent of his interest. He inwardly smiled, enjoying his impure thoughts and the physical reaction.

"I know you didn't just come all the way over to Windsor to eye-fuck that woman." Michael nodded toward the restaurant's exit.

Rocco gave his cousin a knowing smile. "Caught. But that's okay. She was a wonderful distraction." He let out a breath, "You're right; I did have a particular bit of business. I decided to catch up with you in person; it's been too long, but what I need is your professional help. I need to hire a dedicated Information Technology professional. One for sure, but I'm not opposed to one for each office plus an IT Officer."

“I was always surprised you didn’t have more of a staff.”

“Dad could never understand the need. But that breach at Gitterman made him look into it more seriously. He’s on board, and wants this set up like yesterday.”

“You know I’ll be able to do the background check, but I’m not an IT head hunter,” Michael said.

“You may not be a head hunter, but you know the really talented computer experts. I remember when you figured out who was behind the cyberbullying of that gay Ottawa MP.”

Michael smiled. “Not an IT guy. It was a... a friend, a good friend of mine who is now writing for the Windsor Star.”

“A reporter?” Rocco puzzled.

“*Yeah*, she is. She was freelancing and had a blog. She came to the paper's attention after the work she and I did with the MP’s case.”

Rocco smirked, “Attention of the paper? Isn’t one of your frat brothers at Postmedia? And doesn’t Postmedia own the Windsor Star?”

Michael held his hands up in surrender. “Guilty.”

“I get that she rocked it with what she pulled together for the MP case, but....” Rocco cocked his head and considered his cousin for a beat. "So, Michael, what else is she to you?"

"She is fascinating. And she's worked on a couple of other things for me, and I gotta say I love talking to her. But I've never met her face to face. Not even Face Time or Zoom."

"Really? Why? She's not local, I take it?"

"I'm not sure where her home base is. It can't be all that far away. It wasn't a problem for her to take the job at the Star. She might be doing that remotely, but I'm not sure."

Rocco smirked, "Why the reticence? It's written all over your face that you're more than interested. Why not pull the trigger, meet up with her, invite her for coffee or whatever."

Michael got a faraway look in his eyes. "Right now, she's perfect. In my head, she looks like Elisha Ann Cuthbert. That added to what she's like over the phone or online: smart, sweet, witty. She's my dream girl. I don't know if I want to disturb what's in my head."

■■■

Their evening ended when Michael took a phone call from a client of his security firm. That was okay. They had a good meal and great conversation, and the purpose of the evening, if not the solution Rocco wanted, was at least addressed.

The trip back through the tunnel to the US Customs wasn't too bad. It had been a while since he was in Windsor. The line at the Customs Check Point on the Detroit side was a little more crowded than he recalled from coming home before.

While waiting for an open booth and the U.S. Border Patrol Agent, he was trying to decide on music or a comedy channel when his phone announced, "Frances." That was actually Caraleigh Frances. They sort of hooked up a couple of weeks ago. Maybe. That night was a blur, and it made everything uncomfortable to recall.

She had introduced herself to him at a holiday cocktail party. She was one of a hundred twenty-something women. A little too spoiled, a little too entitled, and a little too unpleasant for anything more than maybe a fuck, but that was a big maybe.

The party was at the Townsend in Birmingham. It was a themed affair with special hors d'oeuvres and cocktails. The evening drink was a cranberry bourbon combination that Rocco wouldn't typically have ordered. It wasn't unpleasant, just not his usual.

That night, Rocco ran into two of his Rugby buddies from U of M. His pals were at the party with several other attorneys from their law office. One of the other attornies, a guy his Rugby buddies called Denton, was working very hard to get the attention of one of the females in that group. Rocco ended up standing next to her and inadvertently picked up her drink. Rocco had maybe two or three sips before noticing the lipstick on the glass. He figured out what happened and turned, apologizing to the woman and telling her he'd get her another drink. Denton practically came unglued.

"Just give it back to her," Denton almost snarled.

"No worries, I can get her a fresh one." Rocco waived a server over, handing off the half-consumed drink for two full ones, one for the woman and one for himself.

Denton was furious. "Give her back the drink I gave her," Denton kept demanding.

Rocco's pals quickly intervened, walking over to talk to Denton. The woman thanked Rocco and excused herself. Denton ignored his coworkers and took off; Rocco supposed he wanted to catch up to the woman.

Rocco's buddies shook their heads and shrugged, making their apologies for Denton's strange behavior, and the three settled back into pleasant conversation.

Another quarter-hour slipped by when Rocco realized he had had a little too much to drink, said goodnight to his buddies, and headed for the coat check. He had just decided to call an Uber when Caraleigh showed up at his elbow, making the offer Rocco knew she had been hinting at a few hours before. He wasn't lying when he explained that he was in no shape for her suggested interlude.

"I have a room here. You can sleep a couple of hours," she offered.

Rocco was dizzy and tired, so tired he could barely make it to the elevators under his own steam. He followed Caraleigh into the room, saw the bed, and fell into it.

Later, it had to be much later; Rocco's cell phone woke him. It was his alarm, not a call or a message. He got out of bed to rifle through his clothes that were everywhere, finally finding the phone to end the alarm. He sat back on the bed, trying to piece the previous evening together. He must have undressed at some point, but he didn't recall anything more than walking into the room. He rubbed his face; he wasn't so fastidious that he carefully folded or hung up his clothes when he undressed, but this? His suit pants at the door to the bathroom, his coat and suit coat at the foot of the bed? This was odd. Odder still was his underwear was MIA, but he still had on his undershirt and socks. His head wasn't clearing all that fast, but he thought with a sense of dread that the girl who led him up here was nowhere to be seen. He got up and found his pants. His wallet was there, and after going through it, he let out a relieved breath. Nothing was missing. "Oh shit," nothing at all was missing, including the two condoms he always had with him.

Okay, not to panic, the hotel probably stocked one or two condoms with complimentary toiletries. He made himself inspect the waste paper baskets but found no condom wrappers in either basket or in either room. He didn't want to process any of that right now.

He looked at his very limp dick to see if there was evidence of possible sex. He wasn't sure what he'd be looking for, maybe crusty pubic hair? God wasn't that gross. He wasn't sure because when had he ever fucked someone and fell asleep? That wasn't part of his hookup repertoire. He normally headed out like his ass was on fire one minute past ditching the spent condom. He wasn't a forensic expert, but if there had been the morning after evidence, he couldn't find any. And his partner in crime wasn't around. It might be helpful to have her answer the burning question.

She also didn't leave a note. That wasn't so upsetting, but he did feel the need to check in on her to verify the activities of the night before because he sure as fuck couldn't remember any more than walking into the room and seeing the bed.

He now inspected himself for other telltale signs. No love bites, nail scratches. None of the smell of sex on him or in the room. In fact, the only odor was the woman's heavy perfume that lingered unpleasantly in the bed. If he fucked her, it had to be a truly pathetic effort.

He decided on a quick shower to help him wake up a bit more for the drive home. It took him another half hour to get himself dressed and out the door. It was a little before nine a.m. when he got home. He had a phone call to make that afternoon, but nothing was pressing this morning. He got out of his clothes, set his alarm, and slept until just after one in the afternoon.

When he arose, later on, he checked his company website messaging portal. He found a less than happy entry from the woman who owned the crappy perfume. "Caraleigh Frances." Rocco read. The subject line read *Last Night.* And she fucking left it on the company message portal where his employees might have seen it – wasn't that fucking fantastic. The message was basically a bitch fest about why he left this morning. She had paid for an additional night at the hotel and was downstairs ordering breakfast while he was *sneaking off.*

She left a call number that he called. His head hurt, and he still felt wiped out. He cursed the party's special cocktail and forced himself to sound normal. She picked up on the first ring with a pouty *hello*. Forty minutes later, he could finally hang up.

He still wasn't one hundred percent positive they hadn't had sex, but she assured him she was on birth control. She was put out that this was the subject of their conversation. She wanted to know when they would see one another again. Was she serious? That was the only thing Caraleigh Frances wanted to focus on. Under the circumstances, he thought it wiser to just get his ass into the doctor for STD testing versus bringing that subject up to her.

He redirected the conversation; this was Rocco's sweet spot. The discussion he had perfected over many years on all sorts of women. He might indulge, but only after making it clear it might be fun; it might be a lot of fun, but no matter how much fun it was, it wasn't going to be twice unless he was very sure the lady's emotional investment was as neutral as his own. Caraleigh would never have a repeat, and he spent the next thirty-nine minutes telling her this - telling her over and over and over again.

That conversation was a few weeks back, followed by dozens of her calls, texts, and emails that he had dodged or ignored. Now, waiting in the queue for the Border Patrol to clear him, the name flashed again, and the handsfree repeated it. *Frances.*

After tonight's dinner in Windsor, he had the Nero's brunette on his mind. It may have been a little crazy to think about her, but crazy or not, it was a very fine thought because the brunette had an allure that Caraleigh and her ilk never would. Rocco got hard again with the thoughts of the Nero's brunette. He adjusted himself. He let out a breath. He looked at the handsfree again; he could have answered the call, but... "hell no." He said aloud to no one. He was getting too old for this booty call bullshit. No matter. He needed to be more circumspect with hookups. He had been living with a hit-or-miss sex life for years now; it was boring the crap out of him. For a liberal and enlightened generation, more than a few clingy women saw their future on the arm of a man they believed should finance their lifestyle.

His mind turned back to the Nero's brunette. She was gorgeous. She had a very attractive softness to her. Tonight really changed nothing, but his thoughts of her held such charm. His next thoughts took him from the edge of lust to a wave of appreciation as he remembered how she stopped her waitperson to say thank you and how she praised the sommelier for the wine offering. She wasn't just a beautiful face atop a smokin-hot body. She was a sweetheart. However, this evening would be the memory of that smokin-hot body he'd take to his bed, along with a hand towel and Astroglide.

■■■

Christina knew every creaky board, the spots where the wood floor was a little loose and groaned under the lightest of steps. She silently made her way into her bedroom. It wasn't that late, but her mother would have already gone to bed, just as likely not yet asleep. It was better that Mrs. Pentelino was tucked away for the night. Christina wasn't up for discussing Neville and this evening's event or non-event, as the case may be.

Well… that wine was pretty wonderful, and even if the meat was too well done for her liking, the truffle butter was a treat. Those parts of the evening made her smile. The rest? Not only wasn't she looking forward to talking about it, but she also didn't want to think about it much either. She'd have to see how all of this unfolded, and she needed her besties with her to debrief.

Chapter 3

Dream Lover

Bobby Darin

Rocco could smell the unmistakable scent of her desire. His cock throbbed, trapped in his jeans. She came up behind him, pressing herself to him and lightly kissing his back between his shoulder blades. She wasn't wearing a top. Rocco knew this because he could feel how tight her nipples were from the winter night. He hoped she wasn't uncomfortable, but he enjoyed the feel of her like this. She began running her hands around to his pecks, down his torso to his abs, and on down further to the waist of his jeans. It made him shiver.

He knew he should stop her from unbuttoning his jeans. He was conflicted; he wanted to feel her soft hand around his hard cock. He wanted her to stroke him just for a minute before taking her inside the Dairy Queen to fuck her. But it was too late; she was making him come on himself. It was too late to do anything about hiding because everyone had heard the bell that went off. No, not a school bell or a church bell; it was... then Rocco found his phone on the nightstand and turned the alarm off.

His dick was as hard as a crowbar, and he was awake enough to know he almost had a wet dream. This was new. Not the morning stiff dick, but the sex dream. He'd have to take care of it, but he'd do that in the shower. He chuckled to himself; he did not know positively if the woman in his dream was the Nero's brunette. He thought it was. No matter, the Nero's brunette would positively help him out in his shower this morning.

Chapter 4

Bad Boys

(You Make Me Feel So Good)

Miami Sound Machine

Rocco's workday began at 4:00 a.m. with a call to an Italian bank in Milan. Rocco never minded the early hour, and he rather liked this task; it made him sharper with his Italian. Not that it was necessary. It seemed everyone in the Italian business world was fluent in English. It was more a point of pride that he didn't depend upon anyone at the bank to transact business in anything more than their mother tongue.

By 7:00 a.m., Rocco's day was in full swing. He had breakfast catered in for himself, his admin assistant, and his relationship managers. It was the perfect way to catch up, but the agenda was actually about Rocco's brother Bruno coming to work at this office of Gagliardi Wealth Management. There would be other meetings like this one, introducing the office to the idea of Bruno before Bruno actually started work.

It was a delicate thing because Bruno could be the proverbial *bull in a China shop*.

The Gagliardi staff knew Bruno from various work-related social events. That meant they probably watched Bruno have too much to drink on those occasions as he provided unplanned entertainment. Like when he dropped his pants to prove he was wearing underwear. Or the time he got a little tipsy, took the mic away from the DJ, and confessed to having a crush on the company's marketing manager's wife. And the one that will forever live on in institutional memory, the 4th of July barbeque when Bruno was caught having sex with one of the caterer's staff.

Bruno took the girl to a bedroom for privacy. However, there was a sleeping baby in a porta-crib in that room. Neither Bruno nor the girl noticed the sleeping baby or the Nanny cam that streamed their encounter to the baby's mother's iPad. The sleeping baby's mother was at a table with several women, including Theresa Gagliardi, Bruno and Rocco's mother, and Nonna Gagliardi, their grandmother. The paternal hell that rained down on the little Poletto, Bruno's nickname, by his father Antonio, was ever after referred to as dad going all Costa Nostra on Bruno's ass.

Bruno's entry into the family business didn't follow the same path that Rocco and their older brother Franco took. Both had been working for the family business in some capacity since they were in high school. Both achieved law degrees as well as financial certifications and licenses. Both had management positions, with Franco primarily responsible for the east side office and Rocco for the west side office.

Bruno hadn't wanted to be involved in the family business. He went off to Waldorf University in Iowa and finally graduated with a degree in general studies after six and one-half years. Bruno came home with more than just his hard-won sheepskin. He also earned a stubborn case of venereal warts, a DUI, and a Facebook page that chronicled his many social activities.

During the summer semester of his sophomore year of matriculation at Waldorf, Bruno got seriously involved with IT geeks. That's where he made another college distinction. This one was in gaming, but along with that, he earned his unofficial Ph.D. in computer hacking. That education came from two exceptionally gifted computer science guys who, much like Bruno, weren't majoring in more than beer and locally grown marijuana.

The three of them, encouraged by controlled and banned substances, planned to start a company devoted to their computer abilities. However, Bruno was the only one of the three amigos to actually graduate. After they managed to stay at the school for four years without a degree in sight, Bruno's buddies were not granted student status and were told to find opportunities elsewhere. Once away from Forest City, they were gone for good, only occasionally answering Bruno's texts. With that part of his life officially ended, Bruno was adrift.

That summer after graduation, Bruno barely came out of his room and lived like some angsty teenage girl continually playing Radiohead and Linkin Park. He'd show up for dinner but didn't engage in more than a grunt here and there. It was Nonna Gagliardi who finally had had enough.

She and Nonno Gagliardi arrived for a Sunday dinner; Bruno came down to the dining room before the blessing was offered. He was dressed in a hoodie and smelled like a gym bag. He silently filled a plate with food, turned, and headed up the stairs. Nonna was incensed. Rocco and older brother Franco had never witnessed their sainted grandmother riled up like this. Bruno hadn't made it to the middle of the stairs when Nonna let loose Italian invectives that really didn't require interpretation.

No one really knew exactly what transpired between Uberta Angelica Pinto Gagliardi and her youngest grandson, but after some door slamming and muffled Italian, Nonna rejoined the family at the dinner table. She looked completely composed and nodded to her son to say the blessing. Some twenty minutes later, Bruno appeared, a showered Bruno dressed in a golf shirt and khakis. He approached the table, faced his family, and said, "Excuse me. My apologies for disrupting the meal. Mother, I'm sorry I behaved *maleducato*." Bruno looked to Nonna. She nodded curtly, and Bruno said, "Please forgive my very rude behavior. I was raised better. I will not forget myself in your home again."

Bruno looked back at Nonna. She regarded him for a moment and then said, "*Sedersi.*"

Bruno was the one Gagliardi who had never taken the time or had an interest in speaking Italian. It was impressive that he did as Nonna instructed and took a seat without someone interpreting.

It wasn't the end of Bruno's missteps and full-blown screwups. Still, he did pull himself out of the funk he had been in. By the following evening, he showed back up for dinner with the news that he would be bartending days at a nearby bar restaurant owned by one of his buddy's parents.

That was Bruno's life for the past couple of months until Nonna came for a second intervention.

This time Nonna showed up after hearing Bruno's degree didn't give him a profession; he was doing nothing more than working a forty-hour-a-week job and only one of those.

This time, she cornered Bruno after a Sunday dinner when she called him into the study. Again, it seemed that the dressing down happened in Italian, which the rest of the family understood perfectly. *Vergogna,* shame. And *pigro*, lazy, were interspersed with other unflattering descriptions of Bruno's behavior in the Italian that no one was sure Bruno understood. And Nonna Gagliardi wasn't only addressing Bruno's work ethic and waste of an expensive education. Oh no, after she was done with Bruno, she called the rest of the family in for Uberta Angelica Pinto Gagliardi's brand of family therapy.

She had them all emotionally on their knees in less than one minute. "It's been years since we lost Caterina. And none of you have come to terms with it," she looked at her son, "we all have let Bruno coast along. I've been to blame as much as anyone. But it has to stop. We treat this boy as if he is still that fourteen-year-old whose sister's accident made him mute."

Theresa fell into a chair and buried her face in her hands. Antonio's eyes misted over, and he stepped close to his wife and placed a hand on her shoulder. Nonno turned from the group to compose himself. Rocco and Franco looked at each other and then at Bruno, who sat on the sofa weeping openly.

Caterina Uberta Gagliardi was just sixteen when the swim team bus she was traveling in was hit broadside by a truck on Moross Road at the I94 overpass. The front of the bus hung precariously over the guard rail when the first responders arrived. Somehow, they managed to get all the girls out as well as the bodies of the coach driving the bus and one other coach before the bus careened onto the southbound lanes of the freeway. It was a miracle that all the girls didn't die that day.

Caterina could never have made it had the hospital been a distance away. Still, it was touch and go for days. The stress on the family was terrible, but the strain on Bruno took a massive toll, and at fourteen, he shut down and couldn't or wouldn't talk for weeks.

Bruno was never the most mature of the Gagliardi children. He was late in almost everything- walking, talking, fine motor skills- but he had Caterina. Caterina was the little mother; she was as encouraging and nurturing as Theresa. Certainly, Bruno loved his mother. Theresa Gagliardi was Bruno's heart, but Caterina was his soul.

Caterina eventually recovered somewhat from the accident, but she never bounced back to pick up her former life, and she died four years later. During her recovery, Bruno was also recovering. He eventually came back to himself enough to return to normal life, and even if it was late, he finally completed high school. Bruno wanted to go to school where his brothers got their undergrad degrees, but Bruno's grades and ACT score wouldn't allow that. The family found a college that would accept him and held their breath that he would be able to acclimate to college life – he did, sort of.

For all the family, Bruno was a fragile being. As horrible as it had been for any of them to lose Caterina, Bruno's loss was exponentially worse.

Listening to Nonna tear into Bruno was shocking and nothing anyone in the family had considered.

Nonna came to sit beside Bruno. She put her arm around him and said, "You don't know who you are or what you can do. You need to discover that. But you don't have to do that alone, *Polpetto*. You may not have Caterina with you, but you have her spirit, and you have your family." She patted his head, "You'll be all right. You're a bright boy. A good boy."

That high family drama was why Bruno would be starting a career at the Gagliardi Wealth Management business.

Much discussion and back and forth happened before it was decided that Rocco would make a place for Bruno at the west side office. This wasn't just finding a desk and computer for Bruno; Rocco had been charged with mentoring his little brother.

On the plus side, Bruno had promised to prepare for the FINRA Series exams or anything else he needed to be a productive member of the family business. Rocco was counting on that to remain the case. Still, he thought other niches were available, which should be explored before trying to fit Bruno into a relationship manager position.

This morning's meeting assured his sales group that Bruno wouldn't be turned loose on the company's clients to execute some ridiculous frat-boy antics. Rocco was confident he made his case without damning or demeaning his brother.

Next, the meeting would be with the accounting group and the office support. That would be a little tougher because the office staff would initially interact with Bruno.

His thoughts were interrupted by a woman clearing her throat and the high-pitched chatter out in the hall. Rocco looked up to see Caraleigh followed by the receptionist, Ava, who was having a panic attack.

"It's all right, Ava," Rocco held up a hand to calm the poor woman.

Caraleigh turned to Ava and, in a genuinely haughty and downright bitchy tone, said, "I told you he'd see me." She stuck out her tongue at Ava and began to close the door to Rocco's office.

"You might want to leave that open, Caraleigh," Rocco said in an even voice.

She shrugged. "Suit yourself," she said as she sauntered over to him, taking her coat off as she went.

Rocco shook his head as he pointed to a chair positioned in front of his massive stone-top desk.

She wilted but took the seat, pouting as she did so.

"What brings you here?" Rocco said, pinning her with an unhappy look on his now stony face.

"You never answered my calls, texts, voice mail messages, or emails. Seriously, I thought something really horrible happened to you. And as your friend, I wanted to be sure you were okay." She sniffed.

"I see. Well, good news, I'm fine. Now, this is a place of business. My friends know never to just show up. They also know how annoying I find it when my staff is treated less than respectfully. Let me spell that out for you. If the receptionist asks you if you have an appointment and you blow past her, be assured that I won't be happy about it because she is doing exactly what I pay her to do. You are preventing her from doing her job," Rocco said with a sour look directed to Caraleigh.

This got Caraleigh's attention. "I meant no harm. No disrespect. I can assure you. I'll... I'll apologize to her on my way out."

"Be sure that you do. And that should happen anytime now," Rocco said, nodding to the door.

"Wait, I had a very good reason for trying to get ahold of you," she said in a rush.

"It better be epic." Rocco folded his arms over his chest.

"My stepfather. My stepfather's company is ready to switch retirement plans. I thought of you."

Rocco mentally went through what he knew about Richard Talmet and his engineering company. It wasn't a huge company, but the firm consistently managed to hang on to its government contracts. With the focus on environmentally friendly construction, they had parlayed that aspect of the company into something worth noticing. There were several reasons why Rocco hadn't personally approached the company. The primary reason was a senior Gagliardi Relationship Manager had the firm on his radar. Rocco wasn't about to step on the man's toes. With more respect than Caraleigh deserved, Rocco said, "Thank you for thinking of our firm. One of our managers has already been in touch with your stepfather."

Her perfectly made-up face fell. "I don't understand. You're not going to personally see to this? You aren't interested in Richard's business?"

"Richard is aware of our services. As I said, one of our relationship managers has been talking with him," Rocco said.

"I see," she straightened in her chair, 'but I could arrange a meeting with Richard to speak directly to you."

Rocco's head suddenly hurt. "Let's leave it to my guy working with Richard already."

She sighed, "Okay, I was only trying to be helpful."

"Noted," Rocco said, standing to offer the signal that she should leave.

She didn't; instead, she leaned forward, giving him a peek at the top of her breasts, and said, "If I can't interest you in Richard's business, can I interest you in a little office erotica?"

He wanted to laugh at the absurdity of this unappealing offer but said, "I'm working."

"Spoilsport. How about lunch? Well, an early lunch?" she asked.

"Still working, Caraleigh," Rocco said.

She grabbed her coat and, in a testy voice, said, "Fine. When?"

Rocco rolled his eyes. "Caraleigh, fixing a specific time would be a date. And I don't date. Remember?"

This was not going well, not going at all how she thought it would. She wanted to scream. This was the long game, she reminded herself. This had to be played just right. "Okay." She huffed, put her coat on, and strutted out of Rocco's office.

He sat there staring at her as she put every move into her ass, walking out the door. It was obnoxious. *Was she fucking crazy? She had to be at least a little nuts to think he'd ever call her.*

Rocco waited another five minutes and picked up the landline. "Ava? That was Ms. Caraleigh Frances. You did exactly what you should have this morning, and I'm sorry for her behavior. Has she left? Good. Did she engage with you at all on her way out? No? Okay. (*Figures,* he said to himself). "Thank you. I don't want you to worry about it; there was nothing more you could have done."

He hung the phone up and thought for a moment. He should have put a remote door opener on the elevator forever ago. That he could take care of before he had another unwelcomed visitor.

Chapter 5

Somebody's Baby

Jackson Brown

"Okay, where's the ring?" Holly asked.

"I thought you said he had a ring?" Marisol joined Holly, patiently waiting for the answer.

"Yes, well, that's a mystery to me. He showed me the ring; he put it on my finger. It was a little big, so he took it back and told me he'd have it resized. I haven't seen him or it since we went out," Christina said.

Marisol picked up the cue and said, “Okay, here’s to your *sort of* engagement.” Marisol held her Pink Circus cocktail, as did Holly and Christina.

“Cheers,” they said in unison, finishing off their cocktails.

Holly asked next, “What’s your next move?”

“I’m not sure,” Christina blew out a breath, “I don’t think it’s up to me. I’ll see him this weekend, and we’ll see.”

“You’ll leave it go until then? You don’t want to confront him?” Marisol asked.

“I don’t think the ball is in my court,” Christina said.

Holly shook her head. “It’s your business; you know we have your back whatever you do.” She looked to Marisol to confirm.

Marisol nodded.

“It’s just that you are owed more than a tepid proposal and a here one minute, gone the next engagement ring. Maybe this gives you the chance to consider Neville and if he should have a future with you,” Holly said.

“You are all about your self-worth with your job and every other aspect of your life except for the men you date,” Marisol said.

Christina began to protest.

"You don't need to respond. Just chew on it for a while," Holly said.

All three were quiet for a beat.

Marisol finally spoke up, "Hey, let's not dawdle. We've got a ten-minute walk to the Theatre. Come on, ladies."

■■■

Rocco sat at the bar with a client; they were waiting for the client's partner to join them. The client rolled her eyes as an anonymous female walked a little too close to Rocco and slipped a bar napkin into his pocket. Then Rocco, too, rolled his eyes, reached into his pocket, pulled out the napkin with a phone number written in a feminine hand, wadded it up, and set it on the bar top to be swept into the bar trash. "Sorry," he offered to Marion, his client.

"Why you gotta be so goddamned pretty?" Marion quipped, "I don't know if I should be offended that she objectified you or disrespected me as the woman in your company?" She carelessly patted Rocco's nicely developed and very hard bicep.

Rocco chuckled, then looked away in time to notice the flash of pink in the bar's mirror. It drew his momentary attention as he noticed an eye-catching brunette at a table in the corner. It took him a nanosecond to place the woman; it was the brunette from Nero's. She was sitting with two other women toasting something. She was dressed in what Rocco assumed were her work clothes. She looked very buttoned up this evening: no lipstick and hair pulled off her face. She was still a stunner. *Huh, small world,* he thought and wondered idly what happened to the boyfriend and the proposal. Or was it actually a proposal? Rocco thought about sending over a drink and then going to the table for an introduction. That would be awkward. What would he say? How could he explain himself?

He forced his attention back to his client as Marion's partner, soon-to-be wife, Kathy, came to sit with them.

Marion and Kathy owned a small chain of day spas in the area and were thinking about expanding. It was all in the talking stages, but Rocco had connections with other clients to bring into the discussion. For the next twenty minutes or so, he explained how Marion and Kathy might approach this and promised to make some calls to set up introductions for them.

The brunette and her friends were gone when Rocco looked into the mirror again. It disappointed him.

A few hours later, after more conversation and a light dinner, Rocco said good night to his client and her partner and took the short walk to the public parking lot. He was almost to his SUV when he spotted her again. She was with her friends, the same women he had seen her with earlier. They laughed about something as they walked to their respective cars. All three were attractive in their own way, but the knockout of the group, the singular beauty, was the brunette. She got into an older Oldsmobile.

"Text when you get home," the petite caramel-skinned woman called.

"Yeah, it's a little worrisome that you're driving to Sterling Heights in that rust bucket," the other called.

Rocco noticed the car again. It didn't actually look like a rust bucket, but it had to be more than a decade old. That fact annoyed him. *Why the fuck would that boyfriend of hers have her drive a car like that? Particularly in the winter when she was so far from home? Maybe after the crappy proposal, she dumped his sorry ass.*

He watched as she drove out of the lot. He had an urge to follow her to make sure she got home all right. Well, that was fucking creepy. He got into his SUV and decided to not do anything so stalkerish.

Maybe Caraleigh's crazy was rubbing off on him. Yes, one whack job around was enough, thank you very much. He again realized that Caraleigh hadn't blown up his phone tonight. He'd take the win where he could get it. Rocco pointed the SUV north and headed for home.

Rocco's home wasn't anything like his parent's or brother Franco's place. Franco wanted the Grosse Pointe mailing address, so he found something middling modest in Grosse Pointe Shores not far from their parent's or grandparent's homes. Rocco's place was just off Square Lake Road near Forest Lake Country Club in Bloomfield Hills.

Rocco wanted something out of the way, private. Something different from growing up the way he did in Grosse Pointe. Grosse Pointe had a very distinct town feel, almost small town. That wasn't the lay of the land in Bloomfield Hills, which Rocco liked.

Rocco bought the four-bedroom ranch on Forest Lake from one of his college friends, a rugby teammate. The friend's parents divorced because the guy's father took up with his dental hygienist. The old guy bought the Forest Lake property to renovate and give it to the dental hygienist as a wedding present. Then the old man dropped dead before the divorce, and the house became the family albatross; they just wanted it gone and were thrilled with Rocco's purchase offer. The asking price was better than good, and the renovations would take the time they would take; he refused to obsess about that. And with little fanfare, Rocco had a new address.

Rocco's home was his cave. He had the country club to use if he needed to entertain. For him, his home needed to be very private; other than the people he hired to maintain the place, no one other than his family had been inside.

Getting home meant a quick shower, answering emails, and going to bed. He got the shower, answered the emails, and got to bed before midnight, but he couldn't sleep. It wasn't a business problem either. Nope. All he could think of was the Oldsmobile the brunette was driving and if she made it home.

Chapter 6

Can't Take My Eyes Off of You

Frankie Valli and the Four Seasons

After tossing and turning, he managed a little sleep. He had a standing appointment with a trainer at the fitness center on Telegraph when he wasn't using the country club gym. He wouldn't blow that off. Whatever else, he needed to burn the useless energy he had collected.

The hand of providence was the trainer had Rocco working with a heavy bag. Where it came from, Rocco didn't know, but that morning he pictured the brunette's dumb ass boyfriend, or maybe he was now her fiancé. Whatever. It was dumb ass's face Rocco slammed over and over again until his arms were wet noodles, and he was panting like he ran a marathon.

Rocco still got to the office early and put in a chunk of uninterrupted work before Bruno strolled in and threw himself on Rocco's office sofa. "Dude, did you see that hottie someone just hired for the accounts payable? She's smokin'."

"I shouldn't have to tell you this..." Rocco walked over and shut his office door, "that comment, besides being middle school level stupid, could find its way into the harassment lawsuit you're gunning for. What the fuck, Bruno."

Bruno had the sense to look sheepish.

"I don't want to sound like Dad about this, but your crap has consequences," Rocco said.

"Okay, let's not lose our shit," Bruno said.

Rocco looked skyward and shook his head. "You're the guy who wants to be taken seriously. You're the guy who is lobbying for a place in the family business. When will you lose enough of your shit, Bruno, to earn that place?"

A blush now stained Bruno's face. He hung his head. "I get it; I do. Can you forget the comment? Can you not say anything to Dad?"

Rocco took in a breath, "If you blow this, it won't happen because I rat you out. Just... just pretend Mom is always in the room."

"*Yeah*, okay. I can do that," Bruno quietly told his big brother.

"You want to start earning your keep?"

Bruno looked up, "Absolutely."

Lunch today is a place in Royal Oak, Nothing fancy. The opposite of fancy. You know the Wadlings? This is a lunch with Norman Wadling. He's got more money than god, but he's not flashy. In fact, it always surprises me that he came to Dad in the first place. He always reminds me of a guy who keeps his cash in a mattress. I check in with him a couple of times a year. Today is one of those times. We have lunch at National Coney Island."

■■■

"What do you want for lunch?" Christina asked Rosemary, the receptionist.

"I'm covered. I brought my lunch," Rosemary told her.

"You can pack it up for tomorrow if you want. Daniel lost a bet, and he's buying all the admin staff lunch today. Thank Dean, for this. I should have led with that. Anyhow, I'm going to the Coney Island," Christina said.

"I love that Chicken Hani. I'll have that with fries, please," Rosemary said.

"Got it. Thanks." Christina wrote Rosemary's pick in her steno pad and went back to her office to call the order in.

It was never nerve-racking for her to drive her car in this weather. It was the Holtzbergs that always had the freak out about it.

Today it was just above freezing, but it was not snowing or sleeting – that was a plus. Since she insisted on going on the lunch run, Dan Holtzberg told her to take one of the company service vehicles because they had four-wheel drive. He was a really nice guy like that.

■■■

By 11:30, Rocco and Bruno found Norman sitting in a booth near the restaurant's front door, reading a newspaper.

Rocco introduced his brother to Norman. This only produced an eye squint from Norman at the younger Gagliardi. Still, Norman was polite while Rocco did his best to keep Bruno in the conversation. It worked. Bruno was attentive but quiet. Norman wanted to discuss moving some of his assets around. Rocco heard him out and began to offer suggestions when the front door opened.

Christina walked in and approached the front counter behind two young patrons.

The woman at the register gave the teen girls a less than friendly reception as she rang their order. They looked rough: one girl with a safety pin in her ear and the other with a bad dye job of bleached pink fried hair. "You're short," the woman said curtly, "you're a dollar twenty-seven short."

The girls may have been trying to look tough, but the two of them now just looked embarrassed. The woman at the register wasn't going to let it go. "Call somebody if you have to, but you aren't leaving until you settle your bill."

Norman shook his head. "What a bitch. Excuse me, I got a buck twenty-seven." He began to get up.

That's when Rocco saw her, the brunette from Nero's and Pinky's.

Before Norman did much more than stand. Christina was handing the woman at the register two dollars and said. "Here you go; this will cover them."

The girls looked at Christina as if she had given them the golden ticket. They thanked her and were gone.

The woman scoffed, “Well, some people got more money than brains.” The woman said loud enough for those around her to hear.

Christina looked closely at the woman’s name tag and smiled. “Maybe, Irene, but I think it’s more that I remember being their age and in the same situation,” Christina said, untroubled by the insult. “I’m here for the Holtzberg order. I called it in about thirty minutes ago.”

Irene stopped short, recognizing the name. She got a little red-faced and said, “Holtzberg. That’s all set for you. I’ll have the boys carry it to your car.”

Christina smiled kindly and handed Irene an envelope, “There’s extra in there for your trouble. Mr. Holtzberg asked me to let you know he appreciates this. One more thing,” Christina pulled a five out of her purse, “please give this to the waitperson who served those girls. I’m guessing they didn’t cover the tip.”

“Oh, sure. Always happy to help. Their waitress was Linda, and I’ll get the boys to carry your order out for you,” Irene said and fled into the back.

The customers closest to the register looked like they were in suspended animation, staring at Christina, a Christina who didn’t notice.

Rocco was dumbfounded; this close, she looked like an angel. She was bundled up with her hat covering her hair, framing her face. He could see now that her eyes were a deep rich brown, and her skin looked like satin with a peachy pink hue, probably from the cold. He knew he, too, was staring but couldn't bring himself to look away.

Two young men came out from the back carrying boxes that had to be full of whatever the brunette had ordered. They silently followed the brunette out the door to a service van with the Holtzberg logo on the side. As soon as they packed the boxes into the van, they ran back for more. There were three trips in all before the brunette pulled more cash from her purse for the young men. It must have been a good amount because both were clearly happy counting the money as they came back into the restaurant. Now, as if everyone simultaneously woke up, the restaurant's ambient noise level returned to normal.

Rocco became conscious that he wasn't only mesmerized by the brunette; his table mates were also.

Norman let out a low whistle. "Was that a movie star? Or maybe a supermodel. I know old man Holtzberg. I've been involved in some of their charitable events. I don't remember her. And I would have; she's a beauty."

Rocco nodded in agreement.

Norman noticed Bruno, eyes wide and silent. “Cat got your tongue?” Norman teased.

“I’m pretending my mother’s in the room,” Bruno said.

■■■

That evening, Rocco couldn’t get home fast enough. The brunette was now his guilty pleasure. He had more information. “Holtzberg,” he said aloud just before beginning the internet search.

He found some but not all he wanted. Her picture was out there, but not her name or her marital status. Did the bonehead actually propose?

Holtzberg, Inc. was a Royal Oak business that designed, installed, and maintained commercial kitchens. He thought maybe the boyfriend owned the company – but if that were the case, the guy was a tool for allowing the brunette to drive around in that old fucking car.

Rocco found a family portrait of the Holtzbergs on their website. It reminded Rocco of his own family. The Holtzbergs were a family of three sons, just like the Gagliardi family. He looked over at his family’s framed photo predominately displayed on his home office bookshelf. It was taken when Bruno joined the business, but it was the same as any family photo taken in the last decade; even when they were supposed to be standing shoulder to shoulder, there was a space between Rocco and Bruno. They never did that on purpose; it was just something that happened. It was the space and place that they would always have for Caterina.

Whenever the memories of Caterina hit him, they hit him hard. He shook his head in an effort to shove the feelings aside. He forced himself away from memories of Caterina and back to his little project. He looked carefully at the Holtzberg sons. None resembled the *douche-canoe* with the brunette at Nero's. He went through the company website and Facebook page. There weren't any pictures on the company's web page, but he struck gold with their Facebook. There she was, and the camera loved her; there were several pictures of her, and all were perfect. She had to work for the company, but he didn't think she was in sales or any development capacity. She would have had her picture and contact information public if she were. He kept going back to the images. In one, she was packing food at the local food pantry. She was also part of the litter crew for Holtzberg's sponsored I-75 clean-up effort. In another, she was decorating the company Christmas tree. That picture was only a month or so old; the others he wasn't sure about, but it seemed as if she had been with Holtzbergs for at least a few years.

Rocco had to end the evening's research, but he did so reluctantly. He wasn't a spiritual person. He had more than the requisite Catholic training, a product of over twelve years in Catholic schools. It wasn't that he didn't believe; he did. Not that it was easy after his sister's accident, her agony of living with her injuries, and her death. He came to terms with it enough that he wouldn't turn his back on the church or blame God. He just didn't see the hand of God in all things the way others did. Running into this woman over and over again should have seemed like an insignificant coincidence, but it didn't. It felt intentional.

He said this to himself and then chided that internal voice, saying, *Okay, but what if she was old and plain? What if she was bitchy? Would you still be looking for supernatural interventions? Probably not.*

That jaded Rocco Gagliardi went to sleep only to find her in his dreams.

Chapter 7

I Saw Her Standing There

The Beatles

Sunday brunches or dinners were fairly standard with the Gagliardi family. Today, however, the family was getting together to celebrate Theresa Gagliardi's birthday.

Rocco's gift was an evening complete with a car and driver to Deori's, the Windsor restaurant, where Theresa and Antonio Gagliardi's had their first date almost forty-six years ago. Rocco made this arrangement for them for birthdays or anniversaries since he understood the significance and had the working capital to pay for everything.

He had the birthday card and had picked up a dessert, a lemon cake his mother liked. He was going to be early, which was fine. He'd be there to help if needed.

When he saw the two women at the side of the road, he slowed, ready to help them with the tire they were trying to change. But the picture was off because there were also two men. The women were changing the tire, and the men were sitting in the car? Was that a Ford Flex? He wasn't positive he should stop under these circumstances. Slowing down, however, gave him the chance to get a better look at the women, at the one woman in particular... the brunette, his Nero's brunette.

As soon as the realization hit him, he talked himself out of it. This had to be the product of thinking about the woman too much. Now, random women began to look like the brunette. In fact, he probably hadn't seen the same woman from Nero's or Pinky's or the Coney Island. This was all very likely a product of his imagination. He passed the stranded Ford Flex. As a brunette- no, not a brunette - it *was* his brunette who looked right at him as he passed by.

He got off at the next exit and made it back around to see the two women at the open hatchback of the Flex. He pulled his Escalade a few yards behind them, got out of the SUV, and walked toward the two women. He saw two men still in the Flex, eyes glued to their respective phones as he approached. If he wasn't sure before, getting the opportunity to see the ass-hat in the car solidified that this was indeed the couple from Nero's. He now looked at the brunette, confirming what he thought. His heartbeat jumped. It was one and the same. If he thought she was something before, that was nothing compared to the goddess that stood before him now.

Wordlessly he got to the back of the Flex, pulled up the truck lining, unscrewed the bolts that held the spare, and found the jack kit. With confident efficiency, Rocco had the jack in place, tire off, and spare on, all the while staring shamelessly at the brunette. It wasn't lost on Rocco that the brunette stared shamelessly right back.

As soon as the flat tire was stowed, Rocco closed the hatchback, took a business card out of his pocket, turned to the brunette, and almost lost his breathing ability. He looked closely at her gloved hands, and then he just did it. He carefully picked up her left hand, removed the glove, and put the glove in her right hand. He smiled at the absence of any ring and placed his card in her ungloved hand. "You deserve more than he will ever give you," Rocco told her, then turned and walked away.

Christina stood clutching the card as Neville got out of the Flex to announce, "The tow truck will be here in forty minutes." With that, Neville turned around and got into the warmth of the Flex once more.

As Rocco pulled back on the freeway, he watched her; she was still staring at him, following him with her eyes as he drove off. He should have gotten her name at least. Stupid. That was really, really dumb. He couldn't say how he managed that major miss. The exhilarating feeling that she wasn't engaged to that idiot had Rocco ready to howl and punch the air.

Rocco ran over their meeting the rest of the drive. She was so beautiful. To have the chance to be that close to her was like cresting the top of a roller coaster. The redhead that his brunette was with was the same woman he saw at Pinky's. Realizing that made it feel like he was getting to know her. Then the unpleasant realization that his Nero's brunette was also with that imbecile. What kind of man would allow his girlfriend to change a tire in January in Michigan while he sat in a warm car? A major dolt.

Thinking back to why he didn't get at least her name, it occurred to him that he was now sure he'd see her again. He really thought that? Yes, he was nuts. All he had to do was get her name – a very simple task he failed. But maybe this was a better outcome. If she called him, he didn't have to feel like a creeper.

Back at the Flex, Christina watched as the Escalade drove off.

"Who was that?" Marisol asked.

"I don't know," Christina said, but her eyes were still locked on the black SUV as it disappeared in the Sunday traffic of I-75.

Marisol took the card from Christina's bare hand. "Why do you have your glove off?"

"I don't know," Christian nodded her head, still following the black Escalade with her eyes.

"What did he say to you?" Marisol studied the card.

Christina now started to come back to herself. "He told me I deserve more than Neville."

"He knows Neville?" Marisol said, confused.

"No. Well, I don't know. I feel like I know that guy, but I can't figure out from where. He's… "

"Hot. Gorgeous. Built like an action hero." Marisol filled in the blank. She looked at the card and said, "He's Rocco I. Gagliardi, Esq, CFA. and a lot more alphabet soup after his name. He is a vice president of Gagliardi, INC Wealth Management services since 1951."

"I don't recognize the name, but he's so familiar," Christina said, turning back to her friend.

"Oh my god, you're blushing," Marisol said.

Christina put her hands up to her face. "I think it's just the cold."

"Okay, come on. Let's get out of this weather. Do you think Neville will want to replace the tire? Garrett and I can take you to the auto show if he does. You really do need to find a new car."

■■■

"You're too quiet," Bruno said to Rocco as he took the seat next to his big brother at the family's massive dining room table. Rocco had been late, which never happened. He had also been preoccupied the entire afternoon. The family had noticed, but Rocco didn't appear to be in a bad mood, not sad or angry, just distracted.

"Is anything the matter?" Bruno asked.

Rocco came out of his fog long enough to say, "I'm fine. Just thinking." Then he latched on to a subject to avoid confessing his lusting after a woman he didn't actually know, "The Children's

Hospital Charity Gala is coming up. Why don't you get a Plus One and attend for me if you wouldn't mind? There's tablespace. We have several clients who will be there. It would be a good thing for you to show your face, so people get to know who you are."

Bruno thought a moment. "I can do that."

Rocco paused, "*Ah*, listen, by a Plus One, I mean someone who knows how to navigate these things. This isn't a first-date event. Be sure she isn't going to drink her dinner, eat with her fingers, or show up in a dress that only just covers her ass. This isn't an opportunity to get you laid. If she's on your arm, she represents our business and our family."

"I get it," Bruno said, now thoughtful.

"It's not a problem for you to show up solo. Better you're alone if you aren't sure about a Plus One."

"I'll do that. *Hey*, is this why you take the less fortunate to these things? Bruno asked.

Rocco rolled his eyes. "If by less fortunate, you mean she isn't a Victoria's Secret model, yes. The woman needs to be conversant in more than TMZ."

"Right," Bruno said.

"I have a couple plus ones. They may not be cover girls, but they know the score. They function as plus-ones for me, and I serve the same purpose for them on occasion. It's a mutually advantageous arrangement. You should start thinking about something similar," Rocco advised.

"How do I… " Bruno looked bewildered.

"Tell you what, I'll call one of my plus-ones to go with you. Here's the thing, I don't like to say it, but you have a checkered past. You'll need to be on your very best behavior. Don't drink a drop, no flirting with anyone, be sure to engage with the people at your table, and you might earn the first girl on your plus-one call list. It will be either Heidi Van Bon or Caitlin Newbaugher."

"Thanks, Rocco," Bruno said sincerely.

■■■

Neville thought it best to get the tire replaced. He didn't like that Christina was going to the auto show without him. God only knew what kind of car she'd decide to buy when she was on her own. He really didn't see the problem with her current car. Her friend Marisol always referred to it as a rust-bucket; Neville had never seen any rust on that car. An oil change and a tune-up would likely address any potential issues. Christina was such a child. She probably had never thought of doing any car maintenance. Just one more thing he'd likely be responsible for once they were married.

This day had gotten off to a terrible start. First, because Christina had decided last week to invite her friend Marisol along, which meant the inclusion of Marisol's boyfriend, Garrett. Neville found Garrett to be preoccupied with sex, distastefully so. Garrett was always talking about it, always eluding to it. Neville believed that this loose talk made Christina uncomfortable. That discomfort translated into her hesitancy in staying over on the weekends, which is precisely what happened this weekend. Neville always had a difficult time with Christina in this aspect of their relationship. She was very reserved and hesitant.

He had hoped that the proposal would help. But Christina acted as if he never made her the offer. He supposed that was in large part that the ring wasn't ready. This wasn't going to be resolved anytime soon because the jeweler who offered free resizing was backlogged. Neville considered that he should make a dinner date sometime this week, just the two of them, to revisit the proposal and iron out some things. But... that was inconvenient. So many things with her were inconvenient. He supposed it would be one more thing he'd need to fix.

■■■

Christina couldn't get Rocco I. Gagliardi out of her head. Marisol and Garrett were totally wonderful, making sure she had the opportunity to see each and every car on display. But Christina couldn't get past the replay of Rocco I. Gagliardi slipping off her glove and giving her a panty-melting smoldering smile. What was that about? All she wanted to do was go home and soak in a bathtub, where she could address the libidinous condition she found herself in. God, she was going straight to hell for these impure thoughts, with a stranger no less.

And what of Neville? What did Rocco Gagliardi mean by the comment? *You deserve more than he will ever give you*. Did he mean Neville? How could he know either of the two men sitting in the Ford Flex was her boyfriend? How could he know she had a boyfriend?

This entire thing with Neville was a very uncomfortable subject. Neville wasn't always easy to deal with, but he had good qualities too. He was always sensible. And the big plus, the thing that made him a great choice to date, Neville was never too pushy about intimacy. The practical aspect of

Neville really was a good thing. Like today. He was absolutely right about getting the tire fixed. Okay, it did annoy the crap out of her that she and Marisol were the ones to scope out the spare tire situation while Neville sat in the car. Well, Garrett did too. And while she would never say anything to Marisol, Christina had always thought Garrett wasn't good enough for her friend. So, when Garrett did something less than wonderful, Christina wasn't surprised.

Still, since the *was it a proposal?* at the steak house, Christina hadn't let herself think about Neville's ring or lack thereof - not in any meaningful way. The answer was clear to her, even if it was shameful. If you couldn't wait to get home to touch yourself while thinking about a man other than the one who seemed to want to offer a ring, you could never accept the ring or even the almost ring in the first place.

The realization had her straightening purposefully in front of a Ford F650 6-Door Pickup. "I know what I have to do," she said to Marisol and Garrett.

Garrett smiled and said, "Sweet, we can do some real muddin' in this guy."

■■■

Marisol dropped a disappointed Garrett off at his apartment. She turned to study Christina. "Are you okay?"

"I'm better than Garrett."

"*Yeah,* he's a little disappointed you aren't going to buy the truck." Marisol headed toward M-59 to take Christina home.

"Sorry about that. I just had a little light bulb moment."

"About?"

Christina smiled wryly. "Neville. I can't marry him. I think I knew it before, but this morning and the brush with Rocco Gagliardi was..."

"Jaw-dropping. Cherry popping," Marisol said,

"Enlightening," Christina said.

"Are you going to call him? Mr. Gagliardi?" Marisol asked.

"What? No. For all we know, he could be a serial killer walking around with a fancy business card."

"*Yeah,* but you said you thought you knew him."

"I've seen him before, but that could have been on America's Most Wanted. He was crazy hot, but he's not why I can't marry Neville. He just helped me gain the clarity I needed about why Neville and I are done."

"Okay, enlighten me."

Christina let out a breath. "I have always felt marriage decisions should be very carefully considered choices. That passion shouldn't be the basis for a lifelong commitment."

"And now that you've come face to face with the prince of passion, that's all changed?" Marisol asked.

"I still don't think wet panties are an accurate indicator of husband material. A husband is someone you can trust to be your partner after he's fathered your children. I still believe that. It's just that now I want more."

"What are you going to do?"

"When I get home, I will call Neville to see if he'll meet up with me tonight and, if not tonight, tomorrow. I can't let this go on."

Chapter 8

Don't Come Around Here No More

Tom Petty and the Heartbreakers

"This doesn't make any sense Christina. None at all. I don't accept this. And I'll be picking you up on Wednesday for dinner," Neville said as he crossed his ankle over his knee and began picking unseen lint off his pant leg.

"Neville, I am sorry this doesn't make sense to you. However, it does to me. I will not be home if you insist on coming over on Wednesday."

"What will your mother say about this? Have you talked to her? Who have you consulted about this? We *are* getting married, Christina."

"I don't need my mother's permission to date, much less consider a potential husband. I talked to Marisol..."

"Marisol," Neville spat the name, "look who she's throwing her life away with. That's who you are taking advice from? Marisol?"

"I'm not taking advice from anyone. I'm perfectly capable of making decisions on my own. And, you can insult me if that's your plan, but you will not disparage my friend. Also, we were never engaged. You never bothered to ask,"

"I gave you a ring."

"*Yeah*, well," Christina looked at her bare left hand and remembered Rocco Gagliardi's reaction to that same hand. That made her smile. Instead, she modified her expression, looked at Neville, and said, "never got it."

"Of course you got it. I just needed to have it adjusted," Neville's said petulantly.

Christina was ready to unleash something, anything, to let him know how genuinely frustrated she was, and then... and then she took a breath. "Neville, we shouldn't do this."

"Exactly. That's what I've been trying to tell you. This isn't productive. I think you need a good night's sleep, and in the morning, everything will be clearer for you." He got up to take his place on the sofa next to her. "We'll get together on Wednesday, and maybe the ring will be ready by that time."

She stood, "Neville, I'm still breaking up with you. I would prefer to skip the nastiness and part ways with some dignity. If we ever run into one another, I'd like it to be cordial. I wish you all the best. Take care, Neville." She was out his front door before Neville found his voice.

If the car didn't start or gave her trouble, she might lose it. It also didn't help that she had to get out of there before rounding up her belongings. She didn't have much there, but her favorite jeans, a tote with hair products, and her grandmother's broach were in his condo.

The car started, no problem, and she headed east and home, thinking about Neville and how the day played out. She wasn't angry with him, annoyed, yes, but not angry. And that was the problem, not just with Neville but with any of the men in her life. There had been others since high school. None of them ever had enough of her heart to break it.

As far as breakups go, it wasn't bad, she thought as she exited his condo parking lot. Well, except for that comment about checking it out with her mother.

That one hit home; it wasn't the first time he had made it clear that she needed a what? A guardian. He thought that. She sucked in a breath. Oh god, other people thought that too. She had more than a few relatives who commented about... well, her ability to manage on her own. Hell, she managed a human resources department for almost 700 employees. *Yeah*, but she was still living with her mother. She lived *independently* with her mother. As she thought this, she could see Holly and Marisol rolling their eyes and suppressing a laugh. Okay, she didn't do a ton around the house. There was a reason for that. Her mother was very fussy about how things were cleaned and cared for. Christina cleaned her own room and bathroom... for the most part. Her mom liked to give everything a supervisory once over. That's what her mother called it, along with the reminder that it was still her Mom's house. Christina thought on it more; she had done her laundry for years, maybe not every time but sometimes. She knew how to do it. And cooking. She had been cooking with her mother, aunts, and grandmothers since she was old enough to crawl into the kitchen. She knew how to cook as well as any woman in her family. She just didn't get to do it regularly.

She sifted through the attic of her memories to recall how it was she had never moved on and moved out. Her brother was out of their house as soon as he cashed his second paycheck from his first job out of college. It wasn't like her mother was precisely crying at the door, begging Calvin to stay. And now that Christina considered it after the subject was brought up when her mother's sister-in-law asked, "Aren't you lonely with no Cal?"

Her mother was playing cards with her two sisters and a sister-in-law. She didn't even blink, just said, *the boy is out of college; he's going to be bringing home girls. I might miss him, but I wouldn't want that in my face. No, thank you.*"

Christina was sure that was right. Cal would want his privacy, but that wasn't all of it. She thought back to her introduction to Marisol.

Marisol McNamara got a paid internship at Holtzbergs during the last semester of her college career. The internship program was something that Christina had developed and administered for the company. It was challenging to snag an internship, and it was no easy grade. Marisol was the right fit and made the most of her time at Holtzbergs.

Marisol ultimately moved on to work in the county government's procurement office but not before she and Christina became great friends.

Marisol's county job meant Christina got to meet, know, and befriend Hollyka Jain. Holi for short, but for her western friends, acquaintances, and coworkers, the name was pronounced and spelled Holly. Holly was also with the county's procurement department.

Both women lived on their own. Holly in her own house and Marisol was renting an apartment. Come to think of it, Marisol had been living in that same apartment when she took the internship with Holtzberg.

It wasn't as if either of her friends were critical of her living situation; it was more that Christina now realized that her Besties acted as if it was odd.

It sort of was too. She made decent money. She could afford something; she wasn't sure what because she never thought past the bedroom she had at Carol Pentelino's house.

She felt like a loser for never thinking about it before. Or maybe the reason she didn't let her mind go there had more to do with the sex she didn't much care for.

Living with her mom gave her a built-in excuse. And she had to admit it was super easy to not stay at a man's place. At least it had been for her. Neville always offered, but hey, easy-peasy – *I never sleep well anywhere but home.* And *my mother will be too worried if I'm out all night.* Oh yeah, *I don't have my toiletries.* If all else failed, there was, *I have too much to leave at your place. I couldn't possibly*. It all added up to the same thing, escaping the odiousness of sex. At least sex with a partner seemed kind of gross to Christina until this afternoon, that is. Well, okay, to be fair, sex by her own efforts was fine, better than fine. And she did get juiced up reading Meghan March and Kayley Loring, and *oh my god*, Diana Gabaldon, to name a few.

But books never made her feel the electricity of *Rocco I. Gagliardi's* touch. How that zinged through her when he took her hand. Pulling her glove off felt like he had stripped her bare. His presence had her spinning out of control.

He was taller than Neville, but that wasn't what slew her. She didn't know what he might look like without the winter clothes, but she had a fair idea, and it was hot. When he told her, *You deserve more than he will ever give you.* The *he* in question should have been a mystery, but in her head, she knew he meant Neville. Really, she wanted to hear all about how she didn't need Neville. The low tambour, the beat of his voice, how it landed warm and thick, with a finality to it, did something to her. But that wasn't all of it. It was just him, his presence. His almost black hair that you could tell he had a little trouble keeping in place. His eyes, his dark eyes that locked on her for nearly the whole time he was there at the side of I75. He was handsome, like that Dolce & Gabbana model Noah Mills, but with dark eyes. But honestly, Christina thought Rocco Gagliardi was better looking. Or maybe it was the voice and the way he smelled. God...the way he smelled. It was a little sweat from changing the tire. A little coffee on his breath and a little mint and cloves. There was a hint of his soap or shampoo, and it all was delicious. He might have been in an expensive car, and his clothes were definitely high-end, but he wasn't a dandified metrosexual. He was anything but uncomfortable with the testosterone he had to have showered in.

And now she was the Amazon rain forest between her thighs. *Great. Just great.* She said to herself as she turned into her mother's drive and parked the old Buick in her mother's garage.

It was still early evening, but it was Michigan in winter when even early evening was night. The door to the mudroom opened, and Carol Pentelino's head popped out.

Christina gathered up her purse with her gloved left hand. The sight of it left her with a shiver.

"Oh, honey, get in here; it's freezing. I've got soup I can heat up for you. It's your Aunt Stella's potato and sausage. It's good this time. She didn't put too much of the bacon garnish in it. Come on." Carol waved her daughter in.

"I am hungry. I haven't eaten since this morning." Christina got out of her outerwear in the mudroom. She followed her mother into the kitchen breathing in the pleasing scents of fresh herbs and the faint smell of the bread baked earlier.

Most homes boast that the kitchen is the heart of the house. The Pentelino's kitchen was its soul. The rest of the Pentelino home was tastefully decorated, not necessarily in what was trending. Still, it didn't look like something from the set of the Brady Bunch either.

The kitchen, however, didn't belong to a particular era or decorating style. It was always painted some hue of yellow once every seven years. The single window over the sink didn't have a curtain. Instead, small flowerpots lined the sill or were suspended from the ceiling, all with various herbs. That wasn't the only thing suspended from the ceiling. Every pot, pan, and anything else Carol wanted standing at the ready hung down within her easy reach.

That sink area had plenty of attention because an automatic dishwasher was missing entirely from the room. Carol used a dishwasher once about twenty years ago. “It’s a waste of space. The only thing it’s good for is hiding the dirty dishes. All you need to do is wash the dishes.” There wasn’t one in this home’s kitchen when Carol moved in, and there never would be.

Carol’s kitchen had a small table. It was so old, made with a porcelain top that Carol liked because it was easy to clean. There were two chairs and one stool; the stool was Carol’s. Almost every meal in the Pentelino home was served at that little table after her father’s death. The space, furnishings, and equipment were dedicated to preparing and storing Carol’s food. The stove and refrigerator were both older than Christina. They still worked, worked great, and were what Carol was used to. She didn’t want to hear about ice makers, water dispensers, or self-cleaning ovens. “It's one more thing to break,” Carol always told anyone suggesting that the kitchen needed an update.

For Christina, the kitchen used to be a source of embarrassment. It was the old appliances or dried meats hanging alongside the garlic braids. However, she was pretty happy that, unlike some of her mother’s relatives, the Pentelino home didn’t have an Italian flag next to the American one; or a statue of the Virgin Mary nestled in a niche in the front yard; or worse, a niche that was really a bathtub set on its end and buried halfway to make a place for the Virgin Mary or St. Francis. One of her uncles had such a spot for Mary, and his garage door was painted in an Italian flag's red, green, and white. Christina was grateful that it wasn't until you got inside the Pentelino's ranch-style house that her mother's cluttered kitchen could be discovered. But as she got older, the kitchen felt warm and comforting. Christina needed that solace and comfort this evening.

Back in her youth, it was hard to be living with her widowed mother. It was difficult to be asked if her father was the victim of a Mafia hit or in prison or if he was living somewhere in Sicily with Michael Corleone. Did they hail from New Jersey with the Sopranos? But that was just a given by the time she got to middle school. The unglamorous truth was that he was murdered in a robbery of the business that employed Mr. Pentelino, the hauling company that a great uncle started and where most of the nephews worked at one time or other.

"So? What's going on with you?" Carol asked as she pulled a small pot down to warm the soup, "is this to do with Neville?"

"I won't be seeing him again," Christina said as she got a soup spoon out of the drawer.

Carol stopped and turned quickly. "You're done with him?"

Christina turned to get the bread and butter. "I'm sorry. I know you like him."

Carol stood in the middle of the kitchen, shaking her head, mouth open. "Like him? Christina Maria Pentelino, if I walked into the worst bar in Michigan, blindfolded, with my arm outstretched, the first man I came in contact with... would be a better man than Neville, that slimy little weasel."

"Mother, I thought you liked him? I always thought he was polite to you."

Carol crossed the short distance to take Christina's face in her hands, "Beautiful girl, I'm not the one he needed to be polite to, to be careful of. What does it matter how he treated me? It mattered how he treated you. And Christina, he didn't treat you like he should have. You didn't need that guy. I am so happy you scraped him off your shoe."

"You never said anything."

Carol shrugged a little. "I might have an opinion, but I'm not the one in the relationship with him. You were."

"What if I had accepted his marriage proposal?" Christina said in horror.

Carol went back to the stove to stir the soup. "I love you, but I can't live your life for you. You have to fall on your nose a time or two before you learn how not to fall on your nose." She went back to warming the soup.

The comment had Christina pick up her thoughts from the car ride home.

Carol ladled soup for her and set it on the table before taking a seat. "What's the matter? You aren't broken up about that boy?"

"No, that's the sad truth of it. I'm more relieved than I am upset." She was quiet, eating the soup with the bread. And after a few minutes, she asked, "Mom, do you think I'm an independent person? A self-sufficient woman? "

Carol gave her daughter an apologetic look. "Let's just say you are mostly independent."

Christina sat up. "What do you mean?"

"There's... I don't know exactly how to explain this," Carol fiddled with the condiment tray on the table and finally said, "there's something you're afraid of; it keeps you painted in a corner. Something that keeps you tied to my apron string. Most kids can't wait to be out on their own, doing their own thing with whomever they want to do that with. That was never you. And I think it's more about boys than it's about anything else. I was always glad you didn't bring boys around that were more interested in what's between your legs than what's in your heart or your head.

"Oh my God, Mother."

"Christina, come on, baby, you're grown. You've been with Neville and others you've been out with. I was with your dad for seven years before we lost him. How do you think you got here?"

"I don't know. I mean, yes, I know how I got here, but I never think of you like that. You're a little old school."

"Believe me, the only difference between now and when I was young is that we never would have worn a thong. You girls have that stuck in your crack; we did our best to keep our underwear out of there." Carol chortled and playfully slapped at Christina's hand, "Don't look so scandalized. You know, my wedding night was not my first time. Your father, God rest his soul, was not my first lover, and I wasn't his either."

"I could have lived my whole life without knowing that, Mother."

"Maybe, but I think you need to hear it. Like I said, I'm glad you didn't bring home boys that only wanted you for one night. But you need to find the guy that makes you want to..."

"Want to what?"

Carol Pentelino shrugged, "Just want to."

"I am so not comfortable having this conversation with you, Mom."

"That's okay, but you should have the conversation with Marisol or Holly."

"That's not a comfortable conversation with them either." Christina took the final spoon full of soup.

Carol held her hands up in surrender. "This is your life. You're a very smart girl. Extra smart for dumping that twit, Neville. Don't go off and get tangled up with another like him, Christina Maria Pentelino."

Christina's eyes rested on the bottom of her bowl. "I think I need to move on from more than Neville, moving out, to be more to the point."

Carol wished she could pretend to misunderstand her daughter. But she refused to allow herself to get misty over this. It was inevitable, and it was the right thing. It just made her long for the days when she had both Calvin and Christina home with her and Al. *Ah*, no help for it. She made herself say the following words, "It's past time,

Christina. You know this, in your heart, you know this."

"I feel like crying, Mom."

"Well, you aren't going to let yourself. You get ahold of Marisol and Holly and talk to them about it. It's time. They have experience at this." Carol patted Christina's hand.

Chapter 9

Right Now

Van Halen

Rocco now knew what his next move would be. The thought of it made him feel like a kid on the last day of school before Christmas vacation.

Rocco left his parents' house so consumed with what he would do tomorrow. The forty-minute ride seemed like it took seconds.

It was Franco who brought up the subject. The family always had Mass said in Caterina's memory, and they all gathered for a very sober family dinner. Franco made the off-handed comment that there had to be a better way.

Then it hit him. Rocco remembered Norman's comments about the Holtzbergs and their interest in charitable endeavors. But it wasn't only that they involved themselves in giving; Rocco knew from looking at their website. Every one of their events looked fun, something you'd happily be involved in. Why couldn't remembering Caterina bring a smile? When he made the suggestion, Rocco waited for the negative response he was sure the idea would elicit. And yet... the faces around the room looked relieved.

To Rocco's shock, Bruno picked up the thread and ran with it. "This is so much better. Right? I hate thinking of how she died. I hate it. It's so *fuc*... it's so terribly depressing." Bruno quickly corrected.

Theresa was nodding in agreement. "When we first lost her, I thought the most important thing was, never forget. As if we could. Rocco, this is a wonderful idea."

"What is your plan?" Antonio asked.

"The scale needs to be more. If we do this, our little annual memorial will be much bigger. We need partners for this. My first task is getting that first partner. I think that's going to be Holtzberg, Inc." And if that meant running into his Nero's brunette? Two birds, one stone.

■■■

The appointment at Holtzberg's wasn't hard to get. Rocco called Norman back to ask if he could drop his name. Norman laughed at him but gave him permission. Rocco wasn't sure if it made a difference, but he wasn't taking any chances, and the appointment was offered for the next day. Yep, it felt just like Christmas.

The Holtzberg's offices and warehouse were just off Fourteen Mile Road. The place was tidy. It was a well-maintained property that looked like what it should – industrial, but just enough.

Rocco caught sight of the car. Her car. This was a very, very good sign, and he took the steps two at a time.

The meeting included Mr. Doug Holtzberg and two of his sons, Dan and Dean. They settled in, and Rocco realized he had not thought this out. He hadn't thought about what he would say. For a moment, he considered making his apologies and sprinting for the door, and then he started to talk.

"We lost my sister some years ago. It was horrible for our family - devastating. She was in her teens when she was in a bus accident and twenty when she passed away. As a family, we always have a memorial. The memorial is a private thing; it's the family having a mass in her honor on or close to her birthday. After the church service, we have a family dinner at my parents' or grandparents' home. My family wants to do more than just remember. We want a commemoration of her life more than a gathering to mark her death. Norman mentioned that you are dialed into charitable events, charities, and so forth. We aren't so much looking for a place to dump cash in Caterina's memory as we are a way to celebrate who she was. I think that's the best way to describe it."

There was a hush, and Rocco looked up to see the old man's face wet with tears.

It was Dean who spoke, "We lost our sister too. She was the firstborn. She died a few days after her birth. My parents had tried for a baby for almost eleven years before Mom got pregnant with our sister. After all that and losing her, they figured it was hopeless. Then Dan here came along, and ten months later I was born; ten months and two weeks later along came David. We," Dean gestured to his brother, "try not to think about the timing," he said ruefully. "The embarrassment of family riches was never lost on my parents. They always felt like the door may have been closed, but the window was opened. My parents have always found ways to express their gratitude. That's what your friend

Norman was explaining, although he probably didn't know the why. I never knew my sister, but I've always felt my parents' pain at her loss. So I get it. Not in the way you do. You have memories of your sister. That makes it tougher, I think. Every charity we contribute to must have one element, or we won't get involved. From what you've described, I don't know if there can be a good fit because we are all and only about *hope*."

Rocco looked down at his feet, pondering this. It wasn't a comfortable consideration. Nothing in Caterina's death felt hopeful. Before her death? Before the accident? Before, everything was hopeful for all of them. He had Francine, looking forward to a life with her. Caterina loved the heck out of being in high school and joining the swim team. After? The after for Rocco saw Francine fall in love with someone else. For Caterina, the after was pain, endless days, months, and years of it. "All she wanted was to be able to live like the accident didn't change anything," Rocco said, not realizing he said this aloud. "She told me once that she could live with the pain if she could just sleep in a bed that let her pull herself to a sitting position."

"They have those beds," Dean said.

"I know, but for whatever reason, her doctors never signed off on getting that for her," Rocco said, "there were a few things like that. I think everyone was waiting for her to get a little stronger, which didn't happen." Rocco leaned forward in his chair, bracing his chin in his cupped hands. "What about an event that allows kids with disabilities to participate as if they had no disabilities? What about a day or part of a day that offers a respite? Would it be in line with the hope you want to inspire?"

The Holtzbergs looked among each other, but it was Doug that said, "Would that be the memorial you want for your sister?"

Rocco sat up and, looking off into the distance, said, "I want to think of her smiling. I haven't thought of her like that in years. She was a really sweet kid, a generous kid. I know she'd love this idea." Now he focused on Doug Holtzberg. "Yes, this is exactly the kind of memorial I want for Caterina."

■■■

Led by Dean Holtzberg, Rocco left the building from a different door, not before setting up the next meeting and not before inquiring after the brunette.

Rocco decided that it was far less creepy if he told Dean about the Coney Island lunch with

Norman and how Norman talked about the charitable work the Holtzbergs got involved with. He used that as the inspiration to come and talk about the memorial instead of admitting he wanted to be introduced to the woman picking up the Holtzberg's lunch that day.

"*Yeah,* that lunch was the result of a bet." Dean laughed. "I won that bet, of course. I get him every time. My brother Dan he's a smart guy, but he never exactly got the idea of a point spread. I try to make any bet about something more than handing me his hard-earned money. That day the admin staff got a nice lunch out of the deal. Sometimes it goes directly to the Salvation Army or whatever charity thing we're doing. Hey, wait, Norman recognized Christina? The woman who picked up the lunches?"

"Norman saw the step van with the company name on it. He never said that he recognized anyone, just the van." Rocco suppressed a real need to punch the air and holler. *Christina. Her name is Christina.*

"I forgot that we made Christina use the tuck when she insisted on doing the lunch run. She's the head of HR and part of our leadership. We are after her to get something with all-wheel drive instead of that grandma car she insists on driving. Sorry, we think of her as family, and we worry. You'll meet; she'll be part of our team," Dean explained.

It was all Rocco could do not to ask for an introduction at that very moment. That might expose him as the creepy creeper. Better not to head down that path. Besides, all he had to do was hang on, and he'd officially meet her. He'd meet *Christina.*

For now, he needed to get to his office, call his parents and brothers and run everything by them.

His father suggested a dinner. "I think your mother would like the Roma Cafe. It's been a while."

■■■

Even in the early dark, Rocco could see the striped awnings of the restaurant. When he was younger, he didn't appreciate the more established Detroit restaurants: the London Chop House, Sinbads, Mario's, Dakota Rathskeller, and several great places in southwest Detroit. They were in buildings a century or older, sometimes in forgotten neighborhoods. This never bothered his parents. The places they liked best were definitely old school. He wondered what Christina liked. Would she like something flashy, less buttoned-down, and more boujee? That thought took him all the way to the valet stand and into the restaurant. His parents and brothers were already seated in the smaller dining room his mother preferred. Rocco greeted his parents, seated himself, and found a glass of Barolo for him as the appetizers were delivered to the table. It made him chuckle. His mother would have already placed the order. She had particular favorites at any restaurants they frequented as a family. She would never presume to order for anyone but herself if the restaurant visit was with friends. Theresa was never bossy or bold unless it was about food for her family.

Tonight it would be the Fresh mozzarella Caprese to start with the Minestrone and House-made Fettuccine. It would take him two days or better to work off the meal because Theresa had asked for cannolis and the Tiramisu.

The dinner conversation was about the offices and office gossip. Rocco was impressed that Bruno wasn't mentally drifting off. Since forever talk about the business, and Bruno was doing something, anything else rather than participating in the conversation. He could see that Franco noticed this too. The little *Poletto* just might grow into something more.

As the first bites of dessert were tasted, the conversation turned to Rocco's plans for Caterina's memorial.

"Norman Wadling told me about the Holtzbergs. They have a business selling and repairing commercial kitchen equipment. They do a lot of charity work and have an excellent footing in the community. Besides that, they are a family business. It's the father and three sons. The Holtzberg parents lost their only daughter at birth."

The Gagliardis were quiet, reflective.

"They made me realize the thing that has been missing," Rocco said

"What? What do we miss?" Theresa asked.

"Caterina's life. All the expectation she created. She was willing to be just that much more for the people around her. And how brave she was showing the way," Rocco said.

Theresa and Antonio sucked in a collective breath.

Rocco went on, "It was in how bright and wonderful she always was. How she," Rocco began to chuckle, "how she'd invite that group of girls from the Y, you remember that, Dad? How she and the girls talked you into learning to do the Hustle? Remember? "

Theresa let out a snort, a ladylike snort, but a snort nonetheless.

"And how she got Mr. Ryan to pick those girls up from Chandler Park," Rocco said, laughing.

Now, the Gagliardis were doubled over.

Franco looked at his family like they were lunatics.

Rocco got himself under control to start the explanation for Franco. "You were at that summer writing camp when this happened. The girls from the Y were black girls Caterina met at some swim meet. They were nice to Caterina and her friends. They were nice girls in general, maybe eight altogether, but Cat was good friends with three of them: Ebony, Cassie, and Latesha. Cat got their phone numbers and started to include them with her school friends, which was fine. Kind of what you'd expect girls with similar interests to do. Except those extra sweet, very tiny black girls scared the crap out of most of the parents. And the more they all hung around together, the more there was what you'd call a cultural exchange. Cat got a really impressive slang vocabulary. They learned every Italian cuss word Caterina knew. Mr. Ryan, Shannon's father, was scared out of his socks about them, and when Cat talked him into picking them up at Chandler Park, Cat had to promise she'd go with him to... to.." Rocco was laughing too hard to finish, so Bruno did. "Cat had to go with him to *protect* him. It was hilarious. Those girls weren't even five feet tall; not one of them was even twelve yet. You should have seen the eye-rolling Caterina had behind Mr. Ryan's back. I forgot about that." Bruno wiped his eyes and said, "There were a million things like that. She was the sweetest badass of them all. Caterina was the best."

Theresa threw her head back, smiling. "Remember the cat walking?"

"Mrs. Marrille? God, that was so adorable." Antonio said.

Theresa turned to Franco. "You were busy with your friends and school; you wouldn't remember this," she patted Franco's hand, "Caterina would visit that elderly neighbor of ours. You remember Mrs. Marrille. Well, Caterina told her she should have a pet. Caterina, at age seven, got ahold of Mrs. Marille's son and talked him into taking her to the Animal Shelter to find a cat. Which they did. The son knew nothing about cats; Caterina knew nothing about cats. We only ever had dogs. So, Catarina went faithfully to the Merrill house every morning and after school to take the cat out for a walk. She just told us she was walking with the cat, not why she was walking the cat. God, it was cute.

Of course, the cat was eliminating in the house. Fortunately, the housekeeper clued Caterina in on litter boxes, but that was after three or four days of cat walking. I hadn't thought of that in years."

"Remember Milo's friend?" Franco made air quotes for the word friend.

"I remember Milo, the neighbor kid, right? Ron and Vanessa Allen's boy," Antonio mused.

"Yes, the Allen's younger son, Danny Allen's little brother. The friend, Buddy, was the red-haired kid with the coke bottle glasses and the stutter that made him painful to listen to. Milo only kept him around to make fun of him. Cat knew Buddy from the school choir. I don't think they were friends exactly, but she knew Buddy pretty well. Caterina would stick up for Buddy with Milo, not that he'd listen to her. Okay, so the Allen's had their annual end-of-the-school-year pool party. Cat was there, and so was Buddy. Milo was having a field day punking Buddy, laughing at him. The big put-down of the day was supposed to be Buddy making a play for some girl. Milo convinced Buddy that the girl really liked him, and Milo talked him into hitting on her. Cat overheard this, and when Milo got distracted, Cat talked Buddy into singing to the girl. She ran home and got Bruno's ukulele. And it's almost like the rest is history because

Buddy was a phenom. He didn't stutter when he sang, and he played and sang like a rock star frontman; the place went nuts. Buddy was surrounded by all the girls begging him to sing for the rest of the evening." Franco smiled at the memory. "Cat did that. Took a potential traumatic bullying event and turned it into a triumph for Buddy. She was something. The biggest heart."

Antonio took his wife's hand, kissed her knuckles, and said, "You're right; we've been remembering the wrong Caterina. I like your way, Rocco. I like it a lot."

"Tomorrow morning, I go back to Holtzbergs to meet with the other principles, and Thursday, we have a lunch meeting at our offices. The idea is to create a day for kids with disabilities where they can just be kids. Just enjoy the day. I honestly don't know what that will look like, but it's more in keeping with who Caterina was," Rocco said.

Theresa reached over and took her son's hand. "That sounds wonderful."

The server appeared with the check for Antonio and the boxed cannolis for the office tomorrow.

Just as elder Gagliardis stood to say good night to their sons, *she* appeared at Rocco's elbow. "Is that your family? I'd love to meet them," Caraleigh gushed.

Cornered. Yes, he was cornered. Rocco looked at her like the very unwelcome intruder she was. He managed to say, "Mother, Dad, Franco, Bruno, this is Ms. Frances, Ms. Frances, my parents, brothers, Franco, and Bruno."

"It's so nice to finally meet you," Caraleigh said dramatically, "we've been involved for weeks, and yet…" she let the statement hang.

Okay, well, he had had enough of this. "That's a bit misleading, Ms. Frances. To clarify, I met Ms. Frances at a Christmas party." Then turning to Caraleigh, he said, "You leave the impression that we are dating. We are not dating, Ms. Frances."

She paled but found her footing. "*Hum*, I suppose it might have a different interpretation in some circles."

"Doubtful. Well, good to see you, Ms. Frances. You should get back to your dinner. Have a good evening." Rocco turned from her.

Caraleigh huffed but left.

"Rocco?" Theresa looked at her son with narrowed eyes.

Antonio provided the save. "We need to get going. I think there is a Red Wing game tonight. I don't want to get caught in the traffic."

"Certainly." Theresa took her husband's arm, and the Gagliardi parents left Franco and Bruno wide-eyed at their brother.

"That was awkward," Franco said.

"Who is she really?" Bruno asked.

"It's like I said; we met at a client's Christmas party, and I made the mistake of being polite to her." Rocco nearly spat.

"I thought you told me I shouldn't flirt with anyone when I'm out for the business?" Bruno said.

Franco chuckled, "I think Rocco just offered sage advice based on his experience. So, yes, not a good idea to flirt unless you want some girl to dive bomb you at a family dinner."

"What he said," Rocco offered. "I need to bounce before she decides to make another dive."

■■■

Caraleigh was white with fury as she returned to her table and her mother without the promised Rocco Gagliardi.

"What happened? Where is he?" her mother, Carolyn, asked.

"He was with his family. He needed to get his parents home." Caraleigh took a sip of her cocktail and then another and another. Carolyn didn't notice, so Caraleigh took a gulp and drained her glass.

"I've always thought Italian men are too close to their mothers. I don't think you should be serious about him. I mean, he couldn't spare a moment to come and meet me? That's something wrong there. He's probably using you to get to Richard. That happens all the time. I have to be vigilant about who I interact with for that very reason. You should adopt the same attitude, dear. You really can't be too careful. And really, you should stick to your own circle. There are so many wonderful young men to spend time with. My god, Richard's company is brimming with them. Why don't you let Richard suggest a boy for you to date? That would be the more sensible thing to do."

"Mom, I'll find my own men. Men, Mom, not boys. I don't want any of those skinny thin-lipped nerds. Rocco checks all the boxes." She held up her hand. "One, he's gorgeous. Two, he's rich. He has his own company, Mom, and you should see his offices. I read somewhere that Dirk Decoursey designed both east and west-side offices. Three, he's never been married, so I wouldn't have to deal with an ex or children. Four. From what I can tell, he knows how to keep it in his pants. Five, I like him better than anyone else. I like my chances. I just have to figure him out a bit more."

"I'd be a little bit careful. Seriously, Caraleigh, there's a reason he doesn't have an ex or two. He might not be as perfect as you imagine." Carolyn pushed the half-eaten plate aside to make room for her after-dinner cocktail. "And he's Catholic too. Isn't he Catholic? I think all Italians are. Your father might not be happy about you marrying a Catholic."

"How is that a problem? This isn't the 50's, Mom. Almost every Catholic I ever knew never goes to church. It's just something that people do to be married in a church. It's hardly a consideration."

"What will you do if he wants a legion of children? Catholics don't believe in birth control. I've heard that's still something they adhere to."

Caraleigh laughed out loud. "I do not believe he's adhering to that particular church code or law, whatever they call it. Besides, I'm guessing he's not really up for children. He's a workaholic. I think he and I will be like-minded in this regard."

"Well, you are old enough to make up your mind about these things. You might do a bit of research about this. Richard has people who do that for him; you should ask." Carolyn raised an eyebrow as she looked at her daughter and polished off her drink.

Chapter 10

I'm a Believer

The Monkeys

Rocco was at the Holtzberg's front door at 6:55 a.m., extending a hand to Dean Holtzberg.

"I always want to apologize for these early meetings my dad is fond of, but you don't seem put out."

"I'm not. I have meetings when convenient for the client, and most of them are day-long busy – before eight a.m. is standard. I'm very appreciative that you've made time for me," Rocco said, entering the building.

Dean led him to a conference room and offered coffee. "*Hum*, I think we forgot to lay out the bagels or muffins. Excuse me a moment," Dean said as he left the room.

Rocco was pouring himself a cup of coffee when he caught sight of her in his peripheral vision.

She stood momentarily in the doorway as she let out a little gasp.

Rocco stared at her left hand. *No ring*. "Good morning." In all the ways he saw this moment playing out, he decided to act as if this was the first time they had met. But there was this part of himself that was inwardly cheering that she recognized him. Hopefully, she wasn't gasping because she didn't want to see him again. He'd find that out in the next few minutes, wouldn't he?

Christina got ahold of herself, "Good morning. Oh my, there should be baked goods for this meeting."

"Well, shit, was that the reason she was gasping? The missing baked goods?" Rocco thought.

"I'll just be a moment." She turned and all but ran off.

Christina almost collided with Dean, carrying a tray of Danishes and muffins.

"That's Rocco Gagliardi in there," she said, wide-eyed and breathless.

“Yep. Didn’t we say it was Gagliardi Wealth Management we were partnering with?”

“No. I’d have remembered.”

“Is there a problem?”

“No. No, not at all. I sort of met him; he stopped to fix Neville’s tire. Saved the day, sort of. I recognize him, but I don’t think he recognized me.”

“Sounds like he’s a nice guy, which is what we, Dad, Dan, and I thought when we met him. So, you crushing on this guy? Is that why you’re all Fanny Price from Mansfield Park?

Well, didn’t he catch on fast? She thought but said, “Should I find it odd that you know Jane Austin's works of fiction? I was surprised. Just surprised. I’ll join you all in a moment.”

Christina headed for her office and her make-up bag. And.... Right. She had chapstick, Gold Bond hand cream, a dried-up mascara tube, and a Jolly Ranchers baggie. The chapstick would have to do.

When Christina returned to the conference room, Doug, Dan, Dave, and Dean chatted with Rocco. They all looked up as Christina self-consciously walked into the room.

“Rocco, this is Christina Pentelino. Christina is part of our executive team and our HR Director.”

Rocco moved a little too quickly, the Holtzberg men noticed, and got himself squarely in front of Christina taking her hand and saying, “Rocco Gagliardi; it’s a pleasure to meet you.”

Despite her dry throat, Christina managed a, “You as well.”

At this point, Doug moved to take a seat, and the others followed.

After Dean recapped the conversation from the day before, he, Doug, Dan, and Rocco sat back. It was Doug who asked Christina, “Well?”

Christina was still pondering. She looked down but answered, “Maybe an event like a carnival.” With that, Christina's face illuminated. She looked up and said, “A day set up with activities for even the most handicapped child. A friend of mine is a physical therapist at William Beaumont. She was telling me about playgrounds built for handicapped children. There are very few in Michigan. Maybe we could see about having the event at one of them to capitalize on the equipment already there. And maybe...” She looked off, and began rhythmically touching her pointer finger to her chin, “maybe we do this to draw attention to the lack of playgrounds for children who are not able-bodied.” Christina stopped herself, realizing she had just taken over the meeting. “Sorry, I get carried away," she said apologetically, "I guess I'm not used to company." She gestured to Rocco.

"God, that's brilliant," Dan said.

Rocco expected her to be pleasant, and he knew she wasn't dumb, but he never imagined this sort of on-the-spot creativity. He managed to say, "Please go on."

"This is why we love you, Christina. Yes, please go on," Doug said.

"There's a YouTube," Christina got up to find the remote for the conference room's monitor, "here, this isn't very long."

The five men watched transfixed as Christina found the YouTube of a PBS News Hour, *Magical Bridge Playground*. Which led to another video of *Harper's Playground* and finally, the video of a Scottsdale, Arizona playground.

Christina looked at the men in the room and said, "You might think about building a playground and have the carnival as its grand opening."

Rocco's face brightened, "That's a great idea."

"I love it. I absolutely love it," Doug said. Then looking at Christina, "This is why we made Christina a part of the executive team," Doug beamed at her.

Christina blushed, stealing a look at Rocco, who was staring at her. It made her blush some more. "I can invite the physical therapist to the next meeting. She can provide some insight into this. If that's okay."

"I think that's a wonderful idea, please do. I'll do some research on what's currently available to figure out a few possible locations," Rocco said, "I'll do what I can to have that ready for Thursday."

"Oh, shoot, I've got the guy from Veteran's coming this morning." Christina jumped up. "Very nice to meet you, Mr. Gagliardi. I'm really excited about the project." And with that, he watched her fine ass move out the door.

"Sorry, I forgot about the Vet's thing she has today," Dan said.

"It was one of her ideas from a couple of years back. One that has worked out extremely well for us," Doug said.

"Hiring Ex-military," Dean offered

"Ex-military?" Rocco asked.

David took up the question, "She realized that while the combat training isn't a neat cross-over to what we do, we aren't armed and no bombs," he chuckled at this, "but there are aspects of it that are like combat. Thinking on your feet, using what is available, that sort of thing. She got in touch with the Veterans Affairs folks to find out if there was a need for employment for returning vets. There is a huge need. She and the Veteran's Affairs manager figured out how to get the community college to offer training on some of the equipment and systems we maintain and repair. We've been hiring from that group for a few years now. They have been some of our very best techs. This morning, the guy she's meeting with is new at Veterans Affairs, and he's bringing a potential hire."

"She's amazing." Rocco mused.

Doug nodded. "What she did this morning is classic Christina. Someone comes up with a concept, and she takes off with it," he chuckled, "Christina is a tremendous asset to our business and to us personally."

"She is so beautiful on top of it," Rocco's eyes followed the path Christina had just taken.

All three Holtzberg sons noticed Rocco's apparent interest, but Dan spoke up, "We think of her as family. Like our sister, to be specific. You aren't the first man to come in here and notice her. She's got it all, but she's not now and never has been that sophisticated when it comes to dating and men. She's not that hit-it-and-quit-it girl. Besides that, she just ended a fairly serious relationship."

"He was a dunce." Dean piped in.

Dan was nodding. "Not that it was any of our business, but I wasn't sorry to see the last of that guy."

Doug nodded. "Beyond the fact that she's been a model employee and a productive member of this organization, she is a quality person: the woman you take home to meet the family." Doug looked over at Dan, "I much prefer that description to the *hit it and quit it*." He looked back at Rocco. "I have faith that you will understand who Christina is if you intend to pursue her."

Rocco looked down at his shoes. Caught like a rat. "I never officially met her until today, but I have seen her before, and I'd be a liar if I told you I didn't find her attractive. I'm not a liar – I find her immensely attractive. That was before that virtuoso demonstration of quick-wit she put on this morning. I very well may be the last guy she wants hanging around. I take nothing for granted. As for pursuing he," he shook his head, "I'm so out of practice I don't know if I know how; my business has been my focus. But I sure would like to get to know her. I'll leave it like that."

■■■

The new hire and the Veteran's contact had just left the building when Christina bounded across her office to shut the door and call Marisol and Holly.

As soon as Marisol picked up, Christina said, "Is Holly there with you? If not, please go get her and put this on speaker. I have to talk to you two right *effing* now."

"Okay, hang on. She's right around the corner," Marisol said. After some shuffling and a door closing, Marisol was back, "We're here."

"Do you remember the guy that fixed the tire?" Christina said breathlessly.

"Rocco something, wealth management? That guy?" Marisol said.

"That guy was here this morning, and if you thought he was hot before, you have no idea how hot he really is. I almost fainted," Christina said.

"That's the glove guy?" Holly asked.

"Yes, the glove guy, and he was staring at my left hand a couple of times this morning too." Christina was now looking at her left hand wistfully. "I will be working on a project with him. Well, he and the Holtzberg boys. We have to meet him on Thursday for a lunch meeting at his office. I'm dying here. What do I wear? What do I do?'

"Do you want us to go shopping with you or do a closet intervention? Your call," Marisol said.

"I don't know. I don't know what to do. You know, wait, this is dumb. I'm not going to do anything. He's so far out of my league; this is just dumb. Never mind," Christina's voice deflated.

"What the hell does that mean? Out of your league? Your problem is you never take inventory. But that's why we are here. Okay, first, be prepared to fire up the Master Card; we are going shopping," Marisol said.

■■■

Rocco couldn't recall a time when he felt so optimistic. That old movie clip of the guy dancing down the street in the rain? *Yeah*, that's how he felt after officially meeting Christina. Christina Pentelino: a mind that could make a man applaud; a face that could make a man sing; a body that could make a man weep. She even had a melodic speaking voice. He could have spent the rest of the day just listening to her. *Christina Pentelino, you are about to be wooed.* He wasn't sure how he would do that, but he would. It would happen.

Getting back to his office, he opened the door to the main lobby and heard the receptionist Ava's relieved laughter. "This has certainly opened my eyes," she said as Rocco started up the stairs to find his assistant Bridget high-fiving Eric, a junior relationship manager. They turned to face Rocco.

"Mr. Gagliardi," Eric nodded in greeting.

Luther Herbert, the office's head of accounting, was heading toward Rocco, a man on a mission.

"Bridget? What's going on?" Rocco said before Luther could get much closer.

"I'll let Luther explain. This started in accounting."

"A hint, please?" Rocco asked.

"Let's just say you need to give your brother a raise, a massive one, and a hug," Bridget said as she took Rocco's overcoat.

By this time, Luther was within a few feet. "A word, Rocco?"

Rocco motioned for Luther to step inside his office.

Without a segue, Luther began, "I was very skeptical when you brought your brother on board. Very skeptical. And I wasn't the only one. Over the past weeks, Bruno has been proving his metal, and I thought there may be something to be made of him. After today?" the older man lifted his chin, "after today, my hats off to you. He's worth his weight in gold. Thirty-point seven million, to be exact. I just wanted to catch you before the others did. The problem really started in accounts payable, on my watch. He's a remarkable boy. Really remarkable." Luther's cell phone sounded. "Forgive me, Rocco; it's the bank." With this, Luther ducked out of the office, leaving a wide-eyed Rocco.

Bridget passed Luther in the doorway. Rocco signaled for her to come in.

She was shaking her head and smiling, "Wow, right? I wonder how many millions of available dollars he saved the company this morning."

"I really need to know what happened. Luther was no help. So, please sit and start from the beginning," Rocco said, sitting at the small table.

Bridget sat down on the sofa and began, "Early this morning, Carrie from accounts payable opened a pernicious email attachment by mistake. She didn't know she did anything wrong until the attachment announced it would shut down our system and would not get it back without payment. After a few minutes, nothing was working. It was like, one by one, computers just seized up. Bruno walked in and found Carrie crying. He looked at the attachment. Then, he told Carrie and Luther to give him a little time with it. Everything was back to normal at about nine, and Bruno gave the office a crash course in computer security. He's been going desk by desk to be sure nothing else is lurking. I don't think anyone understood his abilities. I sure didn't. I feel a little silly now for thinking he only got the job because of his last name," Bridget said, wide-eyed and star-struck. She began to speak again, "I don't know if you've ever been involved in this sort of thing, but I was. Not here, but at our church. They aren't kidding around; these hacker types. They can shut down the system; that's what happened with my church. And you won't get your system back. I don't know how Bruno did it. We have some very tech-savvy church members, and they just threw up their hands and told the Reverend to pay. Of course, those members set things up after it was over, so getting held for ransom isn't as simple next time."

"Do you know where Bruno is?" Rocco asked.

"He had just finished up with Eric. He said he'd catch up with the rest of the accounting staff. He asked that you not turn your computer on until he's been up here to look at it."

"How did he..." Rocco let the thought trail off because, really, how did Bruno learn any of this? He didn't major in systems. Rocco was very sure that wasn't even a program at Waldorf. Instead, Rocco thanked Bridget and promised not to touch a thing until Bruno gave the all-clear.

Just before lunch, Bruno appeared. "Hey, bro, I need a few minutes with your computer."

"Sure, I haven't opened anything." Rocco got up from his desk, and Bruno slid in his place.

After a few minutes, Bruno got up. He stretched. "We're okay, but your antivirus is for home computers – in this application, it's for shit. You need to invest in something a little more than off-the-shelf. And training; Dude, you need to train everyone how to spot malicious emails."

"How do you know about this?" Rocco asked.

"Let's just say I hung with a crowd that was way deep into shit that they shouldn't have been, and I got a first-class education," Bruno chuckled, "we are very lucky we don't have a portal for the clients' accounts. I mean, we should have that. But the way everything is set up, if we did, it would have been compromised a long time ago with the setup you have here."

Rocco sat down on his office sofa and stared at his baby brother, who actually had a handle on this. "So, what do we do?"

"First, we hire an IT consultant," Bruno said.

"Why can't you be the IT person? You seem to know about it."

"I know about some things; I don't know all of it. You need someone who can set up a client portal, knows how to maintain it, understands security, and can develop a continuous training program for the staff. I can help, but in the pool of IT, I can save a drowning man, but I'm no Michael Phelps. And we need Michael Phelps," Bruno said.

Rocco sat forward and asked, "Was it bad? What happened here this morning? Was it as Armageddon as Bridget told me?"

"If the assholes who pulled this had the skill level they thought they had, it would have been a much bigger problem. The training isn't a once-and-done. I gave the staff some rules for the road with emails. You've got a conscientious staff. They aren't lazy, and they aren't stupid. Most of this happens because people don't look at who is sending them shit. The bad guys are always getting better," Bruno shrugged, "so we have to stay a step ahead."

"Start today. Find the best and hire them. Get this handled, and keep me in the loop. As soon as this office is under control, you'll do the same for Franco and Dad. I'll talk to them. And Bruno, thank you."

Chapter 11

I Feel Pretty

Rachel Zegler

"I thought we'd be shopping for work clothes," Christina said, looking at the items just purchased from Victoria's Secret.

"We can, but this stuff," Marisol nodded to the pink and white striped bags, "is what will give you the confidence you need around his hot and wonderfulness."

"I don't really understand." Christina looked between her friends.

Holly took up the question, "Did you ever hear the story about The Ziegfeld Follies?"

"Like in *Funny Girl,* that Ziegfeld Follies?" Christina asked, now totally bewildered.

"You know *Funny Girl*?" Marisol asked.

"Mrs. Holtzberg is a huge Barbra Streisand fan girl. That gets laced through any family event," Christina explained.

"Yes, *Funny Girl,* that Ziegfeld Follies. Did you know that the Ziegfeld Girls were outfitted with totally expensive Irish linen petticoats? Petticoats that no one saw when the women were performing. Flo Ziegfeld did it because he understood what that did for those women. It made them walk a little taller and move a little more gracefully. That's what Marisol is saying. You are a total babe. Everyone who meets you knows this. Everyone except you. And if you are going to get away from the Neville dumb-dumbs of this world, you need to own it."

"How do you know this stuff?" Marisol asked.

"Reading the history of American Theatre when my brother tried to get my parents to give him acting lessons. I was reading up on it to help with his argument," Holly said.

"I never knew Rayaan was into theater," Christina said.

"He didn't get too far, and then he took up the piano. There wasn't an argument to win about that choice," Holly said, then pinning Christina, "the point is to feel like your best self, and it starts with the underwear."

"Okay, I won't argue because, holy moly, this is so pretty," she said as she hugged the bags, "but I have another dilemma."

"All ears, but can we adjourn to the place that makes smoothies?" Marisol pointed to the café, "I need to sit."

After getting their drinks, they took a seat with Marisol and Holly all attention.

"Okay, so I'm going to be moving out of my Mom's. I haven't got a moving date or anything like that. I want to figure out do I rent or do I buy. And where? Where's a good place to look?"

"Wow. Well, it's about time. But wow," Holly said.

Marisol became thoughtful. "The first thing I think you should look for is a rental versus buying."

"She's right. You'll have a better idea of what you want when you do buy a house. Besides, right now, it's a seller's market. Give it a little time before you make a house-size investment. If I were you, I'd look over near where you work. There are a couple of places right off Fourteen Mile. They aren't apartments; they're condos, and there are always condos for rent."

"I know where you mean. That's actually within walking distance to work," Christina mused.

"I'm not saying there and only there, but that's a place to start," Holly said.

Christina took in a strong breath. "Okay. You're right; it's a start."

"Do you want us to help you? We can," Marisol advised.

Christina thought a moment. "No. Thank you, but no. I need to just do this myself."

Marisol's phone chirped with a text. "Sweet," she said and grinned big. "We need to get our asses in gear. I got us an appointment." She stood. "Holly and I will be getting our eyebrows done, but you, my darling, will be getting your who-ha waxed."

"Garrett's sister's salon?" Holly asked.

Marisol nodded. "She can squeeze us in, but we need to get a move on."

"What do you mean, my who-ha?" Christina said.

"This is all part of it." Marisol got her coat on. "You are going to feel totally glamorously sexy. Rocco I. Gagliardi isn't going to know what hit his fine ass."

"Wait a minute. How is he going to know about my waxed who-ha?"

"He isn't. Well, unless you wear a short dress, go commando and relax your knees. And you'd have to be facing him," Marisol looked over at a horrified Christina, "yeah, I didn't think so. Like I said, he won't know, but you will. Now come on," Marisol said as she led a skeptical Christina out of the mall.

■■■

If she wasn't experiencing this personally, she would never have believed it. It was true; wearing the floral bustier, matching panties, and lace top stockings with a full Brazilian made her feel dazzling, sexy, and beautiful. She talked herself out of wearing more makeup than she usually would, and her dress was not sexy; it wasn't even snug. She paired a loose-fitting knit dress with ankle boots and a scarf. She left her hair long but pulled it back with a metal hairband that was nearly invisible. She knew she looked put together but not flashy.

As she walked up to the building, Tanya, her Beaumont's physical therapist buddy, stepped up next to her.

Tanya had dated Christina's brother, Calvin, a few years back. When they broke up, Christina and their mother were none too happy about it, knowing Cal did the breaking up. They told Cal they would be staying in touch with Tanya. He just rolled his eyes at them and said it would be the last time he brought a girl around until he found one to propose to. So far, he was a man of his word.

"You made it." Christina hugged her old friend.

"I did, and I was able to get two of the doctors to join us today."

"That's great."

"It is. The one doctor worked with the county Parks and Recreation people on an accessibility project. That's Dr. Henry. There is another doctor, too; he's kind of a glory hound, but I figured if there was ever the guy to get the hospital to underwrite something, this is the guy to have on your side. His name is Baxter Grandville. You will know who I'm talking about immediately when you see him. He always looks like he thinks he's being photographed."

"Oh, fun. Can't wait," Christina smirked as they entered the building.

Stepping into the entryway, Christina was awed. It wasn't overdone, but Rocco Gagliardi's offices were impressive. The lobby was a two-story affair with a split spiral staircase that led to the second level that overlooked the floor below. It was all granite, marble, and wood, screaming *I'm expensive and won't be going anywhere.*

Tanya looked around and said, "Should I prepare to curtsy?"

"This is my first visit. This is what I want my wealth management company to look like if I ever had the wealth to manage," Christina said.

As Rocco exited the elevator, both women were busy looking at the Murano blown glass chandelier. Christina felt his eyes on her as he walked over to greet his guests. He wasn't smiling, but she got the feeling he rarely did. Instead, there was a warmth to his countenance as he said, "Good morning." Not ignoring Tanya, but definitely directing his attention to Christina.

The undergarments and estheticians' treatment were doing their thing. Christina was oozing the confidence she worried she lacked as she introduced Tanya and explained that there would be two doctors joining them through Tanya's efforts."

"I hope that doesn't throw the lunch plans off," Christina said.

"It doesn't. I'm impressed that you could get doctors here on such short notice." Rocco said.

"I have a confession," Tanya looked between Christina and Rocco. "Dr. Henry is a personal friend and always interested in this sort of project. Getting him here wasn't ever a problem. I pulled out a picture of Christina here for Dr. Grandville, and he cleared his calendar."

Tanya giggled, Christina looked confused, and Rocco stiffened.

Tanya looked over at Christina. "*Yep*, still the same, Christina. No idea that you could turn the heads you turn."

Rocco looked at his Nero's brunette; she was a beautiful pink blush and so uncomfortable it was almost funny. He wanted to tell Christina he thought she was beautiful, that she was breathtakingly beautiful the first time he saw her in Nero's and at Pinkie's, then at the coney island and for sure when he stopped to fix the tire. *Yeah*, creepy. He also wanted to poke this Dr. Grandville in the eyes with his fists, but that couldn't happen. However, he did decide to keep Christina as close as he dared. That meant getting her upstairs and settled before the good doctor showed up. "Well, ladies, shall we?" Rocco gestured to the elevator.

■■■

Rocco's efforts to keep Christina away from Dr. Grandville paid off. This wasn't all that easy. The doctor was slippery, and he openly flirted with Christina. That didn't go unnoticed by anyone in the room. Rocco was incensed. When that happened, Bruno picked up on his brother's energy shift and sent him a text that Rocco covertly read.

Bruno: Dude, why didn't you tell me she's your girl? I would have fixed it, so Dr. Dumbass's seat was as far from Christina as possible.

Rocco: too late now.

Bruno: Doesn't matter. She's not into him. Look at her face when he opens his mouth – it's like the guy farted. Besides, the posse from Holtzberg looks like they want to beat the crap out of him for even talking to her.

Rocco began to read the room in earnest. The Little *Polpetto* was right; Dr. Grandville wasn't enjoying much celebrity. Not that the doctor appeared to notice.

Christina's beautiful face *seemed to blanch whenever* the doctor opened his mouth. Still, Christina was now aware, just as Rocco was, that the douche nozzle didn't come to the table empty-handed. He was the keystone to having the hospital on board. Rocco noticed the Holtzberg men. *Yup.* They didn't like him, but no one could afford to blatantly offend the doctor.

By 1:00 p.m., the action items were assigned; the next meeting was scheduled, and the meeting closed. Bruno was instantly at Christina's side, ushering her from the conference table through the never-used side entrance. Rocco didn't think Bruno knew the key codes around the office, but he clearly did.

As he rose to speak to the Holtzbergs, Rocco got a text message from Bruno letting him know Christina would be in his office. Rocco wanted to laugh out loud at the audacity. Instead, he spoke to Doug Holtzberg to let him know Christina's whereabouts.

Doug gave a tight nod to Doctor Grandville, turned to Rocco, and said, "Thank you. She'll need a ride back. You'll take care of that?"

"Yes. I'll take care of it personally," Rocco assured.

Doug smiled warmly. "Thank you. And thank you for getting in touch with us about this project. It's going to be something special."

Bruno appeared in the conference room doorway and made a beeline to Tanya handing her a note. He then turned to intercept Dr. Grandville, leading him out of the conference room as if Bruno was stage manager at a rock concert.

Rocco could hear women's voices and laughter coming from his office. Mimi Rangel, the administrative assistant who handled HR for this office, and Christina were amiably chatting like old friends as Rocco stepped into the room.

Bruno zipped past his brother to stand next to Mimi. "Hey, sorry," he nodded to Christina and turned to Mimi, "can you help me, please? I'm supposed to give Luther the tax file, but I don't know which shared drive I need to be looking at."

"Oh, of course, no problem," Mimi said to Bruno. She turned and said, "Christina, so glad to meet you. We should do lunch, *yeah*?"

"We should," Christina fished out a business card, "you call me, or I'll call you."

Bruno and Mimi left Rocco and Christina alone. Both were quiet, silently watching the two retreating figures out of the office and down the hall.

"Why do I feel like the last ten minutes were taken from a Marx Brother's movie?" Christina said, not looking even a little annoyed.

"You know Marx Brother's films?" Rocco asked.

She cocked her head and eyed him.

Rocco cleared his throat, just a little uncomfortably. "My brother believed he was on a rescue mission."

She chuckled. “That Dr. Grandville is rather taken with himself. I don’t think he understands. I will ask Tanya to explain that I’m only a foot soldier for this project. In any case, I do have to thank your brother. Grandville was annoying.”

Rocco liked her take but offered no more about Doctor Dickface and instead said, “I hope you don’t mind that I’ll have to drive you back to work,”

“I don’t want to disrupt your day any more than I already have. I can uber.”

“It’s not at all a disruption. I was hoping to catch up with you,” Rocco said as he drank in the sight of her. She was spectacular.

“Yes, I was hoping to catch up with you too, Mr. Gagliardi, wealth manager, charity sponsor,” she leveled a look coupled with a smirk, “tire fixer. I’m a little curious about that last item on the list of your talents.”

Rocco lowered his head and looked sheepishly up at her through the longest thickest eyelashes Christina had ever seen.

He knew it had to come up, but he wasn’t ready to have that conversation with her. Not just yet. “Ms. Pentelino, would you indulge me, please? You are due an explanation. May I suggest we have that discussion over dinner in six weeks?”

"In six weeks? Why six weeks? And what date exactly?" She asked.

Rocco straightened to his full height, looking more like he was preparing for Christina to land a blow. "February 14th."

"Valentine's Day? Seriously? What if I have plans for that day?" Christina said.

"If the plans are with family members, we could amend dinner plans to February 15th."

She shook her head, but she was smiling. That had to be a good sign, he guessed.

"What if I have a significant other?" She lifted an eyebrow and smirked at him.

He narrowed his eyes, only considering for a second, then said, "I don't believe you do. I don't believe you would have indulged me this long if you had a significant other."

Christina smiled. "You're right. Fine, I will hear this explanation of yours on the 14th of February."

"Until then. Are you free next Saturday?" he asked.

She began to say something, then stopped, "I don't...I shouldn't..." she started, then asked. "What is it you have in mind?"

"Dinner."

"Dinner?"

"Yes, dinner," he steeled his gaze and said, "at Nero's in Windsor."

She took in a breath; *of all the places, she thought.* This was probably not a good idea, and that look on his face made him look dangerous. "Okay. Yes," she said tentatively.

Bruno arrived in the doorway with Christina's coat. Rocco took it from him and helped Christina put it on.

Bruno gave Christina a mock salute; then, he turned so only Rocco could see him and waggled his eyebrows as he headed out of Rocco's office.

Rocco rolled his eyes at his baby brother but gifted him with a rare smile.

That warmed Bruno. He hadn't been around either of his brothers all that much. Rocco hadn't had a girlfriend around since... since they lost Caterina. Bruno didn't really pay attention to what Franco or Rocco did, particularly not back then. Bruno knew everyone thought Francine was hella gorgeous, but Bruno remembered Caterina really hated Francine there at the end. Caterina told Bruno not to be *taken in* by either Francine or their cousin Roberta. Bruno didn't get it back then. Now? Now it was obvious to him that Roberta and Francine had a thing for each other. It didn't surprise Bruno that Rocco wasn't eager to get close to a woman after being burned like that. Now? Now, it looked like Rocco wanted to get into the race, and Christina seemed to Bruno like the perfect starting line. Francine may have been good-looking, but Christina was hot AF and had the body to make a priest's clerical collar awfully tight. She knew how to handle herself if the meeting today was any indication.

Midway down the hall, Bruno heard Rocco's voice. It was low and deep. Nothing out of the ordinary there. But there was something else about it, something different. It reminded Bruno of his father's tone when his dad spoke to Bruno's mother. A tenderness reserved only for her. Bruno turned around to see Rocco guiding Christina out of his office. Rocco's face gave the whole thing away. Bruno suppressed a belly laugh, and in a voice too low for anyone else to hear, he said, "Brother, you are so done for."

■■■

"Get the fuck out of here," Marisol said.

"I'd say what she said, but I don't talk like that then kiss my parents," Holly said, "but, no kidding? Did you ask him to take you there?"

"He picked the restaurant," Christina said,

"What do you think inspired that?" Marisol asked.

"He didn't offer any explanation. And I was too stunned to question it. Besides, what would I say? Oh, and by the way, my last boyfriend sort of asked me to marry him at that particular venue. The last thing I want to bring up is Neville and the ghost proposal of dinner dates past."

"Hey, have you heard from S'Neville?" Holly asked.

"S'Neville?" Christina looked between her friends, who instantly put their heads down. "No way, you call him S'Neville behind my back?"

"Has he?" Marisol asked.

"He texts here and there. I delete them. If he hasn't gotten the message, sooner or later, he will. I find it endlessly fascinating that he texts me now that we aren't together. Something he rarely did when we were," Christina said ruefully. She then broke into a fit of giggles.

"What?" Marisol wondered.

"S'Neville, that's funny," Christina said.

"I never thought you'd be yucking it up this soon after your breakup," Holly said.

"I think it's because I wasn't all that invested. I got that pearl of wisdom from my mom about this, and then there are the significant life events I'm living through," Christina said as she produced a receipt from the Sleep Number store.

"What's this?" Holly asked.

"The receipt for my new bed." Christina was now scrolling through her phone gallery. Then held up the iPhone for her friends.

"What are we looking at?" Marisol said, squinting.

"This is my new front door," Christina handed the phone to Holly, who scuttled closer to Marisol. "Keep scrolling. The next picture is of the kitchen; then it should be the master bedroom sans the bed-the bed that's being delivered in three weeks."

"Wait, you moved?" Marisol looked at Christina as Holly kept scrolling.

"I moved," Christina said with an air of smug satisfaction.

"When?" Marisol asked.

"How?" Holly went through the pictures once more.

"I mentioned that I was looking for a nearby rental at work. Doug knew someone with condo rentals not even a quarter-mile from the office. The guy Doug knew was a very nice man. Anyway, he showed me the two condos he currently had for rent. The one I loved, he said, was difficult to rent because it was a carriage house unit. That's just a fancy way of saying it's over the garages of the other units, and there is a flight of stairs to walk up. I love it." She gushed. "It's two bedrooms and two baths. There's a big eat-in kitchen with a fireplace in the living room and in the master. There's a balcony that overlooks the pool. And there is a laundry room in the garage, my garage. I didn't have to do a credit check because of Doug Holtzberg. That meant I could practically move the next day. Dan and Dean had two guys take a truck and move me in."

Holly's mouth hung open. "You're all moved in."

"Unreal." Marisol shook her head. "How do you like it?"

"I'll like it better when my bed is delivered because I'm sleeping on my twin bed from my mom's house. And I need to do some decorating and get the rest of my clothes. I only took my winter clothes. I haven't had the chance to like it or not like it, not yet. There's been so much to do. Not that it's a bad thing. I like setting things up the way that I like them. I never considered that before. I never knew. I sort of hated that. At Mom's house, unless it's in the kitchen, everything is either in a drawer or closet. I like having my toiletries out where I can reach them when I need them. I like having a dedicated space for my sewing, so I don't have to put it all away when I'm done for the evening. I have the second bedroom for that now." Christina looked up to notice her friends, eyes a little wide and mouths open.

"What?" Christina asked.

"You went from zero to sixty in a nanosecond," Holly said.

"Not that there is anything wrong with that. It's wonderful, but how come you didn't let us in on any of this?" Marisol asked.

"It all happened so fast and during a workweek. I started to hit pause, but then I thought, why? It's not like I can't move if I hate it. It's a six-month lease, not a thirty-year mortgage. And... not that I'm happy to admit this, but Neville's comments really got to me."

"Why? What did he say?" Marisol asked.

Holly huffed, "The *didn't you ask your mother* comments." She turned to Christina, "Right?"

"Yes. Right. I did talk to her about it. Not a should I; shouldn't I, but we talked, and she did encourage me. When the opportunity presented itself, it was me, myself, and I that made the decision. It felt pretty good, I must say," Christina told them.

"Okay, boss lady, when are we invited over?" Holly asked.

"Sunday. I'll need to debrief the Nero's date with you guys," Christina said as she got up to order another round.

"What if he's not out of the condo that early?" Marisol said, earning her a pinch on the thigh from Holly. "Ouch. Hey."

"Don't go pressuring her. One mountain at a time," Holly said.

Chapter 12

I Want You to Want Me

Cheap Trick

Nigel threw his head back and laughed.

Neville scoffed and said, “I’ll remember this when you get your ass handed to you.”

This brought on more laughter, and a couple of hardy guffaws before Nigel settled enough to respond, but he did respond, “First of all, she didn’t strike you. No punches were exchanged. She didn’t clean out your bank account; she didn’t embarrass you with your peers. She did nothing more than call it off. That she didn’t call it off the second after you took back the engagement ring is a testament to her goodness and character."

"I never took back the engagement ring. I was having it resized," Neville sniffed.

"Unless you were switching out that crappy little diamond chip for something more in keeping with an actual engagement ring, brother, you are lucky her family didn't come after you."

"I don't want to talk about the goddamned ring. I want some help."

Nigel eyed him, "To do what exactly?"

"I want to understand the real reason she did it."

"What did she tell you?" Nigel asked.

"She said the relationship wasn't working for her, and she didn't want to string me along when there was no future in it," Neville said disgustedly. "What does that mean anyway? The relationship isn't working."

"Seriously, Neville, you don't see it? You treat her like she's a dolt. From what I hear, she's involved in a huge charitable effort, AND she's part of the management for Holtzberg's. One of my friends at Crain's, who knew you dated Christina, said they are doing a feature on her because she's snagged a *Thirty under Thirty* award. I know you were too busy disparaging Holtzberg's and her role there, but you'd be alone thinking that her job was something disposable."

Neville laughed dismissively. "Crain's is probably just promoting Holtzbergs or their charity; it has to be a Holtzberg thing. They are heavy into their pet community projects. It was that and not Christina, I can assure you."

"God, when did you become such a petty little...."

Neville stiffened.

Nigel caught his brother's reaction and stopped himself. Nothing good could come out of finishing that thought. Instead, he said, "I'm sorry it didn't work out with Christina, but there is a world beyond her. Next time you'll find a better fit."

"I don't want another girl. I want Christina," Neville ran his fingers through his hair and said, "she won't do well in the spotlight. She'll be too anxious to be able to handle that type of attention."

"Neville, did you ever consider that you don't really know her?"

"That is the entire problem. I am the only one who does know her. Thank you, you've clarified what my next move is," Neville said, punctuating the comment by getting up and taking his leave of Nigel, who shook his head.

Chapter 13

Wonderful Tonight

Eric Clapton

Rocco thought she might still live with her folks. She gave off that vibe, sort of like a few of his female cousins; their fathers didn't even want them to go to colleges out of the area. When he thought about it, almost all of his female cousins were sent to college more like finishing school so that a potential husband could appreciate a well-educated potential wife. Christina had more going on than that; she was more than just arm candy.

This got him thinking about Caterina and if Caterina would have been polished up to get her married off. He laughed inwardly. Even though his mother and dad were as old school as they were, Caterina would never have put up with it. Instead of having her in some completely inconsequential job at the family business, Caterina would have found her own way.

That made him consider Bruno. Bruno was initially in that same place, an utterly inconsequential job at the family business, but... But Bruno was more, and he was proving it all the time.

Rocco's smile was as much from the happy thoughts of Bruno as the radiant Christina opening her door as Rocco was about to ring the doorbell.

"I'm ready," she said as she locked the condo's deadbolt and turned to follow Rocco to his SUV.

She was bundled up, but, as wrapped up as she was, the coat cinched at the waist showed off her curves, and the hat framed her beautiful face. Tonight she was wearing lipstick: nothing too dramatic, just something different than he recalled seeing on her before. She didn't wear much makeup in general – she didn't have to. She had a healthy glow to her. With a clear complexion, dark eyes, and eyelashes that outlined those beautiful eyes, she didn't need more. This close, he took in her scent. It was subtle, he noticed before, but only when he was close to her. It smelled clean and uncontrived. He wanted to hold her at arm's length just to drink her in and still hold her close to feel her warmth and take in her scent.

He helped Christina into the SUV. She was so hot. His cock got a little hard just being next to her. She was built differently than his usual hookup type. This included Francine. Christina was taller with a more generous body, an adult woman's build. He had to acknowledge he was far more attracted to Christina's body type than the other. He pondered that for a moment. Was it Christina herself, or did he purposely choose women who didn't check all the boxes to keep them at a distance? He may never know the answer to that question, and for now, he didn't need to. For now, he'd just enjoy the evening and the woman.

This evening, crossing the border to Windsor via the tunnel wasn't much of a hassle. They were walking into Nero's just before seven o'clock.

He wasn't sure why he wanted to get her back to Nero's. He had several different thoughts on the matter. On the one hand, he wanted to see if the venue sparked a memory of that night. On the other hand, he wanted to give her a wonderful dinner experience to replace that other time with that other man.

The reservation included Rocco's request for a table by the window. They watched as an ore carried cut its way through the iridescent winter waters of the Detroit River. Christina hummed her appreciation of the view, the river, and Detroit's skyline.

Rocco ordered the Nero d'Avola wine before he recalled that she would think it was the house wine.

Christina sampled the wine and nodded her approval. "Your house wine is truly wonderful," she said to the sommelier.

"This isn't the house, ma'am. The house is fine for a less discriminating palate. This particular wine is usually overlooked but one of my favorites," the sommelier said.

"I may have misunderstood. I was here once before, and I know this was the same wine I had then – it is wonderful. I probably misunderstood and thought it was your house." She took another sip and smiled at the sommelier.

Rocco toyed with the idea of fessing up. He was just about to rat himself out when Christina looked across the room to the table she had occupied with that bone head ex-boyfriend. Rocco cleared his throat but was interrupted by their waiter. The waiter introduced himself, began explaining the specials for the evening, and talked a bit about the desserts.

Christina listened intently and asked, “What would you recommend?”

The waiter smiled. “The rib eye with the zip sauce. It’s perfection.”

“Sounds great. May I have that medium-rare?” She then stopped cold and looked at Rocco for approval.

It made Rocco want to find the dick head ex-boyfriend and slap the snot out of him for causing Christina to believe she needed permission to order her own dinner. *The fuckhead.* Rocco said to himself, but to Christina, he said, “Order what you like the way you like it, Patatina; oh, order the Black Truffle Butter.”

Her face lit up, and she did include that wonderful delicacy.

After Rocco had ordered and the waiter left them, she looked at him and asked, “Did you just call me potato?”

He winced and laughed self-consciously, “I meant no disrespect.”

“I didn’t take it like that. I was just giving you a poke. My mother’s maiden name was Gentile. My grandmothers’ maiden names were Conti and Alfano, respectively. My mom is second generation, and so was my dad. I understand the endearment. I may not be fluent, but I've had a lifetime of hearing Italian. I understand it and probably can even write it."

"I know we don't know each other very well, but I've had the feeling that you and I have a similar cultural background," Rocco smiled.

"I get that about you too. I sometimes feel I have to suppress the parts of myself that people might find a little too Italian, even with my closest friends. This, with you, feels really... I would say comfortable, but it's more than that."

He sat back, let out a breath, looked at her, and said, "I never put it into words, but I have thought that same thing so many times. And it's liberating to not have to censor myself. It's very *at-home* with you too."

She blushed.

"I don't mean to make you uncomfortable. You're blushing," he said.

"I'm a blusher. But not all my blushes are born out of embarrassment or discomfort. This," she pointed to her cheeks, "is from my pleasure in hearing you say that."

The waiter came by to refill their wine glasses just before the first course was served, and then there was a suspension of any heavy conversation.

The dinner they shared settled into what was the norm for both of them. It was the same as any family meal; the conversation was simple, light, and thoroughly enjoyable.

When the dishes were being cleared away and the dessert menu was presented, Christina said, "I cannot eat an entire dessert."

"Have a little of mine then?" Rocco offered as he ordered the chocolate cake with raspberry sauce.

"This has been a wonderful evening." She stilled, unsure she should share more, but the wine made the disclosure easier. "I've been here before, but that evening wasn't as pleasant as this evening. That had more to do with the company than the dinner."

The waiter brought the coffee and cake and left as Rocco encouraged her, saying. "Tell me if you want to."

"There isn't all that much to tell. I dated a man, Neville Eastburn, for a better part of a year...."

Rocco mentally rolled his eyes, *Neville? He even sounded like a douche.* He said to himself, But he told her, "Go on."

"I don't think I gave the relationship much thought until Neville took me to dinner here and gave me a ring. It was supposed to be an engagement ring. But he never actually asked me to marry him, and he took the ring off my finger about a half-second after he put it on. It was the strangest thing."

"What is this Neville to you now?" Rocco asked, hoping he understood the situation as well as he thought.

She paused and said, "I don't want to say he's nothing. That seems cold for a relationship that lasted the months it lasted. I didn't end it immediately, but that dinner pointed me to the exit with him." She looked down at her hands nervously. "I ended it the afternoon after you changed the tire."

This piece of information made him want to yell some victory anthem, pick her up and carry her off to claim her. He kept it in check.

"I know we've agreed on your explanation happening on Valentine's Day. I can live with that agreement, but I really wish I understood your reaction to me that day," she said.

Rocco would pretty much do anything for her, but he quietly told her, "Please indulge me."

She nodded, "It will be as we agreed."

"But… " Rocco turned to her and took her hands, "between now and then, I'd like to see you."

"See me? More than at the meetings for Caterina's Memorial?"

He sighed. "I'm not good at this, Christina. I'm not conversant in the language of dating or relationships. The last real relationship I had was like a decade ago. My focus has been on my family's company. When I do go out, it is for our business. I want something different with you. I want to get to know you, to date you. I hope you can look past my clumsiness at this and make time for me. If it's a hard no for you, I'll understand, and that will have no impact on what we do for the event for Caterina's memorial."

From the moment he took her hands in his, she felt the electricity between them. It should have forced the *hard no* from her, but instead, she found herself unable to do more than nod her agreement.

No to the no. He wanted to celebrate. But now, it was his hard cock he had to deal with. He felt like some kind of an animal over it, beastly, and thought if Christina knew, she would be out the door, and the whole thing would be for nothing.

The table shielded her eyes from his lap, and the obvious erection his pants did nothing to hide. Rocco calmed himself and brought up the one thing he wanted to settle this evening.

"There's a playground equipment group in Muskegon. They sell product lines, but they have the capability of fabricating as well. I contacted the owner earlier this week to discuss the type of equipment we're interested in for the playground we want to build. He, Mark Jefferies, invited us for a visit. I'd rather it was just you and me, but if you can't come along, then I'll ask Doug or one of the sons to go. But, I'm hoping you'll agree." Rocco said.

"What day were you thinking of going?" she asked.

"I've got a pretty full week, so Mark agreed to a Saturday visit. Next Saturday."

"That's actually better for me too. Sure, I'll go." She smiled, still blushing.

Chapter 14

The Dream's in the Ditch

Deer Tick

Living with his parents should have felt uncomfortable. It didn't. Bruno's room was the same one he had as a boy. He liked it. It felt safe. When Caterina was released from the rehab hospital to come home, her room was moved to Franco's old room, closer to her parents. Franco's old room was next to Bruno's. The move didn't have the same significance to anyone else as it did to Bruno. In his head, he understood why Caterina took over Franco's old room, but in his heart and soul, he believed she was moved nearer to him so he could be near her.

Until the day he was shipped off to college, he was Caterina's companion. Not that it was easy watching his sister slowly but steadily fade. She knew it, and from the day she was released from the rehab hospital, she was the only realist about her situation. Something that made everyone around her uncomfortable and angry. Bruno was downright depressed. Caterina dealt with him every time the angsty Bruno showed up. "If you are going to behave like this is a bigger problem for you than it is for me, there's the door," she told him.

He'd think about that every now and then. Caterina might have been the sweet little Gagliardi lady. Still, she wouldn't tolerate her parents treating her like she was a baby, her big brothers acting like she was so fragile she'd break, or the little *meatball* acting like someone crapped in his Cheerios. That was Caterina's speak for him feeling sorry for himself.

She was so brave, and he was a chicken shit. No one ever came out and said it, but Caterina and Nonna came the closest to landing that punch.

When Nonna appeared in his room that day after he got home from college, telling him he stunk and to clean up so that he was fit to join the family for dinner, it wasn't her words that hit the mark. Nope, it was the tone and delivery – just exactly like something Caterina would say when she had had enough of his shit. And just as if it was Caterina, it always came in twos. It was their way. First, Caterina would chide him. It would be a little swipe about some dumbass thing he was doing that she noticed and didn't like. Bruno would do the minimum to get her off his back; things would normalize. And that would be that... for a while. Then it would become evident that he didn't fix the problem, just whitewashed it. Caterina would go nuts with him and unload both barrels. After one of those second confrontations, he'd acquiesce and straighten up, and even if he didn't get it just right, it would be close enough.

Nonna's verbal beat down wasn't nearly an ass-kicking as what Bruno would get from Caterina but definitely in the ballpark. Weirdly, Bruno loved every minute of Nonna's tirade. He closed his eyes during the worst of it, and Caterina was right there.

As for Nonna's anger and disgust, he knew she was right. He had been a big baby. Part of it was his way of saying to himself that he was justified in his actions. He was hurting, and if he was hurting, everyone just needed to back the fuck off.

Nonna may not have read him right, but that didn't matter. What mattered was he needed to stop it. First, stop the pity party, and then, the big one, he needed to stop acting as if working with his family was caving in and not being his own man. It wasn't an immediate epiphany, but by the time he had a week under his belt working at the west side office, he knew two things. One, it wasn't his family that made him feel like an outsider – he had done that to himself. Two, he had something to offer, something to contribute. He may not be the business brain that Rocco was or have the talent with marketing that Franco had, but he was smarter than he thought before. He had skills. The people at the office initially acted like they weren't happy he was there. Over the weeks, it had changed. Bruno knew it had. It started out small, but after the first month, he was invited to lunch by some of the relationship management group. Mostly it was the younger guys, Bruno really liked them, and they had started to include him in their client meetings.

Rocco was very happy about this; Bruno heard that piece of information from a few people, including Rocco himself. Even the older women who treated him like the turd in their punch bowl when he was first introduced were nice to him. The one woman, Annamaria, who had been there since

Eisenhower was president, now brought him cannolis every Friday. She also showed him how to generate a report that Rocco had asked for. Annamaria helped him become proficient with the Access program to create another report Bruno wanted. She was the last domino to fall in his quest to fit into the office.

During his first week on the job, he could hear her bitching about him in Italian. Bruno was not fluent, not at all, but he knew enough to be offended by Annamaria's verbal jabs. At first, he thought he would tell Rocco about it. That thought went through his mind, and he heard his sister's disgusted dismissal.

It wasn't that this was an isolated occurrence, hearing Caterina telling him off. It occasionally happened during the first few years she was gone, but lately, she was giving it to him full tilt, mainly since Nonna gave him the second smackdown. It happened when he acted stupid or was a baby; then he'd hear Caterina. *Brain donor,* she'd say, or if he was acting like a baby. It was, *ah, go suck a pacifier.*

The first couple of times he heard her annoyed him, but lately, he loved it, particularly since she also told him when he got it right. Then it was, *See, you aren't always an infant,* or *I knew you had more brains than God gave a goose, little*

Poletto. That might have made him cry, but that was before. Now it made Bruno smile.

Chapter 15

First Day of My Life

Bright Eyes

Marisol had the scones. Holly had a thermos full of tea. They made themselves at home in Christina's living room as Christina lit the fireplace.

"This is really nice," Marisol said.

"It is. I love the master bathroom. So many places have the dinkiest bathrooms. You did good, girly," Holly told her.

"Yeah, and the kitchen is my personal favorite. You have plenty of room, and I'm jealous of the counter space." Marisol arranged the scones. "So, spill, girl. Was going to Nero's, weird?"

Christina smiled that rare smile that showed off her dimples. “It was wonderful. I even told him about Neville, and it wasn’t awkward at all. That surprised me. I liked that he didn’t bash Neville.”

“No. Bashing S’Neville is our job.” Marisol pointed between Holly and herself.

“What did he say about Neville?” Holly asked.

“He wanted to know if Neville meant anything to me. That was as far as that conversation got. I felt like he understood the entire Neville thing. Anyhow, the evening was great top to bottom, and we are going to see a playground manufacturing company this coming Saturday.” Christina sighed.

■■■

That Saturday morning, Rocco’s senses woke up the minute he walked into her condo. It was the kitchen's warmth and the delicious smell of the baked goods. It was like, just like, his Nonna’s kitchen.

Christina had greeted him at her door, asking for a moment. He followed her up the stairs and into a small vestibule that looked into a comfortable front room. He followed Christina into her inviting kitchen.

Christina now faced him, “I hope this is okay; I baked cornetti for us, and I’m bringing some coffee too.”

Rocco was a little stunned and very pleased. "I was planning on stopping for breakfast, but this is perfect to tide us over until we find a good place. Thank you, Christina, this was thoughtful, and it smells so good; I don’t want to leave your kitchen. Can I help with anything?”

She was blushing again. “I need to pack everything up. That will just take a minute.” She smiled prettily and filled a cloth tote.

Rocco marveled at her. It wasn’t that the women of his acquaintance were selfish or less than mindful. They were perfectly socially acceptable. However, not a one of them would have thought to bring anything more than themselves, much less coffee and baked goods. If they did, he knew the baked goods would not be fresh out of their kitchen’s oven at the crack of dawn.

He and Christina were in Rocco’s SUV and on the road a few moments later. They drank the coffee for the next couple of hours, chatted, and ate Christina’s heavenly cornetti with blood orange marmalade.

Rocco's plan was to stop for breakfast, but he found himself outside MDJ Playscapes more than an hour early.

"Christina, I'm so sorry; the time got away from me, and we're here. We are really early; I thought we'd need extra time for breakfast," Rocco said.

"I'm not hungry, but I'll just get a coffee if you are."

"I'm not hungry either; that was an exceptionally fine breakfast. My Nonna would be impressed. But now we have time to kill," Rocco said.

"Can we drive into town? It's supposed to be really pretty. Lots of public art," Christina said.

"Sure, perfect. How do you know that? Have you been here before?

"Nope, never." She covered her face, embarrassed. "I haven't actually been to many places, so if I get to go somewhere, I always Google wherever it is. Like the ten best things to see in... well, in Muskegon. That's where I read about the public art."

"That's a savvy move." Rocco smiled over at her. Yep, she was blushing. "So, where have you been, and where do you want to go?"

"Well, let me see. I've been to Windsor, Canada," she said, winking at him, "I've only been to places in southeastern Michigan and Windsor."

That surprised him. "Where would you like to go?"

"Where wouldn't I like to go?" She let out a breath. "I want to go to Italy. I want to go to the village where my grandparents came from, Tagliacozzo. I want to see Rome, Florence, and Venice, of course. But I want to visit Tagliacozzo. After that, I want to visit just about everywhere in the world. Where have you been?'

"I've had to travel because of our business; I've been to many places, but not in the way I'd prefer. I've been lucky enough to have visited where my great, great grandparents hail from. I've been to Italy a few times, and I don't think I will ever get enough of it."

"I'm jealous. But someday, I'll get there. Oh, look there on your left. I think that's the sculpture in the center of town."

■■■

The time flew by, and Rocco pulled the SUV into the MDJ's' Playscape parking lot a few minutes before the appointed time.

Mark Jefferies met them at the door, and for the next three hours, Rocco and Christina got an introduction to the world of playgrounds.

They had lunch with Mark and were back on the road. The conversation was good, and Rocco wouldn't have cared if the drive lasted hours more. And then. Then his phone announced *Vonda,* as in Vonda Pathenger's name, popped up on the screen.

He hadn't heard from her in a while, not that he was upset about that. Vonda's calls were almost always an invitation to hook up, but she had been good about taking no for his answer. And the answer, even before seeing Christina that first time at Nero's, was a definite no. He could make this short; he took the phone off hands-free and greeted Vonda in his most professional voice. Her response was a knowing but annoyed, "It's a bad time, isn't it? Call me; I need something for one of your clients."

Rocco almost referred Vonda to Mimi but decided against it. Instead, telling Vonda, "Sure, but Monday, *yeah*?"

The call ended, and Rocco took a quick look over at Christina. She probably hadn't been paying attention. She seemed busy with her own phone. He got the SUV's handsfree in place and put his phone in the holster for the rest of the way home.

They were almost at Christina's door when the handsfree phone announced *Frances* in Suri's voice.

Rocco quickly declined the call. But Caraleigh would not be put off. She called again, and an embarrassed and rattled Rocco swiftly tried to reject the call but instead answered it. Realizing his error, Rocco took the phone off Hands-Free and said, "Yes, How are you?" Not waiting for Caraleigh to respond. "I do need to speak with you. May I call you back?" Again not waiting for a response, he said. "Thanks." And this time, he did find the correct button, ended the call, and turned off the phone.

He turned to Christina, whose face said she wasn't buying it. *Fuck*, Rocco thought, then he cleared his throat and spoke. "That's someone I ran into at a Christmas party. She had recommended our firm to a family member. But I don't need to deal with that today." It wasn't a lie, just not the complete truth.

Christina looked dubious but accepting. Then went for a subject change, "It was a great idea visiting with Mark today. It gives us some answers. Thank you for including me," she said as she prepared to leave Rocco's SUV.

"Would you let me take you to lunch one day this week?" Rocco hurriedly asked.

She turned to him, blushed a little, and said, “Sure, what day were you thinking?”

“How about Tuesday?”

“Okay,” she said as she began to exit.

Rocco got out and moved to help her from the car.

Neither noticed Neville’s Ford Flex parked across the boulevard.

Rocco walked Christina to her door. He decided to be deliberate with her, intentional and measured. Rocco wanted to be invited into her condo, but a simple kiss on each cheek in the way of their Italian roots would have to do... for now. He pulled her close and kissed her. He waited until she opened her door before saying, “I’ll come for you at noon on Tuesday.” Rocco then turned for his SUV and the conversation he’d be having with Caraleigh.

■■■

Neville watched in shock. He didn’t believe that she had actually moved out of her mother’s home. He would never have found this out had it not been for the Facebook post Marisol put up a few days ago announcing *visiting my bestie Christina at her new address!* This was complete with pictures of those horrid women friends of Christina's. After Neville discovered that news, finding where Christina was now living wasn't too tricky. But there was a part of him that had difficulty with the concept. Christina wasn't the type to feel equal to the kind of independence she'd need to be living on her own.

Neville called that imbecile Danielle, one of Christina's coworkers, to get the details. Neville was cheered to discover that Danielle wasn't aware Christina had broken up with him. Danielle also didn't think it odd that Neville was asking where Christina was now living; Danielle was such a moron, but he was able to get almost every single detail out of the woman, down to Christina's new address and her landline number.

He thought he'd just come by to scope the place out when he watched in fascination as Christina got out of that big boat of an SUV. It looked like something a pimp would be driving. What was she doing? How far had she sunk since she ended things with him? More's the pity. And when the goon walked Christina to her door and kissed her, all the color drained from Neville's face, but he managed to get the car's license number.

He wouldn't confront her now. He'd do some more research. He'd find out who this thug goombah was. He'd have more ammunition before taking the subject with Christina ... again.

■■■

When Rocco turned his phone on in the absence of Christina, there were several more calls and now a string of texts from Caraleigh. He decided to get a little closer to home before he called her, and like the plug had been pulled, a new text came through. He turned off the phone to concentrate on driving and think about Christina, his new favorite daydream.

The trip home happened in only a few minutes. He needed to get some gas. As soon as he turned into the gas station, he turned his phone back on. The number of texts and calls from Caraleigh was almost frightening. He didn't have to dial her; oh no, she was calling as soon as the phone powered up.

"Caraleigh," he said, making an effort to be as neutral as possible.

"There you are. I thought you had been hurt or something. I am on my way to your house." Caraleigh's shrill voice made it possible not to use the phone's speaker option.

Rocco suppressed the growl forming and said, "You should turn around," but then realized, "what do you mean you were on your way to my house? How do you know where I live?"

She laughed. "Okay, maybe not where you live exactly, but I'm pretty resourceful. Don't bet against me. I can be at your doorstep in a matter of an hour."

He let out an exasperated breath, "You are not coming over. That's a statement of fact." He got out of the SUV, credit card in hand, to pump the gas. "Look, Caraleigh, there is no future with me. I've explained this to you before, so I'm surprised you continue to contact me."

"You don't have to be rude," she spat.

"If being rude will make the point, I'll be rude," Rocco said.

"This is because you're seeing someone else, isn't it?" She pouted.

"My personal life is none of your business. Now, after we hang up, I will be blocking your number. You will be escorted off the property if you show up at my office. I sincerely wish you all the best, but do not, Caraleigh, do not contact me again." Rocco hit the end button. Now so angry, he wanted to hit something.

Caraleigh lifted her head, looked, and looked again. The romance gods were absolutely smiling down on her. It was a sign because there he was at the gas station mere yards from where she was parked at the Square Lake and Telegraph Road strip mall where she was retrieving her dry cleaning. She thought he might live close by her mother and Richard's home just south of Square Lake Road. Before another moment passed, she redialed him.

Rocco should have thought better of it, but before he could, he picked up in time to hear Caraleight say, "I don't think you fully appreciate the clout my stepfather has, Mr. Gagliardi. I don't think you understand just who you are dealing with," Caraleigh cooed the harsh words.

"I am done." He hit the end button, and this time, he blocked the number.

Rocco was still trying to calm himself down when the phone rang once more. If this was Caraleigh again, he would lose his mind. He checked the number. "Bruno?" Rocco asked tentatively.

"Dude, are you okay? You sound a little..."

Rocco sagged into his seat, "I'm fine. What's up?"

"Mom mentioned she called a couple of times and couldn't reach you. That's what you get for having your phone on 24/7. I was dropping off some print work at that shop you like in Auburn Hills, so I figured I was close enough to check in on you and send Mom a proof of life picture, but if you're okay...."

"How close are you?"

"Like, maybe fifteen minutes out."

"Have you had dinner?" Rocco asked.

"No. You want to go to dinner?"

"Yes, Why don't you meet me at the Country Club?" Rocco said.

"Sure."

Rocco called his mother, reassuring her. The effort helped him calm down. He finished filling up the SUV and spent some time cleaning the front and back windows. That also gave him a moment to burn away some of the adrenalin from his Caraleigh encounter.

By the time he got back into the SUV, he was better settled driving the short distance to the Forest Lake Country Club.

Rocco was already seated when Bruno walked in and found him.

This was new for Bruno; he hadn't hung out with his brothers before. That was mainly because Bruno was closer to Caterina. And, if he was honest with himself, Bruno knew some of his habits and quirks were off-putting to Franco and Rocco. Rocco's invitation made him feel like he might actually be ready to sit at the adult table.

Rocco waved him over and got up to embrace his little brother. Another gesture that made Bruno feel like he was in the club, as it were.

"I thought you were in Muskegon today?" Bruno said as he seated himself.

"I was. I took Christina. We met with the owner of a playground manufacturer. It was a worthwhile trip. I didn't get much further than tracking that equipment maker down. I'll see if there are others at a drivable distance."

Bruno knew that just a few months ago, he would have focused on the fact that Rocco had taken Christina. That was the old and immature Bruno, so he asked his brother. "Did the manufacturer have what we are looking for?"

"Some of it, but they fabricate too. He, Mark Jefferies, really spent the time to get us familiar with what is available and what might have to be fabricated specifically for our project."

"I keep thinking this stuff is off the shelf, but it isn't, is it?" Bruno waived off the server, deciding against anything more than wine with dinner. Another adult decision. Bruno could see that Rocco was really engaged in the conversation with him; that was a rarity too.

"I don't have a total read on this yet, but I think almost everything that will truly be useful will happen because of the architectural elements and custom fabricated equipment. The next big move will be hiring an architectural firm. This is such a specialty project we may have to go out of state for the right firm. I don't know that for sure, just that it's possible. I'm a little concerned that Dr. Grandville sees this as a way to reward his friends by hiring his favorite architect, a firm that the hospital doesn't even use, which I found interesting. We'll be addressing that in a future meeting,"

"It's kind of a big deal, right? Why aren't you setting Doctor dumbshit straight, like now?" Bruno gave an audible *Tchah* to his question.

"Even if we could afford to insult him, we won't. I've worked this out with the Holtzbergs. We have a list of potential architects that we will request qualifications from. The committee will shortlist the firms. The doctor is only one vote, and since it's Holtzberg cash paying for the design work, they will have the last word on the subject."

Bruno nodded. "I hear Nonno. *Don't take advice from the man with no skin in the game.*"

"Right," Rocco smiled, "I never thought you listened."

"I listened. I just didn't see myself doing what you guys are doing."

Rocco sat back. "Are you sorry?"

"You mean sorry that I'm in the family business?"

"Yes, Are you?"

"I thought I would be. I thought all of it was a yawn. I thought if I had to be involved, I'd only do it until I could get back to my real life," Bruno's eyes brightened, "I don't know if I love it like you and Franco do, but I love being a part of it."

"Not to get too far ahead of anything, but you've become the best surprise. I don't know where you'll end up. It depends on what you gravitate to. You're really good at people-related things. That's the bedrock of our business. It's people, not money. That's what sets us apart. And, Jesus, Bruno, the work you're doing with the IT department . . . it's great."

Bruno was pleased with the assessment. Having popular Franco and businessman Rocco as older brothers made it seem like Bruno's only place was the back seat. This nod from Rocco felt momentous.

Dinner was better than pleasant for both. It was primarily about the office with a side dish of Caterina's memorial and a dash of other family gossip. Bruno never realized that Rocco could or would gossip. Rocco could, but it was after a more substantive conversation happened, and Rocco needed a glass of wine or two.

After dinner, the brothers walked to the valet stand, making plans for the coming week, when Rocco caught sight of Caraleigh across the road. She quickly got into her BMW, probably thinking Rocco didn't see her.

Rocco appraised this brother. No one would think they could be twins, not up close. At a distance was another thing. They had the same coloring and just about the exact same height. "Do you mind switching cars?" Rocco asked his brother.

"I can, but why?" Bruno gestured for the nearest valet to join them.

Rocco nodded to the BMW across the street. "You remember Caraleigh? Roma Café? She's angling to find out where I live. She must have followed me here – God, what a pain in the ass, not to mention creepy."

"I see. Sure. We'll figure out switching back later," Bruno said and politely explained to the valet what was needed.

Bruno got in the SUV, and Rocco hung back, out of sight. As Bruno drove off, the BMW pulled out behind him.

When Carleigh's tail lights dimmed in the distance, Rocco began chatting with the guys at the valet stand, asking if they noticed the woman in the BMW. There was some snickering and a little eye-rolling. Finally, the group's boss said, "When she figured she wasn't going to get in, she was trying to pay us off to see who you were having dinner with."

Another one in the group of four piped up, "She wanted to know if you bring women here. She told me she would pay me if I kept track. Gotta say that chick is whack."

Rocco did a swift calculation hoping he had taken care of these guys since he got the membership to the country club. There was going to be a nice little something and a call into the management to commend the service. "Thank you, all of you." He handed the valet a tip and went over to the valet boss. "Thanks again." Rocco pressed three large bills into the man's hand. "Take your crew out on me." Rocco left before there could be a protest.

As Rocco pulled into his garage, he thought about where Bruno would be on his trek back home to Grosse Pointe. He figured about now Bruno would be just past Twelve Mile. He imagined driving that stretch himself and looking over to his right and recognizing the approximate spot where he stopped to change the tire. He had driven by that spot a few times since that Sunday. It made him smile. He then let his thoughts go back to earlier that day, their trip to Muskegon and all things Christina.

He liked how she didn't put up some artificial barriers when he asked her out. She did that again when she accepted his invitation for lunch on Tuesday.

He knew she wasn't a pushover; he knew her affirmative responses weren't offered to be easy. He knew that because she wasn't calling, texting, or dropping in on him. She actually *was* hard to get. That was a truth told by actions. Unlike other women of his acquaintance, she wasn't demanding or even suggesting his next move. That might change. He wouldn't mind if it did, but for now, he was extremely happy she wasn't angling to make this like some sort of a chess match.

Once he got into his home, he took a shower, helped himself to some bourbon, and made himself comfortable. He scrolled through the pictures on his phone, finding the ones he took of Christina today under the guise of taking photos of the equipment Mark Jefferies showed them.

Two pictures were especially good: one of Christina, listening intently to Mark as he described the production process for the wheelchair swing. Christina was turned at the waist so that the image was of her generous backside and the profile of her breasts. The other picture was of her face. It was supposed to be a picture of a raised sandbox. The sandbox wasn't in the picture at all. Rocco zoomed in on Christina's beautiful face. God, she was so pretty; she would be a photographer's dream. She could have been a model with those eyes that weren't desperate for makeup, her translucent skin, and kissable lips. In the picture, she was laughing at something Mark had said. Rocco let it go because he was busy getting a photo of her. Mark hadn't overtly flirted with Christina, but it was a near thing. It stopped immediately once Mark understood Rocco's dark.

Rocco flipped back and forth between the two pictures of her. She was special. He wasn't about to miss his chance with Christina Pentelino. He would double down on cleaning up his unfinished business. He would win her, all of her.

■■■

Caraleigh kept up with Rocco's SUV from the moment he left the Country Club, and even after he headed south on I75, she lost track of him as soon as he passed Fourteen Mile Road. She was so sure he lived in Bloomfield Hills, and it had even been suggested that he lived within walking distance of Forest Lake Country Club; she was sure she had that right.

Nothing she had tried was working with him. She needed to figure out a different strategy: something that would get her in front of him and didn't rely on chance; something where she could demonstrate her value beyond recommending potential clients for his firm.

She needed to do some research and find a better path.

■■■

Neville slammed the cell phone on the granite countertop hard enough to shatter the screen and immediately cursed the person responsible for his frustration and thus his cracked cell phone screen.

"God damn you, Christina. I should return the ring and get myself a replacement phone," he bellowed to an empty room.

The truth of the matter took him back to the problem at hand: his golf buddy, the guy who worked for the Sheriff's Office but wouldn't look up the license plate to get Neville the name of the thug Christina was with this afternoon. Why this was a problem wasn't clear to Neville. They did it all the time on television. Neville suspected his golf buddy was not the buddy Neville thought he was, pulling such a prick move and leaving Neville in the lurch.

The phone remarkably still worked, and Neville's next call was to his brother.

Nigel saw his brother's name come up and decided to let it go to voice mail. He would take a side trip and swing by Neville's condo when he finished dropping off his last boxed food delivery to the 94-year-old woman living just outside Oxford, a task he was doing very late in the day.

Nigel's weekends were devoted to a little charity he developed. He got involved because one of his coworkers told him about the senior food program that didn't have the resources to deliver on the weekends. He didn't do anything immediately, but sitting at a Rochester restaurant with his dinner date that evening made him wince. Nigel couldn't shake the idea of people depending on food deliveries having to forgo weekend meals.

One of his best friends was a pastor at a large church in Lapeer. It didn't take a lot of strong-arming to get Peter the Pastor involved. After that, it was mild arm twisting, and Nigel had the program off the ground and paid for. The big push was finding volunteers to make the deliveries. He knew he couldn't ask others to do something he wouldn't do himself. So there he was Saturday and Sunday, usually from late mornings to early afternoons.

In the beginning, it was the joke between Peter and Nigel that the delivery schedule was the convenient excuse not to attend church. Not that Nigel would be a regular churchgoer to Peter's or any church. Something that Peter occasionally brought up to Nigel.

A couple of weeks in, and Nigel didn't see it as penance for missing church or a drudge. He found he liked the people he delivered to. After a year, a few of those folks passed on. There were always more people to fill in the schedule, but he did feel the loss. Still, he decided the positive in getting to know them was worth more than the pain of losing them.

Nigel has several favorites he delivered to on his weekend route, but this old dear was his number one.

She was living in a trailer parked on her nephew's property. The trailer wasn't much to look at on the outside, but Abbey Jones-Faber kept it clean as a whistle, neat as a pin. So many of the people he delivered to had challenges getting out of bed. They couldn't see as well as they might and had trouble getting around. All that meant their personal hygiene was sketchy, and daily chores didn't always get done.

Abbey's trailer smelled like fresh coffee in the mornings and clean laundry in the late afternoon. Nigel was never closer than a few feet, so he couldn't say for sure about her personal upkeep, but he thought she used a liberal amount of soap and baby powder. She may have been inching toward one hundred, but she was quick-witted and fun to visit. He called her Westminster Abbey or Downton Abbey, and she called him Nigel Godrich. The first time she called him that, he did a double-take. "Okay, Downton Abbey, how do you know that guy?"

She thought a second, shrugged, and said, "He's the Radiohead guy, right."

Nigel stared at her, mouth open.

There she was, all five foot zero of her bent over with osteoporosis, pinning him with eyes that needed new glasses and cataract surgery as she placed a balled-up fist on her hip and said, "I've got the internet on my phone. I stay current," she told him with a slight *Pfft*. It made him chuckle any time he thought about it.

Today, she was at the door the minute his foot hit the first step up to the trailer.

"I've got green tea if you have the time," Abby said as she shuffled toward the trailer's kitchen area.

"Sorry, I'm so late. I've got the time, thanks. What I want to know is if you are trying to distract me by offering me tea because you know I can whip you at cribbage?" Nigel taunted.

"Didn't I teach you a lesson with rummy?" She said as she brought the teapot to the table.

"Your play was suspect, madam," Nigel said as he unzipped his coat and shoved his gloves in his knit hat.

"Keep telling yourself that, Nigel Godrich. Now, come over and sit." She pointed to the chair and poured the tea.

"So, Downton Abbey, what's new and exciting? Did your nephew ever get his car running?"

"Didn't I tell you? My nephew moved. He's in Florida for the winter. He and this new wife of his are snowbirds now. They got a place in The Villages."

"Really? Isn't that the STD capital of Florida?" Nigel took a sip of tea.

"I thought you were far more enlightened than that, Mr. Eastburn. That is a myth perpetuated by an overreach by the New York Post. Statistically, Sumter County, where The Villages is located, is at the bottom of the list for their infection rate."

"The internet?" Nigel lifted an eyebrow.

"Of course. I had heard about the *Gomorrah of Central Florida*," Abbey said, adopting the cadence and tone of a fight promoter, "I wanted to see what Gary, my nephew, was getting himself into. The story should have been New York Post does lazy reporting, but..." she threw up her hands, "the toothpaste was out of the tube, so to speak."

"They should hire you to run down the veracity of the news they want to report."

She waived an arthritic hand. "Those hotshot news organizations have every option to research; I don't know if they are too lazy or arrogant to bother with a fact audit. Or, maybe it's more that they only come up with stories that support their opinions."

"I'm sure you're right. I dated a woman who wrote for a living," Nigel said.

"I'm sure you weren't averse to her being too fast." The old lady winked.

"Don't think you can embarrass me, Ms. Jones Faber; not going to happen. And yes, she was a little ADHD, and yes, that worked to my advantage."

"I thought so. You're a commitment-phobe," she said, but just as quickly added, "no, no, you aren't. If you were, you wouldn't be delivering food to people who probably don't remember getting their dinner week to week. You aren't afraid of the commitment, and a fine-looking specimen like yourself wouldn't be without company. So, what's you story? If that's too personal, blame it on my age, but answer the question."

He sat back, considering. "I don't really know. I don't mind my bachelorhood, but I wouldn't turn my nose up at a relationship. I suppose it comes down to not yet meeting the right one, and I refuse to settle."

"Did I ever tell you I was married four times?" she said earnestly, "and I have eight children."

"You have eight children, Abbey?"

"Only seven now, Robbie died in Viet Nam. My oldest are twins, a boy, and a girl, Patsy and Patrick, Junior. Both live in Washington State. After the twins is my son Rick; he's a retired cop in South Bend. Jimmy is South Beach, and Anthony is in South Dakota; those are my souths. I have two news: Kenneth and Ron live in New Hampshire and New Haven, respectively."

"None in Michigan, then?"

"Not a one. I followed my last husband here when I married him. The nephew is actually my ex-husband's nephew. Stan's family gave a care for me. If not, I'd be in a homeless shelter, I expect. My own children are rather annoyed I'm still alive and breathing. It would have been better for them if I hadn't outlasted the money I had put aside for my retirement. All my husbands are now dead. The first and the last were great husbands, the other two?" she shrugged, "the other two were not, but life never worked out that well for either. Sometimes Karma's a bitch, and I went to both funerals in a red dress and my best pearls. That was before the dress didn't fit, and I had to hock the pearls. After losing my last husband, I decided to dial the romance back and take care of any itch I needed to scratch with modern technology. That would be online porno and a vibrator. That's been working out fine."

"You leave me a little awestruck," Nigel chuckled.

"I didn't tell you all that to impress you. I told you all that to say, if you need someone to hear you out, give you advice if you want it, I come with loads of experience, and I'm not judgemental," Abbey said.

"I'm not the one with romance issues. When I'm ready to jump into the deep end of the pool, I will. But my brother? My brother is the guy who needs a willing ear; he'll never take advice, I'm afraid."

"Is he as smart and good-looking as you are?"

"*Ah*, thanks. I think he would pass muster in the looks department. He does okay career-wise, and I'm sure he'd be well above average if he took an IQ test. His problem is he really thinks he is the sun, and the woman he had been dating should be an orbiting planet."

"Was dating?"

"Yes, was. I don't know for sure, but she's probably moved on, and my brother refuses to accept that she could."

"Well, it's hard to live without the sun," she raised an eyebrow.

Nigel chuckled. "He, my brother, has been texting me all morning."

"Does he know you deliver meals Saturday and Sunday?" Abbey asked.

"He does. He believes his life is far more important than anyone else's." Nigel let out a mirthless laugh at this.

"I see. Hard to believe he's your brother, but I was always stunned at how different each of my children was from each other."

Nigel blew out a breath. "I'm going to have to face the music with him today. I'm afraid of his next hair-brained scheme to win her." Nigel sat still, clapped his hands down on his thighs, and stood. "Wish me luck. I'll report back tomorrow."

■■■

Nigel had read the situation correctly; Neville was in high drive, furious that Nigel was feeding people who, according to Neville, would be better off in a morgue. The words never stung; Nigel had a lifetime of rolling his eyes and shaking his head at Neville.

"Any nasty comments, and I'll head home," Nigel told his brother.

"Well, what do you expect from me? I'm in a crisis here," Neville spat.

"Okay, take a breath; I'll be there in about half an hour." Nigel quickly ended the call before Neville got another word in.

In less than thirty minutes, Nigel turned onto Neville's street. Briefly, he thought he'd circle the block before pulling up to Neville's door. He shook his head to clear his thoughts; *well, sooner here, sooner gone*, he said to himself.

Over the better part of an hour, Neville reviewed his recent discoveries about Christina: the new condo, living on her own, and the man she had been with.

Nigel listened and was only mildly surprised at any of it. He wouldn't tell Neville that he always found it strange that Christina was still living with her mother. Nigel had met Mrs. Pentelino. She never struck him as a clingy parent or someone that needed a caretaker. Christina had the resources to manage her own place. She was an exceptionally bright person who brilliantly managed a demanding career. There was nothing that made it critical to stay living with her mother. Of course, none of this resonated with Neville, so Nigel didn't press.

Neville's witnessing Christina with the man that had dropped her off at her new place was another matter. This needed to be addressed.

"I understand that you aren't done with your relationship with Christina, but, brother, she's obviously done with you. I don't know if she's moved on with this guy you saw her with, but you aren't part of her life as far as she's concerned. Sorry, but she's moved on."

Neville looked like his head would explode.

"I wish this wasn't upsetting to you. I'd let it go if it were me. Even if you convinced Christina to come back. Is she who you really want?" Nigel reasoned.

"Weren't you the one who went on and on about what a great girl Christina is?" Neville threw himself onto the sofa.

"She may be, but if she's not invested in you, why would you want her?" Nigel sat forward in the chair, facing his brother. "It seems to me she isn't of the temperament or world view you will be happy with long term. From what you told me, you want a stay-at-home wife. I don't see Christina as the girl who would be happy staying home."

"That is the entire problem; she doesn't understand herself," Neville sniffed.

"And you understand her?"

"Yes, I do. She's like a wayward child, rebelling. Don't you see that? She's left home and thinks she can live independently."

"And she can't?"

"That's right. She can't. Not in the long run. It's those so-called friends of hers. They probably put her up to this. And you should have seen that thug she was with. It was very disturbing that she let herself fall into the company of that grease ball. I intend to find out who he is and take that information to Christina's mother." Neville pounded his fist on the arm of the sofa just a little too hard; he winced.

"Neville, this is a little obsessive. You could find yourself in legal difficulties. You need to rethink this."

"I'm not about to follow anyone around. I just happened to be there today. I haven't been stalking Christina, and I won't start now. I have the license plate number of the sleazeball boyfriend. All I need is a name. I'm sure I won't have any problem finding out enough to tell Mrs. Pentelino about her daughter."

"I see. So that's why you called me over? To run the plate?" Nigel shook his head.

"I tried another source before I called you." Neville screwed up his mouth in anger at the thought.

"I'll bet you did. Okay, look, I'll get you the name of the car's owner, but that may not be the same person driving the car. You get that, don't you? And, even if it is, I want you to promise me you'll talk to me before you do anything with the information."

"Of course, you have my word." A giddy Neville all but applauded.

“Give me a minute,” Nigel said as he began dialing. After several minutes and some conversation, Nigel's head swung up, and he eyed his brother. “Thanks, Randy. I owe you one.” Nigel ended his call and walked back to talk to his brother.

Neville stood up, crossed his arms over his chest, and straightened. “Well?”

“Is your computer fired up?” Nigel said as he walked to the condo’s second bedroom Neville used as his home office.

“Should be.” Neville followed.

Nigel seated himself at Neville’s desk and began a Google search. “Pull up a seat,” Nigel said to his brother.

As Neville pulled a stool over to sit before the computer’s dual monitors, Nigel found the website he was looking for. Gagliardi Wealth Management’s website came into view. “I’m not positive they will have a contact page with photos, but... *ah*, they do.” Nigel said as he pulled up the page that listed the company’s principles. “Rocco I. Gagliardi,” Nigel said. “The car’s registration listed this man as the owner. Is that the guy you saw?”

“I knew he was some mafia-type.” Neville sneered.

"Hold on. The Gagliardis are as much mafia as the Mike Ilitch's. The Gagliardi family has been in the US longer than our family. They are pillars of the community, very wealthy, very respectable, and very, very much solid citizens. If you run around telling people that Rocco I. Gagliardi is a thug, anyone who knows Rocco Gagliardi or the family will think you are nuts. Besides, you really don't know if Christina is involved with him. All you know is that Christina has her own place, and apparently, Rocco Gagliardi gave her a ride home," Nigel said.

"He kissed her," Neville said petulantly.

"If he did or didn't, that is not our business." Nigel stopped and took a long-suffering breath; this would not go the way Neville wanted. It wasn't that Christina was the type of woman to be swayed by a big bank account. Still, if what Nigel knew of Rocco Gagliardi and the Gagliardis in general, an intelligent, dignified, and uber respectful Rocco would have a far better shot with a woman like Christina than his whiney self absorbed brother. "I think you need to take this as a life lesson and move on."

"What possible life lesson is watching Christina throw away her life supposed to teach me?"

“To start with, not all women hold your world view, and you either need to court the woman who does or change your attitude.” Nigel looked at his watch. “I have an appointment; I need to be across town in another hour.” He looked at Neville with kind eyes, “I’m sorry this didn’t go how you wanted. There is life after Christina. Hey, why don’t you call Nava? Didn’t she have some friend of hers that wanted an introduction?”

“I will not be reduced to having my sister play matchmaker for me.” Neville began walking Nigel to the front room to collect his coat.

Nigel prepared to face the January cold and was almost out the door when he turned and caught Neville in a three pat man hug. “What do they say? If you want to get over a woman, get another one under you. Crass, but probably sage advice,” He said as he headed to his car.

Neville hurried back to his home office and pulled up the picture of Rocco Gagliardi. “Solid citizen, my ass. You, Rocco Goumbah, are nothing but a sleaze bag dressed in a five-thousand-dollar suit. And I’m going show you as the fraud you are.”

Chapter 16

We Should Be Friends

Miranda Lambert

"*Woohoo*, look at our little Miss Bollywood," Marisol applauded, and Christina joined in.

Holly walked out of her bedroom and made her best impression of a model on a catwalk. Her dress was mustard yellow with red beading around the high front collar and framing the plunging back.

"My god, Holly, that color is perfect with your skin. Put the heels on," Christina said.

"I don't know about the shoes." Holly raised a skeptical eyebrow.

"They are perfect," Marisol said.

"They are," Christina chimed in.

Holly pushed her toes into the shoes. "It feels like I'm walking on stilts. It's awkward."

"That's why you need to practice with them; you've got to February 14th," Christina said.

"You'll need a coat, and I've got just the one," Marisol said.

"Your black satin kimono?" Christina asked.

"Yup." Marisol smiled.

"I'll swim in it," Holly said.

Christina shook her head. "You won't. It's not meant to be fitted. It's beautiful. It's dressy, and it's warm," Christina inclined her head to Marisol. "She must really like you to lend it to you.

Holly turned toward Marisol. "Hey, what will you wear if I've got this?"

"Don't worry your pretty little head over it. I've got a fake fur...

"We don't call it fake fur; it's ethical fur," Holly said.

"Okay, I have an ethical fur coat that is warm and looks great," Marisol said.

Holly turned toward her bedroom, "I have to get out of this dress before I spill something on it," she said as she disappeared down the hall.

Marisol pinned Christina with a smirk, "Okay, you need to spill it."

Christina sat down hard on one of the love seats in Holly's living room. "I don't know. I like him, but… I don't know."

"Why don't you know? You say you like him, right? He's obviously interested in you. What's the hesitation? Hey, are you afraid for us to meet him?" Marisol took a long sip of her flavored water and offered Christina the bottle.

Christina took it and sipped before answering. "I do like him, and he's really attentive without being pushy, but I get the feeling if I were to let myself get involved, I'd be part of a stable of girls he dallies with."

"Why? What happened?" Marisol asked as Holly walked back into the room and took a seat.

"There have been a couple of… well, not anything in my face and not red flags necessarily, but things that I find a bit unsettling."

"Like?" Marisol asked.

"Like talking with Mimi, his HR manager at his office. She told me about some woman that came in demanding to see him. I guess the woman insulted the receptionist Ava, which is almost unforgivable because Ava is such a sweet girl. Anyway, when Mimi asked Ava about it, she said it looked to her like some lover's spat," Christina frowned, then went on, "another of the office's admin, Bridget, told me that women will make appointments to see Rocco just to come on to him. Mimi mentioned that too. How he, Rocco, was never an HR issue because he always kept the female staff at a respectable arm's length. But women clients were a constant problem, not that he encourages them, just that there always are aggressive women who use client status to hit on him. So many that Rocco's staff has rules of engagement to deal with them. Then, on our way back from Muskegon, he got calls. The phone announces the name at the same time, and the screen flashes the name of the incoming caller. There were a couple." Christina arched an eyebrow. "There was a Vonda and a Frances. He was flustered in a way that a person gets flustered like they are hiding something. I told him I didn't mind if he had to talk to clients. He just blew me off." She let out a long tired breath, then said, "But, he invited me to lunch this week; we're going tomorrow. I don't want to tell him to get lost, but it seems to me that he has more of an appetite than I'd be able to satisfy."

"Maybe all the office drama happened way before you. And maybe they were clients on the phone, and he didn't want work to get in the way," Marisol said.

"Maybe," Christina let out a breath, "Okay, I know this will sound crazy, but every guy I've ever dated I had a feeling about. Neville, for instance, long before I ever went out with him, I had a feeling about him, just a nagging feeling that it was a wrong move to date him. I don't have the same feeling about Rocco, but something doesn't seem entirely honest. Like he's not one hundred percent upfront. And he is not exactly an open book."

"It's buddhi," Holly said with a shrug.

Marisol and Christina looked over at her, waiting. Holly got up and went into the kitchen, telling her friend I'll get more flavored water. She returned, handing off the water bottles. Holly sat once more and said. "It's Sanskrit. It's a spiritual awareness in Hindu terms. In everyday bread and butter terms, it just means you have an understanding born out of something like intuition. You should pay attention to it."

"Honest? How is he not honest?" Marisol asked.

"It isn't that I think he has ever lied or tried to mislead me. It is more that he doesn't share. I mean, I'm talking about my past, such as it is, but he never offers anything about his personal life. I know he's got one from talking to Mimi and Bridget."

Holly narrowed her eyes. “Have you asked?”

Christina thought a moment, “I haven’t. All he’s ever said is that he only socializes for business reasons. I know he’s not dating,” she made air quotes, “his clients. He’s got boundaries if Mimi and Bridget have it right.”

Marisol shrugged. “You need to ask about it. You should do that.”

“I will. I’ll see him Tuesday,” Christina said.

“And you see him when that committee meets too. Right?” Marisol said.

“*Yeah*, how often is that?” Holly asked.

“At least once a week. But that’s going to change a little. Rocco and Doug found the site, and as soon as they close on the property, we’ll need to select a firm to design the park. When that’s handled, the committee will need to focus on marketing to other donors and finding a construction firm. I could be wrong, but I don’t think it will look like the original committee once the design work is done.” Christina said, “besides, I have a major event coming up, Career Day. That’s going to be my focus.”

“Busy, busy,” Marisol said,

“You still like living solo?” Holly asked Christina.

"I love it. I thought the shine would wear off, but it hasn't yet. I think if I had to shovel my own driveway, I might not be so smitten, but so far, so good. I think this is better for my mother too. I guess I cramped her style. I think she'd had overnight company lately. I'm not about to share this with my brother, and I don't want to think about the details, but I'm really glad for her."

Chapter 17

Sweet Dreams

Beyonce

Christina's scent lingered on the bed linen. Rocco took in a strong breath, and his dick swelled. He thought about getting up to find her and bring her back to bed but decided to wait for her. He rolled over and found her lying on her back, mere inches from him. Her breasts were soft mounds of tempting flesh topped with rosy nipples hardened into stiff peaks like those gumdrops, the sugar-covered kind. He licked his lips; he could taste the sugar. Her eyes were half-closed, and she was moaning softly. It was almost inaudible, but he could just make it out; she was breathing his name; he waited a moment to be sure that was what he heard. It was.

He rolled to his side and propped himself up, leaning on his elbow, to watch her. What a sight. She was so fucking hot, but this was... man, this was scorching.

Her lips were full, cheeks were flushed, and she was breathing hard, almost panting. He thought about reaching over to touch her, but he then realized she must not know he could see her. Was she touching herself? God, yes, she had her hand between her legs, and she was tenderly circling her clit with her fingers. He thought about what she tasted like. It would be that mix of salty musk. As if she could hear his thoughts, she brought her fingers up, and for just that second, he thought she would let him taste. Instead, she put her fingers in her own mouth and hungrily sucked them. That was all it took. Rocco's hands found their way to his cock, and in a matter of seconds, he came so hard he saw stars. Rocco finally caught his breath and realized he needed the take care of Christina. He reached to find her and pull her closer to him, but the bed was empty. He sat up quickly as his phone's morning alarm went off, and he saw the evidence of his nocturnal tryst all over his stomach.

Chapter 18

Like to Get to Know You

Spanky and Our Gang

Rocco spent way too much time deciding on his clothes that Tuesday morning. He had no client appointments, just a client dinner that evening. Today would be spent with the accountants preparing for the outside auditing firm to come in next week. He didn't have to be dressed to the nines. He wanted to send the right message for his lunch date with Christina. He wanted to look successful but not stuffy. He laughed at himself for being such a girl about his clothes, but he still did it.

Finally, he decided on a sports coat instead of a suit. It was below zero this morning, and he grabbed a pullover at the last moment and left for his office.

As he pulled into his office's parking lot, he saw a Mercedes GT-Class he didn't recognize. He parked his SUV and started for the front door when he noticed a man almost his Nonno's age get out of the Mercedes to chase him down.

Rocco waited at the door to greet this very early visitor. The man approached and extended his hand. "You are Rocco Gagliardi, I presume."

Rocco took his glove off to accept the hand offered. "I am. And you are?"

"Doctor Donington. I know it's presumptuous of me to just show up, but my schedule is hectic, and I'll only need a moment of your time, may I?" he gestured inside the building.

"Of course, my office is just up the stairs," Rocco said, moving toward the elevator.

"This actually will not take that long." Doctor Donington pointed to the receptionist's desk and said, "I understand you have partnered with the Holtzbergs and the local hospital to build an accessible park for the disabled."

"That's true." Rocco nodded.

"I am here to offer the support of the Remington Foundation." The doctor retrieved a business card and handed it to Rocco. "I don't know where you are in the process, but we have resources and personnel to offer to grant recipients."

"We have selected the site and are about to nail down the designer. Our challenges are money and marketing talent," Rocco offered.

"I'll need the details, but we have anywhere from $500,000.00 to $2,000,000.00 in grant funding for a single project. We also have our own marketing group if it will help." The Doctor smiled.

"I'll send you the details." Rocco offered his hand again, and the doctor took it.

"Great, I think this is going to work out well." The doctor pulled on his gloves and was out the door.

Rocco watched the man as he got into the Mercedes and drove off. Rocco made his way to his office; he'd put someone on this. No way would he turn his nose up at that size donation.

Rocco felt good about the morning, and then there was another message from Vonda. The Vonda messages and texts were beginning to annoy. Rocco had already sent what Vonda asked for when she called before, disturbing his ride home from Muskegon with Christina.

Vonda had been a sometimes beneficial business associate and an okay hookup. The plus with Vonda was she had never before been demanding, not as a business acquaintance or the occasional sex partner. When she called, she was direct with an invitation to meet, usually, at the apartment she kept not far from his house. That was convenient. Once they had been at the same event in Lansing, Vonda had invited him to stay over at her home in Okemos. That stay was the last time Rocco had been with her. It had been an uncomfortable evening with this weird forced coupledom that he had no wish to repeat. When he left Vonda's house in the very early hours that morning, Rocco decided that if she called again for anything other than business, he would beg off. Rocco did hear from her office every now and then, asking for or offering business-related favors. That was as far as he wanted to take it. His goal with her would be to maintain the business end of things. He mentally tucked all that away to concentrate on what needed to get done before he could see Christina.

Rocco felt comfortable about the upcoming audit, the subject of the morning's meeting. Bruno was there bright and early and sat in on the meeting. He was quiet; Rocco smiled to himself about that. A reflective Bruno? God, who knew?

At 11:30, the meeting group decided to order lunch. "Sorry, I have to pass," Rocco said as he began to move out of the conference room.

It surprised Bruno, and he caught his brother's arm as he passed. "Lunch with a client?"

Rocco leaned down, smiled, and quietly said, "Christina." Then gave his little brother an affectionate pat on the shoulder as he left.

■■■

Rocco spotted her just inside the entryway. She was looking at her cell phone with an unhappy expression on her face. It still was a beautiful face, Rocco thought, pulling up to the front of the Holtzberg offices. He hastily got out to open the car door for her.

She threw the phone into her purse, looked up, saw Rocco, and her face transformed. She came toward him, all smiles now.

He decided not to ask and exchanged hellos with her as he helped her into the SUV. He returned and settled in the driver's seat; her phone rang again. She looked murderous until she noted the caller and politely asked, "Would you mind?"

"Not at all." Rocco turned on to Fourteen Mile.

"Hey, Marisol. Can I call you later? I'm on my way to lunch. Okay," she took in a breath, "yes, I'm with Rocco, and yes, I think it's got a base note of sandalwood. *Ah*, no. I won't be doing that." She looked over at Rocco sheepishly, "Sure, Friday's open. *Yep*. Tell Holly, please. Bye."

"What won't you be doing?" Rocco asked.

Christina paused, "I'll tell you when you tell me about the flat tire event,"

"All in good time, Ms. Pentelino, all in good time. So, tell me what she asked."

"Okay, I mentioned to my friends that you always smell nice."

That had her blushing like crazy; Rocco inwardly laughed.

"Marisol, the friend I was with the day you changed the tire, thought so too. She wanted me to *sniff* you to figure out the cologne you wear. Whatever it is, it seems like it has a base note of sandalwood."

"I don't wear cologne. It's just soap or maybe shampoo," Rocco explained as they pulled into the Coney Island parking lot.

"Okay, good to know." Christina lightly giggled.

The restaurant was busy; still, they got a table right away. Rocco wanted to be closer to the front door, but as cold as the day was, the middle of the restaurant was far better.

The server came by, a young man who recognized Christina. “Hey, you're from Holtzbergs, right? I remember you from a few weeks back.”

Christina smiled. “That was a huge order. My boss treated everyone to lunch that day.”

Rocco sat back. This was working out. He wanted to remind her of that day.

“Nice.” The server leered down at Christina, but Rocco made his presence known to the horny little shit, and the kid straightened and said, “So, what can I get you?”

“I’ll have the chicken shawarma, no fries. May I have hummus instead? And hot tea, please.” Christina slid the menu back behind the condiments.

Rocco was ordering; she watched him. God, he was seriously hot. Masculine in a way that should scare her to death. *What am I supposed to do? Oh yeah, get him to open up a little.* That was supposed to be the plan for this lunch.

Rocco tucked the menu away and appraised her. “What’s going on this Friday?” he asked a distracted Christina.

“Oh,” she gestured dismissively. “My friend Marisol and our friend Holly try to get together at least once a week outside of yoga. It’s usually something low-key. This week it will be vegetarian at Holly’s house. Holly is Indian, so she serves all things vegetarian.”

Rocco shook his head. “I’ve tried it. Indian cuisine, I don’t know. Is that something you like?”

“It grows on you. But, enough about me. We never talk about you, Mr. Gagliardi.”

He smiled at her. “That’s by design. I’m not very interesting. I work. My family members are my close friends,” he shrugged, “not very exciting.”

“I don’t agree.” It was her turn to smile, “Your family seems pretty interesting. Your brother Bruno is....”

“He’s a character,” Rocco smiled, “he’s the family pet. Our Nonno dubbed him the little *Polpetto*.”

Christina laughed. “That is so cute. I’m sure Bruno wouldn’t appreciate it. I think it actually suited him better a few weeks back. He’s... well, he has changed.”

“You see that?” Rocco asked.

"I do. Not that there was one thing wrong with him before. He saved me from that perv, Dr. Grandville." She smirked.

Rocco seemed to growl.

She ignored what she feared she may be misinterpreting and said, "Bruno has gotten older in the past few weeks. He's still a really charming guy. Lots of emotional intelligence; it's just that now, he fits into your office better. He's sort of grown into the character of your business."

"I think so too. When Bruno started with us, I was really nervous about him. Don't get me wrong, I love my brother. It's just that he never showed any interest in the family business. I thought it would either be Bruno leaving almost as soon as he got there, or he'd just coast. I don't exactly know where he best fits, but he will fit somewhere and be an asset." Rocco smiled.

"You have another brother too, right?"

"My older brother Franco. He and my father run the office on the east side; my dad is easing out of the business, and Franco runs the day-to-day operation."

"What other family do you have? Are there nieces and nephews?" she asked.

"Rocco smiled but shook his head. "You know about Caterina. It's just my bachelor brothers, my parents, and grandparents."

"Cousins, then?"

Rocco stiffened, cleared his throat uncomfortably, and nodded. "There are cousins. Not a legion of them, but a few. None here in Detroit."

Christina looked surprised.

"Is it different with your family?" Rocco asked.

"Very different. We are tripping over our extended family. My mom gets invitations like once a month or more. There is always something: weddings, showers, First Communions, Christenings, birthdays, anniversaries, and every other family something. It's nice for her; she's always flattered that she's remembered by my Dad's family. My mother believes that is because the family circled the wagons after my father was murdered."

"Wait. Your father was murdered?" Rocco looked at her; the shock registered on his face.

Christina sobered and nodded. "My dad always worked an extra job or three. He and my mom were saving for a house. His Aunt and Uncle owned a hauling company; my brother runs it now. My dad was a carpenter by trade, his day job, but he worked at the hauling business nights and weekends. Back in the day, the company was in a pretty rough part of town, and they, my Aunt and Uncle, had been regularly robbed. The people who stole from them vandalized the trucks and equipment. My dad talked a friend of his into putting cameras in and some other security equipment, but that hadn't been done, so Dad was sleeping at the company's office to guard the place.

The best they figured was that the thieves came into the office, and my dad put up a fight. They had guns, and my Dad didn't. He was shot once in the chest, straight into his heart. No other injuries. The coroner told my mother he didn't suffer. I was a little over a year, and my brother was almost three when we lost our father. My

That Aunt and Uncle didn't have children, and they felt responsible that my Dad died guarding their property. They always took care of us as much as my Mother would let them. When they passed away, they left everything to my mom. My brother was in college earning a business degree at that time. Instead of selling the business, my mom gave it to my brother Cal. The house mom inherited is the one she's living in, and the cash from the estate paid for my schooling. I also got the car. It was like brand new, and I still drive it. I get dividends from my brother, which I told him never to do, but he's stubborn. My mom gets them too, and she's refused him, but...." Christina gestured with her hands in the universal sign for a lost cause, "my mom is a beautician. She likes to work, and I don't see her quitting the salon, but she has an income from the inheritance."

The server brought their lunches, and Christina realized she had been talking non-stop. "Oh god, I'm so sorry; I didn't mean to monopolize the conversation."

"You didn't. I asked. Christina, I am so sorry for your loss. That had to be unbelievably hard for your mom. I have a world of respect for your mother. Thank god for your Aunt and Uncle. Even so. I know how hard it is to lose someone."

Without thinking about it, Christina reached over and covered his massive hand with hers.

It would have pleased him, but the look on her face made it clear the intention was to acknowledge his pain. That made his heart hurt. He slowly placed his other hand over hers.

It was a sweet gesture, and it made her smile inside.

"Thank you," he said quietly, brought her hand to his lips, and kissed her knuckles.

His kiss made her blush. The kiss was soft and tender. She was sorry when he set her hand down and focused on his lunch.

The server made a big production out of recognizing Christina, bringing the other young man who had brought all the lunches to the Holtzbergs' step van that day. After they finished and got up to leave, Christina walked past the bank of booths closest to the cash register. She paused as if remembering something, shook her head, and proceeded to the door.

Before Rocco dropped her off at the Holtzberg office, he made sure to ask her out for a Saturday dinner.

She accepted, and Rocco headed for his own offices to prepare for his client's dinner this evening.

Her office phone rang the minute she got back to her desk.

"There she is," Marisol nearly sang into the phone.

"Your timing is flawless; I just walked in," Christina said, taking off her outer clothing.

"Well, any further along on the getting to know his hotness?"

"It's weird. First of all, I have it all planned to get him to open up about himself, and I end up doing a personal information tsunami. And, don't laugh, but this is the second time we've been someplace that I feel I've been before... with Rocco. It is so strange. We are going out on Saturday night. And I told you about Valentine's Day, right?" Christina said, sitting down and opening her computer.

"Yes, you told me. Hey, we probably need to go shopping for your St. Valentine's Day massacre, the night you get Rocco's arrow right in your...."

"Hold up. I can't be cannonballing into that lake just yet. There is nothing certain about any of this. I just broke up with Neville," Chistina said as she gave a cursory review of her emails.

Marisol ignored this. "We still should go shopping. I want to be in something fabulous. Garrett has promised a St. Valentine's Day to remember. So, where is his Italian hotness taking you?"

"I'm not sure. I'll probably find out this Saturday. This needs to go slow. I don't want to get deeper into this too quickly. The playground project is moving forward very nicely. We are almost in the home stretch of planning. Once we get past the next few weeks, my attendance at the meetings won't be required, and if it all goes to hell with him dating-wise, it won't be another failed romance in my face."

"I don't know if I like this fatalist side of you, Christina. That's Holly's specialty. You're our Polyanna."

"I'm just... I want to avoid another Neville. Actually, Rocco is nothing like Neville. I just want to avoid a mistake."

"I hear ya, sister," Marisol said, "Friday, we will discuss this and maybe plan a trip downtown Birmingham to that cool little boutique."

"Friday for sure. Remind Holly. Hugs," Christina said as she turned back to her computer to get lost in work.

Chapter 19

Dancing With Myself

Billy Idol

Neville had been skulking around Rocco Gagliardi's offices. He discovered an adjacent parking area next to the Gagliardi Building with a barrier of pine trees partially obscuring the view both to and from where Neville's Ford Flex was parked.

Neville was getting the lay of the land. He didn't want an ill-timed confrontation and come out of it looking foolish. He was still doing research on this fraud Rocco Gagliardi. Nigel had reminded Neville to be careful slinging around insults about a man that the business community had almost obsessive goodwill towards. This didn't cause Neville to stop; he was silent about his opinions around brother Nigel.

This afternoon there was another watcher. The watcher was on the small side, the very small side. It took Neville a few moments to really look. He, she, Neville wasn't sure which because the kid had some serious outerwear: ski pants and a coat with a scarf covering the face and a knit cap pulled down to cover his or her hair.

After another ten minutes, the workday was ending for several of the staff members in the Gagliardi office, and a steady stream came out of the building until Rocco exited too.

The kid suddenly rushed behind a tree and pulled out a camera. As Rocco left the office, the kid took a picture or maybe a video. It was strange but none of Neville's concern. Just as Rocco Gagliardi drove out onto Woodward in that white-trash Cadillac of his, the kid bent over at the waist, breathless. The knit hat came off, so did the scarf, and Neville could now see it was a girl. A very young girl, it appeared, with dark hair and the olive complexion that spoke of Mediterranean heritage.

She leaned against a pine tree and spent the next few minutes scrolling through her camera.

Then she put on her hat and scarf, headed toward Woodward, and crossed the street to one of the few bus stops in this section of the boulevard.

Neville's attention to the other watcher was fleeting. Still, it was enough reminder that he needed to head out too.

■■■

Caraleigh left her father's house in a fury; she got into her car and slammed the door. Caraleigh threw her head back and screamed as she pounded her fists on the steering column.

She didn't see him very often; usually, if she needed extra cash or wanted a favor, her doctor father could help her.

That is what she was angling for today. One small request. If Beaumont Hospital was represented in Rocco's project, why couldn't her dad's hospital be part of it too? That wasn't the sum total of the support she wanted from her dad, just the critical start.

He not only refused, but also he told her she wasn't allowed to be involved in what was a very thinly veiled effort to use his position with the hospital as Match.com.

She screamed until her throat hurt. Frustrated tears began to well in her eyes, but she refused to have this setback ruin her makeup.

She had already contacted Fred Donington about Rocco's project, and it looked like Rocco had taken the doctor up on the foundation's offer. She had absolutely every intention of following through with this, no matter what her father had to say.

Chapter 20

One Kiss

Dua Lipa

"Oh, I love this place," Christina said as she and Rocco walked up to the entrance of Pinky's Rooftop. Rocco smiled a nervous smile unseen by Christina.

They were seated at the same table Christina, Marisol, and Holly toasted her almost proposal some weeks back. This didn't go unnoticed on Christina's part. As soon as the server took their drink order, she cocked her head and smiled at him. "I was sitting at this same table a few months ago with my friends. This should bring back an awkward memory."

"An awkward memory of what?" Rocco asked.

She let out a breath. "It was right after Neville proposed, well, sort of proposed. We, Marisol, Holly, and I didn't plan to meet to celebrate. I didn't know he was going to do that. We had planned a girls' night. Neither of my friends is, well, were, big Neville fans. Anyway, that evening I told them what had happened. They did what best friends do; they said everything best friends say. Like I said, neither of them are Neville fans, and my telling them about what happened just underlined another reason for their shared acrimony toward him."

Neville. Rocco said to himself. Then he carefully schooled his expression to remain perfectly impassive. Just hearing that little fucker's name made Rocco want to find him and beat the shit out of him. Instead, he just repeated the name, growling it in his head.

"They made what might have been a not-so-nice evening a great memory," Christina said,

The server brought the cocktails.

Christina had suggested a somewhat over-the-top cocktail for Rocco, which he now eyed suspiciously.

“It’s bourbon. You like bourbon. I know. I’ve watched you drink it.” She noted.

Rocco sipped the drink and made an ‘it’s okay’ smirk.

“Told ya,” Christina said as she sipped her Pink Circus.

“Does he... Does Neville call you?” Rocco sort of hated himself for wanting to know, but he wanted to know.

“He did for a while. It wasn’t productive,” she gave a slight shrug, “I blocked his number. He called on another phone a time or two, but he’s backed off.” She gave him her best no-nonsense face, “Now, we’ve covered my less than fabulous dating life. I think I’d like to know about yours.”

Rocco was mid-sip and momentarily startled. Coughing before he composed himself and then was saved by the server bringing him water and staying to take their food order.

As soon as the server left, Christina lifted an eyebrow.

Rocco cleared his throat, “Can I get a pass for a later day?”

“We already have one of your passes for a later day, Mr. Gagliardi. Why the mystery? Just what sort of skeletons are there in your closet?”

Rocco looked at her. "Dating life? No. I haven't had a dating life since college," Rocco said, hoping to close the conversation.

"You, what? You have never been in the company of a woman since college?" Christina's attention was now laser-focused exclusively on him, and it felt very uncomfortable. "What do you mean exactly?" Christina narrowed her eyes at Rocco.

Rocco cleared his throat. "I occasionally have a plus-one for situations that call for me to bring a woman along." God, that sounded utterly douchey, and it didn't ring true. Rocco squirmed, trying to find the words to explain. "I haven't had anything more than very casual arrangements with women." He said almost into his shirt.

Still, Christina heard him, "Is what you are avoiding telling me that you only have sexual relationships?"

"Not relationships," he said too quickly. He softened his tone and strove for somewhere between the truth and the dressed-up version of the truth he might offer to his mother. "I've tried to keep things simple regarding my social life. I haven't dated."

"So, hook-ups then? Your connections with women are nonexclusive hookups?" she asked.

The image this called to his mind seemed to be a tad unsavory. “I have not been romantically involved with any of the women I ...” he cleared his throat uncomfortably, “I haven’t had a serious relationship since college. My connections with women have been casual,” Rocco said.

“I don’t mean to get too personal, but you’ve had the picture window into my dating past, so I think I’m not totally out of line asking just how many hook-ups, say, in the past year are we talking.”

Rocco was shocked at the audacity of the question. But she was right; over the past weeks, he led her into several discussions about just who and what. “I never kept a count,” he said, thinking it was the more gentlemanly answer.

“I see,” was all she said.

He was spared by the arrival of their dinners. Rocco gratefully embraced the suspension of the conversation; however, the quiet turned too quiet. Christina was picking at her meal, deep in thought. Or maybe it was something else. He sure as fuck hoped it was something else so they could drop the discussion about his sex life. Well, he was the idiot that had turned every date with her into a dive into her past relationships.

After the dinner silence, the server returned to take an order for dessert. Christina was, as always, polite to the server but declined anything further.

Rocco handed over the payment in the bill folio, thanked the server, wished her a good evening, turned to Christina, and said, "There's a nice little pub around the corner. I'm told the wine selection is exceptional. Would you like to try it with me?"

"You mean now?"

"I was hoping that if you don't want to stay here, we could try it now," Rocco offered.

Christina squinted her eyes and nodded her head slightly. "I think we need to finish the conversation."

Rocco looked pleadingly at her.

Christina was not to be deterred and asked, "Getting back to the previous discussion, when you tell me you don't date, but you have been dating me. I suspect you want the weight of that to make me feel more important to you than the women in your past. If that was the message, it's lost on me. The message I'm getting is this: you have experienced lots of women, so many in fact, the number eludes you. I can tell you with some certainty that the extent of my sexual experience, not lovers, events, over my lifetime is barely in double digits."

Rocco stilled, not sure he was happy or unhappy to hear this.

She went on, "It isn't just that your past is a road littered with former lovers. It's how does a woman like me ever compete with that? There's a good reason I haven't had a legion of lovers, Rocco." Christine leaned in, looked him in the eyes, and said, "I have never enjoyed it, and I have made sure to choose men that don't seem to want or enjoy sex much either. Not until you that is."

Rocco's mouth fell open.

"Rocco, thank you. Thank you for this evening. You have always been a wonderful companion, and I've always enjoyed the time I've spent with you, but this has to end. I never should have accepted that first date. I'm not in the same league as your other women, not their abilities or interest. I never will be. I'm in over my head. Way over my head." With that, she put on her coat and picked up her purse.

"Christina, please? Where are you going?" Rocco stood and began putting his coat on. "Wait. If you want to go home, I'll take you."

"No need, Rocco; I'd prefer to find my own way home," she said as she walked away from him.

Rocco was speechless, watching her walk away. “Oh, fuck, no,” he said more to himself than anyone near enough to hear.

She was out on the street starting to place a call when he caught up to her.

He silently took the phone out of her hand and pocketed it.

Christina gasped.

Rocco was shaking his head. He took her hand and led a shocked Christina to the side of the building. He stopped abruptly, pulled her close, and roughly kissed her. She didn’t immediately relax in his arms, but she didn’t push him away either.

He repositioned her, an arm around her waist and his other hand cupping the back of her head. It wasn’t a soft kiss and not so insistent that it felt sexually aggressive. But it did feel sexual, and it wasn’t passive.

Christina felt like she could quickly lose herself in his warm lips. His tongue invaded her mouth; unlike others, it was welcomed, exciting, and sexy. She could taste the bourbon, the hint of buttery spice from his dinner, and what had to be the taste of Rocco; it tasted good.

The kiss went on until Rocco realized that his erection might make everything he wanted her to understand seem a lie.

"Christina, if I bring you, I take you home." He then softened his voice and tenderly held her face in his hands, telling her, "We need to have a frank talk. Tonight took me by surprise. That's not to say you aren't owed the information. Because you're right, I didn't think about it, but you're right; it would seem that I've been grilling you. It wasn't my intention, well, I wanted to know, but it wasn't just about your past boyfriends," he almost spat the word, "God, Christina, I want to know all about you. From how you grew up to why you have that knitted shawl on the occasional chair in your front room instead of your sofa. I find you a fascinating subject and one that I want to be an expert on. I'd like to blame the clumsiness on my inexperience at dating, but it's really more that you are very interesting to me, important to me. A hell of a lot more interesting than I am. I mishandled it, but I promise you we will have a frank and earnest discussion, and I will answer any questions you have. Just give me the 14th, please," he kissed her again, "Please? Don't throw me away, *Tesoro*," Rocco said, holding her close.

Christina let out a shaky breath and nodded.

■■■

The ride home was quiet but not tense. Rocco stole as many glances at her as she did at him. When they got to her place, he walked her to her door, pulled her phone out of his pocket, kissed her with more intention than just a good night kiss, and said, “Next Saturday. Please?”

“Next Saturday. What time?” Christina asked.

“The reservation is for 7:00. I’ll pick you up at 6:30. Okay?”

She nodded, “Okay.”

She had climbed the stairs and chanced to look out the window. “What am I doing? she said to no one as she hung her coat up and took off her boots.

It was early enough, so she called Marisol. The phone rang long enough for Christina to grab a glass for the wine she was about to pour.

“I thought you were out with his hotness tonight,” Marisol answered her phone.

“I was.”

“Okay, well, I know why I’m doing nothing more than folding laundry, but why are you home so early?”

“I think we just had a fight. I broke up with him and left the restaurant.”

"You need a ride home? I can leave in five minutes. Where are you?"

Christina let out a breath and took a sip of the wine. "I'm home. He refused to let me get my own way home. I was dialing you when he stopped me. He refused to accept my declaration of ending it with him. And we are going out again on Valentine's Day as planned."

"Why did you want to break up with him?"

Christina groaned in dismay, "He's too much for me, Marisol. We finally got around to talking about him, and it was my worst nightmare come to pass. According to him, he does not date, and he doesn't do relationships."

"So, what's he been doing with you?"

"I think I'm supposed to believe I'm different," Christina said.

"Why is that such a stretch for you?"

Christina laughed a humorless laugh. "He's drop-dead gorgeous. He's good company; no, he's great company. He's wealthy, and he's hot. I'm supposed to believe that I'm the pink unicorn? I don't see it. He's used to sleeping with women who don't expect anything more. According to him, it's always casual. His last girlfriend was in college. How do I compete? I am anything but casual, and sex with me can only be a disappointment."

"This is where your lack of regular normal sex partners sets up to misread things. Honey, *you* are drop-dead gorgeous. You are smart. You are nice, a sweetheart. And, Christina, you are hot. If I didn't like dick so much, I'd make a play for you. You have been with three too many boys, and none of them had any testosterone. You've got a man in your midst. He's flawed. What man isn't."

"Is he really flawed? I don't know; I think I'm the one who's messed up. If this was you instead of me with him – it wouldn't be a problem."

"He's not interested in me. He's had his sights on you since, well, since he fixed Neville's tire. And he hasn't altered his course once with you. If he was only interested in bedding you, he would have made a big move the first time he took you out. I'm not saying you have to do anything with this guy, and if you didn't like him, it would be one thing. But Christina, I think you are just waiting for the other shoe to drop, and it hasn't, so you found a way to make a problem where one doesn't actually exist," Marisol gave that a second to sink in, "I know not everyone loses their virginity by a certain age. Not everyone has multiple sex partners. It's just that logically, Christina, most people have cashed in their Vcard in their teens; the older you are, the more opportunity to have multiple partners. He's what? In his thirties? That's a window of more than a decade to slip his Italian sausage into a Focaccia bun or two. It doesn't make him faithless. I don't know if I've ever told you about my first real boyfriend."

"No. And this is surprising because I know a ton about Garrett." Christina snickered.

"*Yeah, yeah, Geez*. It didn't happen until my senior year in high school. Anyway, my first was in high school. And honestly, that first time was the best of my life. It was my boyfriend Adam's first too. We had been together for like two years before we did the deed. And then, a week later, after our senior prom, he had sex with Mallory."

Christina gasped. "I thought she slept with your college boyfriend."

"Oh, she did. But before college-Alex, was high school-Adam."

"That's enough to put you off a Master's degree," Christina said.

"Yes, well. I've got Garrett prepped for meeting her; if it can't be avoided, he'll be ready for the tempest that is my sister. But back to the point. Adam was completely inexperienced except with me. The first chance he got, he became the faithless prick he became. I think you need to go on this next date and see. Isn't this the date he promised to explain the tire fixing affair? I want you to go on that date just to get this potentially interesting information."

"He promised. I suppose. In so many ways, this feels right, And you are probably on the mark that I'm looking for something to make my worst fear a reality."

"Well, pour a glass of wine and take a hot bath. I'm calling Holly for a girls' night. Let's go out on Friday or maybe something lower key at Holly's place. She'll serve something uneatable made with vegetables. That way, we won't overeat to be ready for dinner on Saturday."

"Good plan."

Chapter 21

Daughters

John Mayer

The day was warmer; the drift of snow that created a sort of berm dividing the Gagliardi parking lot from the one Neville was spying from was beginning to melt. This was the third time that girl showed up too. She wasn't as bundled up as she had been. Neville called to her. She looked over without moving from her spot.

"I know why I'm watching Rocco Gagliardi. But why are you?" Neville thought of this as more of a fishing expedition; he didn't actually expect an answer. To his shock, she walked a few paces toward the car; blinking, she said, “He’s my father.”

Chapter 22

All I have to Do Is Dream

Everly Brothers

Rocco decided to surprise her with a noon-time visit. He wasn't positive where her offices were. This place was a maze of hedges to just get to the front door. But he soldiered on until he found a small space between the shrubs. He could squeeze himself through it. He tried, but that wasn't working; he was too big and bulky. He might damage the hedge; he now realized the hedge was his hedge, and if he forced his way, he would be ruining something that was his. Rocco stood paralyzed, weighing his options as his lunch hour ran out. Then he saw her. Christina was standing on the other side of the hedge, and she was naked. This made the time problem so much worse. He needed to cover her before anyone else could see. He needed to get to her fast, but the sight of her was bewitching; he could only stare. She was on her knees, bent forward, weeding a garden patch. Every time she leaned a bit more in that position, he could see the lips of her labia between her legs and her breast swaying as they hung down with her nipples hard and almost dragging in the upturned soil. It made his cock hard, so he began stroking himself. He enjoyed seeing her like this as he kneaded his cock and massaged his balls. He could feel his orgasm building, his spine-tingling as he increased his speed. Then he heard men's voices in the distance. They were coming; they would see her like that. They'd see her tits; see her pink cunt. He stopped abruptly and made his decision. He tucked his hard dick away and took a running start bursting through the hedge, ready to scoop her up and carry her off. But he couldn't get beyond the shrubs. He began to panic, fighting his way through to the other side, reaching, pulling, and twisting himself to work his way out of the branches that obscured his way.

All the thrashing pulled the sheets loose so that when Rocco was awake enough to take his hands off of his dick and reach for his phone, the bedding was a tangled mess, the evidence of the fight Rocco waged with it. He'd sat up shaking his head; there was a lesson or a warning or something useful in that dream somewhere, maybe. He looked down at himself. God, he was used to a regular piss hard-on, but this was fucking absurd. Ah well, nothing he wasn't taking care of in the shower.

He had to admit rubbing one out each and every morning might be adding to his calmer demeanor. That would be helpful when meeting with the representatives from the hospital today.

Chapter 23

We Are the Champions

Queen

Bruno sat back and watched as the last of the Beaumont party left the conference room. His brother was like a maestro at this shit. Bruno imagined Franco was similarly graced with the same abilities; both were lawyers. And they were blessed with natural leadership abilities courtesy of their father and Nonno Gagliardi.

Today's performance nailed down three critical pieces to Caterina's Memorial project. First, it outed Dr. Grandville's attempt to force Jasper Construction down the committee's throat.

The Doctor dropped the bomb a week or so ago by telling Rocco and the Holtzbergs that Beaumont's support was conditional based on who would do the construction.

Bruno knew it didn't sit right with anyone else at the meeting. Still, the proclamation was Grandville throwing down the gauntlet for Bruno. He left that meeting with the decision to research the hell out of Dr. Grandville and the Jasper owners. He'd do it on his own, and if he found anything, then and only then would he mention it to Rocco.

In the beginning of his sleuthing, it looked like there wasn't any sort of nefarious connection. That was the first day or so into his search, but then Bruno found a Linked-In post from late last year. It was Gretta Jaylen, the Jasper owner's daughter, gushing over Baxter Grandville's wife, Kaye. Kaye liked the comment, so it was included in her feed.

Bruno began to pick up the scent and discovered that the two had gone to school together and had been in the same sorority. There wasn't enough in the Linked-In post itself to make the case that nepotism was at work for this project, but there was a path of bread crumbs to follow. Bruno began the search anew, this time focusing on Gretta Jaylen and Kaye Grandville.

This approach was a more straightforward path. It wasn't only Gretta and Kaye; there was a pattern of using Sigma Delta Chi connections in business, *a good ole boys'* business model, now employed by the ladies.

Gretta Jaylen's family firm was the contractor, Candice Collette was a partner in a commercial architectural engineering firm, and Heidi Richter worked for a commercial real estate company.

The way this had been packaged by Dr. Grandville for the Holtzbergs and Gagliardis was a singular solution. Jasper Construction had property, a design team, and a contractor. It was a turn-key answer. It did make the entire process seem effortless; just add the marketing and *Semplice,* and *finito,* everyone could be on hand to cut the ribbon.

Rocco hadn't said much during the meeting when Dr. Dickhead made his initial pitch. He did, however, have an entire conversation with Bruno, Christina, and the Holtzbergs afterward. During the next meeting, it was Christina who threw the first cold water on Dr. Dungbreathe's plan. She began by asking if the contractor company would *outsource the site work* because she noted that their website didn't list site work as one of their work capabilities.

Dr. Dopeface seemed offended that Christina did background checking. When Dr. Douchepants said *he'd have to ask*, Christina politely pressed on. This time asking if the design firm could send over information on projects they had completed similar to other accessible playground projects. And this was when Dr. Dumbo went off his nut, losing his temper with Christina and accusing her of trying to *feather her own nest by forcing out-of-state design firms and mom-and-pop construction firms ill-suited to a marquee project like this one.*

Bruno thought Doug Holtzberg was going to come unglued, and Rocco? Fuck, Rocco might have been silent, but he had his alpha male out for anyone who wanted to look at him. Most notable was the death glare Rocco gave Dr. Dingleberry.

Both Doug Holtzberg and Rocco held it together, but it was a very close call.

Unintentional as it was, Bruno thought it a perfect strategy. The meetings were always recorded, and a Dr. Dumbass snarling at a very polite young woman asking perfectly logical due diligence questions would not play well if it was made public.

Bruno sincerely thought that would be the end of Dr. Doinky, but Rocco disabused him of that notion.

"He's not done playing his hand," Rocco cautioned. Rocco wondered aloud why Dr. Dragon's breath went ape shit on Christina. But Bruno knew precisely why. That's when Bruno knew he needed to offer up the internet research he had been doing. So Bruno handed over the carefully documented information to a very pleased and impressed Rocco.

Rocco had Buno sit in on a meeting with the Holtzbergs to give them Bruno's research and plan their next move. Bruno was surprised that this would not be a confrontation with Dr. Dribble.

"I know it would be more dramatic to have the *you ordered the code red* moment in the committee meeting. But how it will be handled gets it done so it can't come back at us to deal with again," Rocco explained to Bruno.

Thus, the information Bruno found was shared with Beaumont management sans Dr. Granville. That was followed by a meeting with representatives from Beaumont, also minus Dr. Dorkface. Bruno would be along with the Holtzbergs, Antonio, Franco, and Rocco to meet with the Beaumont group. Bruno didn't think he'd be included, but Rocco all but dressed him in an overcoat and pushed him out the door, saying,

"Come on, little *Polpetto*, you are the hero today. Come and enjoy the spoils of the battle."

The meeting lasted long enough for the three major players from Beaumont to sign off on the committee's pick of a design firm and their approval of the property purchase that had already happened. The design firm would be under contract before the construction company was selected. The results of all this would be the subject of the next committee meeting two weeks from now.

As the meeting with Beaumont Hospital dispersed, the CFO from the hospital stopped Doug Holtzberg and Antonio Gagliardi to apologize for Dr. Dicknose's handling of the matter. He praised the men for finding qualified partners and finding and securing the property and reaffirmed the hospital's commitment to the project.

After that, Doug Holtzberg told Antonio how much he appreciated the hard work Bruno had done to uncover the information about the Grandvilles and their plot to enrich Kaye Grandville's friends. "That was masterful work. And it saved the time and effort it would have taken us to cut the hospital from the project and replace their monetary support. That would have been the plan B. I'm thrilled we don't have to execute it."

Bruno saw the look on his father's face. It made him blush. That look had been reserved for Franco and Rocco for the times that his brothers brought honor or acclaim to the family. It was emotional for Bruno, but he stoically enjoyed his moment.

Antonio clapped Bruno on his shoulder and said, "Franco is sorry he didn't keep you with him at the east side office. You are doing great things, Bruno. Rocco keeps me filled in. I think we need a new nickname for you. You aren't the little meatball so much anymore."

■■■

The appointment to hand over the Foundation's check for Rocco's charity thing would be Friday morning. Caraleigh decided to be the Foundation's representative and do it by herself, just her and a photographer to capture handing over the check to Rocco.

She was really disappointed that the Foundation's involvement was limited to turning over the grant money. It turned out that the project was just the sort of thing the Foundation had been looking for. Fred Donington called her to thank her for bringing it to his attention.

Caraleigh thought she'd have to do some convincing to get the group to award a sizable amount. Instead, the grant was the two million dollar max without one word from her. She did press Fred to allow her to make the presentation to Rocco. Two million dollars should make an impression on Rocco. Once Rocco understood her part in the foundation's grant, he would have evidence of how vital a partnership with her would be. The bow on the package was the maximum amount. Caraleigh knew that Rocco and the committee had only been aware that the amount was significant. Caraleigh could imagine Rocco's reaction when he looked at the check. All those zeros. Delicious.

Caraleigh also knew the old woman with the bad dye job who wrote for the Foundation's newsletter and did their press releases. Betty-blue-hair had already interviewed Rocco, some other old buzzard, and a doctor who specialized in physical therapy from Beaumont hospital over the phone. The press release and the newsletter article would include the photo Caraleigh intended on getting with Rocco standing next to her. That one picture would be worth a thousand words, and really it wouldn't be too late for a Valentine's Day date; as corny as that was, she was still a girl after all. After she gave him the money for his charity, Caraleigh would suggest a dinner date.

Caraleigh still would have to run the gauntlet and get by that little bitch at the reception desk in Rocco's offices, but she had a plan for that too. She would have the Foundation call to announce the arrival time, and the photographer would come in first so that she would tag along. Simple. And when she walked in to hand over the check, Rocco would have to see her, to talk to her. Besides, he'd be grateful and amused at her pluck. This would be the start of the next chapter of her life.

Now, all she had to do was pick out the perfect outfit to be ready for the picture. The picture that would announce to the world her status on Rocco's arm.

■■■

Rocco buried himself in work. He did that so he didn't think too much about the coming Saturday and Christina. He made sure to stay in touch with her throughout the week. Nothing heavy or unusual; they had exchanged text messages almost daily over the past weeks. Things about the playground, but now there were other connections. Christina and Mimi from Rocco's office were lunch buddies, which put Christina in touch with other people in Rocco's office: Bruno, for sure, and Rocco's administrative assistant Bridget. Since Christina understood and could read and write in Italian, Rocco would send her anything he thought might interest her. In the past several weeks, it had been a fun something to do. Now? Now, it felt like his lifeline to her. Whatever else, he should have his answer tomorrow.

Before last Saturday at Pinky's, he thought coming clean about how he actually met her might creep her out to the point she wouldn't want to see him again. He knew that was a possibility. In the beginning, had she decided it was too close to stalking, even if he wasn't actually stalking her, he was prepared to let it go, to let her go. Now? Now, no and hell no.

Last Saturday was upsetting, but it clarified his position perfectly. The sight of Christina walking away confirmed for him that any *take it or leave it* was an impossible outcome. There was one steady thought running through his head; she was his. If there was any letting-go, it wouldn't be his choice.

He sure as fuck didn't want to think too much about her previous lovers. God, that was fucking disturbing, and he hated it, but it was just that he was still trying to wrap his head around the fact that she didn't like sex. That was a concern, but Rocco didn't for a moment see it as insurmountable.

She was right about his experience. He had enough of that experience to know he affected her. As far as Rocco could tell, the only difference was that Christina wasn't a slave to her baser instincts, but she sure as shit had them. He knew it from the flush of her cheeks, how she pressed her thighs together, to the subtle scent of her arousal that made his cock hard. If that last boyfriend indicated anything, it was that she had purposely dated self-centered little boys. He could do better. He would do better.

He wasn't sure how to bring that subject up, the sex subject. Still, the point of the evening would be to man-up about being a voyeur at her evening with that fucking Neville and seeing her before officially meeting her. It would mean laying his feelings and intentions out for her to accept or reject. If it was a rejection, he'd need to regroup and find a different approach.

But first, he had to get through today; it was a full day. The check presentation by the Remington Foundation was this morning.

Rocco had thought about this how it might be handled. That brief meeting with Dr. Dorington was followed by a fairly rigorous vetting process.

That made Rocco put aside his initial concerns. Once he looked into the Foundation, he was impressed and shared the meeting with the Holtzbergs and Dr. Henry from Beaumont. Dr. Henry was familiar with the Foundation and encouraged Rocco to pursue the award.

The notice that they had secured a grant came by courier along with the request for an interview. Rocco knew the amount could be a half-million to two million. Since this was treated so formally, he figured it was at least a million. That was very helpful, and if this was handled well, it would pave the way for additional contributions. There was a newly formed Caterina and Friends; End of the Rainbow (CaF) W(c) (3) Charitable Organization to accept donations and manage the playground once it was built. The Foundation's money would not only support the current project, put into the CaF for grounds maintenance and equipment upkeep and repair, and the next playground project. It was all coming together.

The check presentation was a big deal. Rocco decided to make sure the right note would be struck.

Chapter 24

My Mistake

Diana Ross & Marvin Gaye

Caraleigh was wearing an Akris grey suit with her Fendi coat with the mink trim. She had timed her entrance perfectly and walked in the front door of the Gagliardi Building right after the photographer *Carrie what's-her-face,* the Foundation's go-to photographer. Carrie was perfect because one of her strengths was settling people down. She was a master at it. And right now, she was engaged in a conversation with that little twit at the reception desk and some other woman.

Caraleigh walked in, and Carrie announced, “There she is.”

Ava didn’t get a good look at her. Carrie and Caraleigh were strolling to the elevator when Caraliegh heard the receptionist calling someone to say that the Foundation people were on their way up – no mention of Caraleigh by name – this was a very good thing.

Caraleigh and Carrie were shown to a comfortable reception area near Rocco’s assistant’s desk. They were offered something to drink for what was described as a short wait. Caraleigh declined, but Carrie got up to get her own.

“Just point me in the right direction,” Carrie offered pleasantly.

Bruno walked up and introduced himself to the photographer and said, “Come with me; we have cannolis too, and they are....” Bruno offered a fingertips-kiss joyfully tossing his fingers in the air and gestured for Carrie to follow. She did. This left Caraleigh alone to arrange herself on the chair facing the assistant.

Bridget didn’t bother about Caraleigh and went about her work making phone calls easily overheard by Caraleigh.

“Hey, Angie, didn’t you say you had the direct number for Moderesto’s manager? Yes, I need it. I have to make a change to Rocco's reservation tomorrow night. *Yep*. Got it. Thanks."

Caraleigh sat up a little.

"Good morning," Bridget said in a cheery voice into the phone. "May I speak to the manager? Oh, even better. Thank you.... Good morning Mr. Decoursey; it's Bridget from Rocco's office... I am. Thank you. Rocco asked to please serve the Nero D'avola 2010 or 2015 instead of champagne tomorrow night. It's a favorite for both Rocco and Ms. Pentelino. *Yes*... Christina Pentelino. She's a doll. You'll love her. Oh, yes, absolutely. Think Odette Annable. *Um-hum*, that girl. But prettier, probably way smarter, and for sure nicer. I would not be surprised at all, and it would be the wedding of the decade. He's never acted like this before. Oh shoot, I've got another call. Thank you. Yes, you too."

Caraleigh was stunned. She composed herself, but she let the news run through her mind. *Doesn't fucking date? Right. The liar*. Well, he was still single and up for grabs. Let the best woman win. She would make her play. Let's just see who will be having dinner at Modernesto tomorrow night, and she will have the champagne, thank you very much.

At that moment, Bruno was coming down the corridor with Carrie and another guy who looked like an NFL lineman with arms so big he could pop the seams of his suit coat. Bruno handed off the small tray of cannolis to the behemoth and motioned Carrie into a conference room. Bruno then approached Caraleigh.

Bruno recognized her from the Roma Café and hesitated for a moment. "Good Morning. Caraleigh Frances, right? Are you here from the Foundation? I believe we've met before."

Caraleigh stood almost coming to Bruno's shoulder in her sky-high boots. "Met? I don't think so," she said carelessly.

Bruno smirked and passed it off. The only thing that mattered was the check she was presenting. He nodded toward the doorway that Carrie and the other man disappeared into. "We thought the light in the conference room would be best for the photo. Thank you for coming in this morning. We would have come down to the Foundation's offices, but this kindness we appreciate," Bruno said politely.

As they entered the room, Carrie motioned for Caraleigh to stand in front of an abstract mural behind the head of the conference table.

"Miss Frances, can I have you here, please? I want to check the light." Carrie positioned Caraleigh and took several pictures before she reviewed the work. "Okay, great. Miss Frances, if you would stand on the left and Bruno, can you stand here, please? Great. Okay, Miss Frances, please hand off the check and shake Mr. Gagliardi's hand. Awesome. Just a couple more. Bruno, my camera loves you. Perfect. Oh, yes, right there, please. Beautiful. Just perfect." Carrie checked her camera, quickly scrolling through the pictures to ensure she got at least a few good ones. She turned to her subjects and said, "Thank you both."

Bruno looked at the check for the first time. "This is very generous of the Foundation. Thank you, Miss Frances. I know the Holtzbergs, my family, and Rocco will be very pleased."

"Speaking of Rocco, Where is he so we can take the picture?" Caraleigh asked.

"Rocco isn't here this morning. He called Dr. Dorington to request that I accept the check in his place," Bruno said.

Caraleigh went pale. "I thought you were just standing in so Carrie could get the light and the background right. Rocco is the recipient."

Bruno squared his shoulders and looked down at her. "No, Miss Frances, Rocco is not the recipient; this began as a memorial to my late sister. Thanks to the Holtzberg family, Beaumont Hospital, and now the Remington Foundation, the charity that bears my sister's name, is the grant recipient. We are all very grateful for the Foundation's generosity," Bruno said politely.

From across the room, Carrie was sipping her coffee and sampling a cannoli. "Caraleigh, come have one of these. They are to die for. "

"I don't want that crap," Caraleigh said. Then turned to Bruno and demanded, "Where's Rocco?"

"He's with a client this morning," Bruno said in a tone far nicer than Caraleigh deserved.

"Client," she spat, "is that the euphemism for the little whore he's currently fucking?"

Bruno looked at her with a professional gaze that gave nothing away. "We are genuinely happy the Remington Foundation has expressed its interest in our endeavor. We hope you have a pleasant rest of your day Miss Frances."

"You're dismissing me? She shook her head in disgust." Oh, I'll go, but tell me this. How did Rocco find out that I would be here today? I'm assuming he didn't have the balls to face me, and he sent you," Caraleigh said, on the verge of angry tears.

Bruno smirked. "We, and this includes Rocco, thought it would be Dr. Dorington here for the picture. I don't think Rocco had any idea you were a staffer at the Foundation. So, no, Rocco was unaware that you would be here this morning.

Sorry, you got the JV team." Bruno gestured to himself with a good-natured laugh.

"One more thing. This girl. This Christina Pentelino."

Bruno narrowed his eyes.

"*Yeah,* I know her name. Just how long has he been seeing her?"

"Rocco's personal life is no one's business but his. His relationship with his girlfriend is private."

"Oh, no. Rocco doesn't do girlfriends. Rocco doesn't do relationships. Rocco was very clear about that." Caraleigh crossed her arms in a challenge.

"I think, Miss Frances, you need to understand the context. Rocco doesn't do girlfriends or relationships *with you,*" Bruno said, lifting an eyebrow, "now, I'm sure you have other places to be." Bruno leaned over and pushed a button, saying, " Donny, can you come into the conference room, please?"

In a matter of seconds, Donny the behemoth came into the room again, nodded to Carrie, and strode to Bruno's side. "Mr. Gagliardi?"

Bruno gestured to Caraleigh. "Donny, show Miss Frances the way out, please?"

Chapter 25

Wanted

Hunter Hayes

He knew she would be beautiful this evening. Christina was always beautiful. Maybe it was the way she had her hair tonight. It was swept up off her neck; there was something about that; it made her look vulnerable. Her dress was simple, and in a sea of fire engine red and little black outfits, Christina looked like a goddess in a close-fitting winter-white dress. There was nothing scant about it: not low cut or sporting a slit to reveal her legs. No matter, Rocco sucked in a breath when she took off her coat. She smiled at him as she gently took his arm as the host led them to a table in the back.

As Dirk promised, it was a little secluded near one of the restaurant's fireplaces. It was also not an easy exit, just in case Christina might be inclined to bolt this evening. He needed to send a note to Dirk Decoursey – this was perfect.

Rocco had worked out the drink and food service to limit the server's presence at the table.

"Rocco," Christina placed her hand at the base of her neck, "This is such a fabulous place. I thought it was impossible to get a reservation. Thank you."

"I made this reservation some time ago." He took her hand. "I wanted something very special."

"I'd high-five you for the win. But I think this is more of a deep bow place than a high-five place," Christina said.

"The owner is an old and important friend of the family. He wouldn't bat an eye with either," Rocco told her.

"I thought it was Dirk Decoursey who owned this with his foster child?"

"That's right, It's Dirk Decoursey and Bobby Jura. They are the owners."

"I saw Dirk Decoursey when I went to New York with my friends Marisol and Holly. We stood outside for the *Today* show. He, Dirk Decoursey, was there because he had just redecorated a

Penthouse for Sting. I think it was Sting; he came over during a break because we had a sign for Holly's Nanni, her grandmother. It said *Nanni, we made it. Troy, Michigan to NYC in 13 hours*. Mr.Decoursey spotted the Troy, Michigan, and came over to say hello, which was totally nice of him."

"No surprise, he's a very nice guy," Rocco said as the server brought the first course to their table. The salad was Bobby Jura's version of *Frutti di mare* because Christina loved seafood. The main course, a petite filet, another of her favorites.

Christina was never blasé about anything. Something that Rocco loved about her. And if she really liked something, she wasn't shy to say so. She loved the meal from start to finish. Now that the dishes had been cleared away, the dessert wine and the cake were brought to the table, the purpose of the evening needed to commence.

Rocco took her hands in his, "As promised. But this is harder than I imagined because you might be out the door by the end of this. Please promise that you will hear me out completely, and if you don't want me to take you home, I will arrange safe transportation for you, Christina."

"This sounds ominous."

"I'm not trying to be so dramatic, but... he looked away for a moment and thought he saw... *No. It couldn't be.* He looked back to begin. "The first time I saw you wasn't in Doug's office. The first time I saw you was at Nero's.... It was the night you were there with Neville."

Her mouth fell open.

Rocco pressed on, "I was there with my cousin Michael. We weren't trying to eavesdrop. And we didn't hear everything, but we heard enough to know he gave you a ring, and the ring didn't fit. We saw him take it off your finger. About a week later, I was at Pinky's for dinner with clients. I saw you. You were there with your friends having drinks. Later, I saw you leaving to go home. I was parked in that same lot as we parked in last Saturday. After that, I saw you at the Coney Island the day you picked up everyone's lunch, and you paid the buck twenty-seven to help those girls out. I promise you I never followed you. Every one of those times was a coincidence. It was also a coincidence that I passed you in Neville's car that day. I recognized you." Rocco lowered his head, and, looking up at her through his impossibly thick eyelashes, he said, "It wasn't a coincidence that I got off I-75 to turn around and get back on so that I could find you again."

"And that's why.." Christina said, a tad awestruck.

"Yes, that's why I did what I did." He took a breath. "That lack of a ring is also why I contacted Mr. Holtzberg about the memorial for my sister. Now, this will sound a lot creepier than it actually was. One of the people I was having lunch with at the coney island knows the Holtzbergs. We saw the name on the truck you drove that day. He knew my family was looking for a better way to honor my sister. He also," Rocco took in a breath, steadied himself, and said, "he also knew I was attracted to you, and he suggested that I approach the Holtzbergs. Christina, I was so blown away by you during that first meeting when you came up with the charity and suggested how it could be funded and how to give it credibility. I have been in brainstorming sessions and high-powered negotiations; I have never seen anything like that. You are quite literally one of the most brilliant people I've ever met."

Christina blanched, not quite sure how to take all this.

"I don't know how I would have handled it if you hadn't called me out for stripping the glove off you when I stopped to fix the tire. I don't know. But I would have done something because this," he gestured between himself and Chistina, "what's going on between us is important. I can't ignore it. I don't want to ignore it. I thought you were incredibly attractive that night at Nero's. I thought you were a nice girl, a good friend that night at Pinky's, and a good person from that day at the coney island. Let's not forget how you put all the boys to shame when we met formally at Holtzbergs. Over the past weeks, the only difference is you have become more to me." He gave her hands a little squeeze. He took in a deep breath as if preparing himself. "I never thought it was a problem conducting my private life like I did. I never looked at it from anyone's perspective but my own," he shook his head. "seeing it from your point of view, it feels cheap to go to bed with people you don't know or care about. I never had an opinion before, but having to talk about this in front of you, I'm not proud of it... any of it," he pinned her with his eyes, "when you asked me last week for a number, it shocked me. I never counted for two reasons. First, it wasn't anything meaningful for me. I know that's callous, but it's the truth. The second reason is there weren't that many. When I got home last week, I did a lot of thinking about all this, including how many."

Christina winced. *Well, you asked for it.* She thought.

Rocco went on. “I have not been with anyone since sometime before Christmas. It was before I saw you at Nero’s. There were two others before that. There was one, but I’m not positive it was in that calendar year,” Rocco said, now crimson with his confession.

“Rocco,” Christina said, “please, I’m embarrassed that I made such a big deal about it. I think it had more to do with me not feeling all that confident in myself as a potential bed partner for you.”

“First of all, Christina, I can promise you I have never compared one person against another. It’s just not like that; for me, it isn’t. I have never been as invested in a relationship as I am with you. I think if it happens, the mechanics aren’t going to be the game changer you think they are.”

She blushed as deeply as the Nero d’Avola wine.

“Also, and I say this because, A. you’re a very smart, creative woman, and B. I’m a highly motivated man. We could figure out that part of our relationship if you agreed to sleep with me.”

Christina thought about it for a second. Okay, true, She had never made a comparison like that either. She looked up, smiled at him, and said, "I shouldn't be comfortable with this, but I am," she sat back, "I am curious why the Nero's and Pinky's and the coney island?" she snapped her fingers and said, "you thought I might remember, and you wouldn't have to make a confession. Am I right?"

"For the most part. I didn't want you to think I was slinking around being some sort of a creeper," Rocco took her hands, "are we okay?"

"I think we are. I know this was difficult for you, but it's really important to me that you were honest about it when you didn't have to be. I don't know if I would have ever figured it out. For that reason, your admission is a huge deal to me."

Rocco thought a moment."There's something else I need to tell you..."

"Well, well, here you are all lovey-dovey on this magical Valentine's Day." A wobbly Caraleigh was dragging a chair over toward their table. "Yes, I'd love to join you and hear all about this magical romance of Rocco's. The guy who doesn't do romance. The man who won't date or ever, God forbid, gets caught dead in a relationship. Did he bother to tell you that, Christina Pentelino? *Ha*, Pentelino. She's Italian. Is that what I lacked? The missing Italian heritage? Would that have made all the difference?" Caraleigh's alcohol-sodden breath hit Rocco, and his reaction was swift. He stood up, taking Christina carefully by the arm; he kissed her hand and said, "I'm so sorry. We should go," Rocco turned his back on Caraleigh, and Christina did as well and began to follow him.

"Hey, you don't get to turn your back on me, you little bitch. Oh, that's right, you're Italian. I saw the Godfather, so I know all the words, Not little bitch, little dago bitch. Or is it wop," Caraleigh began following Rocco and Christina. "If it's not wop or dago it must be Guinea. That's what Carlo called Connie in the Godfather.

Christina halted; Rocco walked on a few steps before he understood that he had lost Christina.

Christina walked back to intercept Caraliegh. "Are you here with someone?"

"What?" Caraleigh sputtered.

"Did you come with someone who can drive you home?" Christina said in a quiet voice.

"No, because I know Rocco, and Rocco will take me home after he leaves you in the dust. That's the plan," Caraleigh said confidentially.

"Nope, we'll need a plan B for this evening. Have you got a friend you can call?" Christina asked.

Caraleigh gave a loud and somewhat snot-riddled snort. "Are you kidding? Look at me. I'm gorgeous. Women are completely intimidated by me. That's why I don't have women friends. I can't. And men? Men fall in love with me. I can't call a man or woman friend."

"I can see that. Yes. It would be challenging to be in your shoes. Do you have a sister or a brother we might call? Someone you trust? Christina walked Caraleigh back to the table she and Rocco had that evening. It was out of the way and a better place for the *not-for-the-public* Caraleigh.

"Hey, you can't be nice to me. We're in a fight over Rocco."

"*Nah*, Let's not fight over him. That is a Prada handbag. I'll bet it's one of your favorites, right?"

"I got this for Christmas. I love it.' Carleigh hugged the bag to her chest.

"If we fight, the first thing I'm going to do is go for the handbag."

"You would steal my handbag," Caraleigh gasped

"No. I wouldn't steal it; I'd vandalize it," Christina said.

"You wouldn't."

"I would. Listen, I have a much better idea. "

"What's that?"

"Rock Paper Scissors," Christina said.

Rocco stopped short, and Dirk Decoursey and a barback collided with him.

"Okay, Rock, paper, scissors it is," Caraleigh said as she slid down the wall, slumping forward and passing out."

■■■

The next hour was spent getting Caraleigh a ride back to her mother's house. This was something that Dirk Decoursey managed with his night manager,

Rocco was quiet, disturbingly quiet. He did not leave Christina's side throughout the entire misadventure.

Dirk was Dirk. He first figured out who Caraleigh belonged to and then found out that it wasn't his bar that got Caraleigh so liquored up. After that, his time was spent chatting with Christina as they watched over a snoring Caraleigh and a taciturn Rocco.

"Come back. Promise me," Dirk said to Christina as she and Rocco were finally leaving.

"I'll come back as soon as I can. Thanks, Dirk," Christina said as Rocco's SUV pulled under the canopy. A stoic Rocco helped her in for the ride home.

As soon as Rocco got in the car, he was on the phone with what Christina figured to be his brother Bruno.

The conversation centered on how Caraleigh Frances discovered he and Christina would be at Moderesto's. Rocco's theory was she somehow had access to Rocco's phone. Rocco was still on the phone when he pulled into Christina's condo parking lot.

Without any ceremony, Christina let herself out of the SUV. By the time Rocco looked up from his phone call, Christina was inside her condo, turning on lights as she went.

"Shit. Bruno, sorry. Yeah, I'll bring it by tomorrow late morning if that's okay. Thanks." Rocco ended the call, parked the car, and took off for Christina's door.

She appeared after some moments, poking her head around the door that was all but shut to him. "Did you forget something, Mr. Gagliardi?" Christina said, with just a chill in her question.

"I, we didn't, I wanted to... I thought we might talk," Rocco stumbled.

"I thought so too, but your priorities are elsewhere, and I won't take up more of your evening." She moved to shut the door.

Rocco shoved his foot to stop her. "Wait. Please wait."

She stopped and looked expectantly.

Rocco blinked but said nothing.

"That's sort of what I thought." Christina put her head down and began to close the door again.

"Please, Christina. I'm handling everything badly, I know. I'm embarrassed. I don't know how she knew I was there. I don't know how she knew who you were. I feel ... I feel like I let you down."

She abandoned the door and began climbing the stairs in silent invitation. Rocco followed.

When she reached her front room, she looked back over her shoulder and gestured to the most petite chair in the space, the one that Rocco wasn't sure could hold his weight, but he sat, albeit uncomfortably. Christina lowered herself stiffly to the sofa and waited.

Fuck. He said to himself. "I never would have picked Modernesto for our evening if I thought she'd show up."

"Seriously? This is why you think I'm less than pleased with you? For such a smart man, Rocco, you are proving to be a little dense." She tucked her legs under her and crossed her arms in a protective hug.

"I don't, I can't. I'm confused." Rocco dropped his head in his hands.

"You fessed up to your past. I accept that you aren't as pure as the driven snow. We both have ex's. Having a drunken ex show up at a romantic dinner isn't great, but it wasn't the end of the world. I was glad she wasn't getting into a car to potentially kill or maim herself or anyone else. That's not the source of my frustration with you."

Rocco just looked lost. "Just tell me. I'll fix it."

She let out a breath, shook her head, then told him, "After you tell me all about your sordid past and how you were too much of a scaredy-cat to let me know you had seen me before you stopped to help with the tire so then you thought it was a good idea to ignore me while you solved the mystery of how your ex-girlfriend caught up to you at dinner? After expressing my uncertainty about getting physical, you thought being on the phone with your brother was foreplay?"

"She was never my girlfriend."

Christina stood, eyes blazing, and pointed to the door.

"Wait. That's not what I wanted to say." Rocco slid off the chair and walked on his knees toward her. "I don't know why I did that. I think it was because I felt ridiculous over her showing up and that things were out of control. I was just trying…"

"Trying to make me feel less important than knowing how she knew where to find you? Hey, thumbs up, mission accomplished."

"No. Never, not at all. I just thought I needed to find the answer," Rocco added quickly.

"If that is the burning question, Rocco, call her tomorrow and ask."

"I don't want to talk to her again," Rocco said. "I wanted to know to protect you from anything like that happening again. I feel horrible that you had to deal with it. "

"Okay, I can see that, but shouldn't you have said something like, Christina, I feel horrible that my former lover intruded this evening. I am concerned that this was more than happenstance. I feel like contacting my brother to figure out if she's hacked into our system. As much as I want to be with you, I'm concerned about the integrity of our system."

"It caught me off guard. You're right, and you're right about all of it, but that former lover is…, it's not accurate. Can we not assign her that title?" Rocco was now at her feet.

Christina sat down. "Sorry, I'm feeling a little resentful."

Rocco embraced her around her knees and lay his head in her lap. "I'm a clod. Please let me make this up to you."

She softened and began stroking his hair. "I wish I could tell you to leave and go on with my life; I find I can't." She lightly ran her fingers through his hair.

Rocco closed his eyes, savoring the moment, and smiled gratefully. "You were ready to ditch me with rock, paper, scissors."

She laughed quietly, "I was more interested in keeping her out of the main dining room and away from the food service. I could imagine a bowl of gazpacho all over the front of a designer dress."

"Most women wouldn't have given a damn. They would have let me lead them out of the place without glancing backward."

"You wouldn't have let her alone to do whatever mayhem she was contemplating, would you?" Christina asked quietly.

"My protective instincts were about you, but I would have figured out something to keep her from driving, most definitely. You had a better grasp of how to deal with her. I'm not happy with myself about that, and I wish you hadn't had to." Rocco nuzzled his cheek against her, then straightened again, kneeling before her taking her hands, and looking into her eyes. "I had such high hopes for this evening. I thought if you didn't run screaming from the restaurant, maybe we could move this forward."

"Define, move this forward," Christina asked.

Rocco got up to sit beside her. She allowed it and let him put his arm around her. He turned to face her. "I want my shot with you."

"What's that mean exactly? You want to enter my name on the long list of your conquests?"

Rocco threw his head back, "God, I conquered none of those women. Do I want to make you mine? You're damn right I do. I've wanted you in my bed from that first moment I saw you. But the conquest I want is more than that." He stroked her face and gently pushed a few strands of her hair behind her ear. "I know I've made some pretty lame moves with you. I may be a slow learner, but I am teachable. And I'm nothing if not a hard worker." He let out a breath. "I heard you loud and clear about not being a fan of sex. Maybe you'll never be. Maybe it'll be a very reluctant and very scarce favor from you. I'm not so much chained to my passions that I only see you as a fuck."

Christina winced.

Rocco went on, "But I'd like to think that maybe your experiences have been with the wrong man. And that man wasn't willing to put in the time and effort to show you there could be more. I don't know if I'm the right man, but I'm willing to suffer the rejection to see if I could be."

Christina's breath caught. "How do I dismiss that?"

Rocco smiled a crooked smile, "You don't. You embrace it. We label it. Whether I bed you or not, you're with me, I'm with you, and it's exclusive."

"I see. Okay," Christina said reluctantly.

Rocco shifted her effortlessly to sit on his lap, and before she knew it, Rocco was kissing her. It wasn't a seduction but better than nice. He smelled of his soap and the wine they had been drinking before little miss Prada handbag showed up. Christina pushed that part of the night away and enjoyed the taste, smell, and feel of him. It felt a lot like the day he pulled the glove off her hand, and she got a little lost in all of it.

Rocco reluctantly pulled away. "I'll call you tomorrow," he said, still holding her close.

She nodded and disengaged enough to stand. Rocco stood as well. He was a physical presence, all broad shoulders and wide chest standing at a commanding six-foot-plus. No wonder women wanted him. Christina had to acknowledge she did as well, as evidenced by her now very wet panties.

Yes, he needed to leave before she did something untoward.

Several other kisses were perfectly chaste before they called it a night.

■■■

Brunch with Marisol and Holly was arranged via text as soon as Rocco left that Saturday evening. And of course, they would be there tomorrow, but late, very late morning, please.

Both Christina's besties were far more interested in the Rocco soap opera than a recount of their Valentine's Day evenings.

"So, what do you know about this girl?" Marisol asked.

"Nothing more than she's got really expensive taste, and she may or may not have a substance abuse problem."

"Are you sure she's just a hookup? It's a little crazy that someone that causal would be all up in his business while he was clearly on a date," Marisol said.

"I don't think he's misrepresented her. I'm also surprisingly okay about the whole seeing me multiple times and not saying anything. At least I understand why I thought I knew him. It's something else. It feels like there's something... I don't think he's untruthful." Christina sipped the expresso.

Holly cocked her head and lifted an eyebrow. "If you think he's the real McCoy, why do you feel unsure?"

"Exactly," Marisol shifted to look at Christina, "I think this guy is the real deal. He didn't have to own up to those other times. He could have come up with some bullshit about pulling your glove off. I think you are looking for drama that really isn't there. Just go with it." Marisol pointed between herself and Holly and said, "We will always tell you the unvarnished truth."

Holly snorted, "And she won't listen any better than you."

Marisol held up her hand in the universal stop gesture. "I have heard you. I know who Garrett is. A child. A very pretty child. But it's fun not to be all that serious about him. Well, it's fun not to be serious about anyone right now."

"I don't understand why you spend your time and energy on someone you don't see long-term; it's your life, and you know we will always be around to support you," Holly said to Marisol.

"Ditto," Christina raised her coffee cup. "As for me, I could see Rocco long-term. I know he's trying, and I really like that. I just wish I didn't have this little niggling feeling the other shoe will drop."

Chapter 26

Come Rain or Come Shine

Ray Charles

Late Monday morning, Christina returned from a status meeting to find a floral arrangement on her desk. It was four dozen preserved red roses arranged in a hatbox. The card read, *Thinking of you, Rocco.*

She sent off a text, telling him, *The roses are beautiful. Thank you.*

Not a moment later, she got Rocco's return text. *Dinner?*

Sure. But early please, I have a big day tomorrow. She explained.

Even better. I'll be by at 5:30.

■■■

Christina appreciated that Rocco was never late. Early, yes, late, not once so far. And that afternoon, he was there at 5:10.

She had just gotten in the car when he asked, "What are you in the mood for?"

"There's a new Mexican restaurant in Novi that's supposed to be pretty good. Is that too far? "

"Not too far. I haven't had Mexican for a while," Rocco said as he pulled out of the condo's parking lot.

The ride was dedicated to Rocco filling her in on the last of the Doctor Granville show and how the hospital replaced him on the committee. Dinner was information about property sale details, which took up most of the conversation. The ride home was all about the selection of the design team for the playground.

"Was it the group from Oregon?" Christina asked.

"Yes. How did you know? Did Doug tell you?"

Christina shook her head, smiling. "They are the group I thought should get it."

"Really. Why?" Rocco asked.

"Because they have redone more accessible playgrounds than any of the other firms. I think that gives them a perspective of what works and what doesn't. If you only do new projects, you aren't always seeing the flaws," she said,

"They were my first pick too, but not for that reason. Yours, by the way, is a really good reason. I just hadn't thought of it before," Rocco said.

"Why did you pick them?"

"The head designer has a handicapped child. I think this is his passion, not just work for his firm."

"He didn't disclose that. How did you find that out?" Christina asked.

"Bruno, the Sherlock Holmes of the family. I asked him to look into the principles for the shortlist of firms. Due diligence to ensure there isn't a predator or pedophile lurking," he explained.

Christina let out an impromptu belch. "Oh my heavens," she said, "Pardon me. I don't know where that came from."

"I think it may have been the refried beans. But, hey, our Scottish babysitter had the perfect aphorism for that situation. She always told us, *better an empty room than a bad tenant,*" Rocco said in a perfect Scottish brogue.

Christina's stomach now began audibly gurgling. She hoped Rocco didn't hear it. It sure sounded loud enough. Christina realized she needed to hold on tight about halfway home because it felt like the gurgling was now potential flatulence. With a rush, the gas could not be contained; the smell of methane seemed to seep into every corner of the SUV's cab. Christina covered her face and apologized.

Rocco decided to ignore it.

Christina lowered her window to clear the stench. It seemed to help, and she hoped the balance of the ride home might happen without another incident. But it was not to be. Just as Rocco turned on to Fourteen Mile, a second more potent gas found its way loudly out of Christina. She again asked for Rocco's pardon.

Now she couldn't get out of the SUV fast enough. Not only because of the two horrendous farts but also because now it was necessary to get to a bathroom before she humiliated herself with the literal *shit-sh*ow that was eminent. Rocco pulled into a parking space in front of Christina's condo; she quickly found her house keys and sprinted from the vehicle, leaving Rocco behind.

She got into the house and ran for the powder room just off the front room. She kicked her boots off and got out of her slacks and her panties around her ankles when the first of several waves of diarrhea hit. The barnyard smell was halfway down the stairs as Rocco made his way into Christina's condo.

Christina struggled to get to the powder room's light and fan switches when a very large hand reached around the corner and turned both on. Christina was speechless. She then heard him retreating down the stairs, and her front door close to her great relief. Well, the worry over if she should date him was now solved. She felt a wash of disappointment in herself. *But*...It was better this way. She could never face him after this humiliation.

After some twenty minutes, Christina heard the door open and footsteps; someone was climbing the stairs. "Christina," Rocco asked, "are you still in the powder room?"

She couldn't speak. She heard his movements down the hall. Lights being flipped on, and Rocco's rustling about.

"Christina? Are you alright?" he asked.

"I'm, I'm okay," she said in a small voice.

Rocco's hand now appeared as he hung her bathrobe on the door knob of the powder room. "Take your time, but when you're ready, let me know, and I'll start the shower for you," Rocco told her.

Can I just die and get this over with? She thought as she put her head in her hands and said, "Okay, thank you."

After another half hour, Christina's legs were mostly asleep, but she seemed to be over the turgidity and loose bowels. She cleaned herself as much as she could. She said a prayer of thanksgiving that she didn't have to walk out of the powder room with crap-soiled slacks and panties. She washed her hands, put the bathrobe on, and peeked out of the powder room. Rocco was in the front room and looked up.

No, no, no. Oh... my... God. She thought.

"Let me start that shower for you. I've got some medication, and the pharmacy recommended electrolytes, so I got you Coconut Water," Rocco said, sprinting around her and heading for her bedroom.

Her Bedroom! Was her vibrator put away? Christina didn't want to think the evening could be any worse. She walked slowly into her bedroom, partly because she wanted to put off the next round of humiliation and partly because her bum was chafed and raw. She rounded the corner, and the vibrator was not sitting out on her nightstand, to her great relief.

She made her way to the master bath where all six foot whatever of him was carefully laying out a fresh towel and washcloth. He straightened, came close, and kissed her forehead. *Was he crazy? He had to be. If the shoe was on the other foot, I would have been running as fast as possible from the hot mess that is me.*

"Call me if you need anything," Rocco said

Christina stared at the closed door for a moment before disrobing and getting into the shower.

Christina appeared makeup free, wearing a robe covering a lavender pajama set. Her hair was still damp from her shower and piled on her head. She was pink, which could have been from hot water or one of Christina's blushes, he wasn't sure, but she looked beautiful.

"Would you like me to heat some broth? Is your stomach up for that?" Rocco asked.

"I had the coconut water. Let's see what happens with that. Besides, I'm not hungry. Just tired," she said.

"Let's get you to bed then." Rocco offered her his hand.

She took it, hoping that the sooner she was in bed for the night, the sooner Rocco would be out the door, and her social agony would end. She wasn't going to try to play hostess to Rocco; she was bone-deep tired, and completely mortified. She all but fell into bed.

Rocco tenderly tucked her in and kissed her cheek. She thought he would now leave, but he stopped in the bedroom doorway after a few moments, considering something. He ducked back down the hallway flicking off the lights as he retraced his steps. When he came back into the bedroom, Christina thought she heard the swish of clothes coming off, but that couldn't be. Then she listened to the sound of a zipper and felt the dip of the mattress next to her. She held her breath, but he wasn't touching her. She felt the heat of him near her, and his breath ghosted against her neck and shoulders.

"Goodnight. Sweet dreams," he said.

"You're staying?" she gasped.

"I am. I'm here in case you need something. Just settle back, relax and get some sleep," he told her.

She was too tired to argue. After a few moments, his breaths evened, and in a few more moments, she heard his light snore, and she, too, fell asleep.

Christina slowly came awake, feeling Rocco's very solid and hard body spoon-like at her back. His head was tucked into the crook of her neck, and her head rested on his outstretched arm. His other arm was slung carelessly around her waist. She could feel his warm thighs against her legs as she became more awake.

Her thoughts raced. She felt his penis, his very large, very hard penis, wedge itself firmly in the cleft of her bottom. She stilled and stayed that way when he got out of bed.

It was too early to have ambient light illuminate her bedroom. Still, she saw Rocco's shadow pass by to make his way to the bathroom. She heard him groan and yawn, the toilet flush, the water run in the sink, and the door opened to hear Rocco begin to retrieve his clothes and dress. In a matter of minutes, he was leaning down to kiss her.

She then sat up in bed.

"Are you well enough to go into work today?" he asked.

"Feeling like it or not, there's too much going on not to." She yawned and stretched.

"Okay, but let me bring you dinner," he said.

"That's... well, brave of you. Very kind but brave, after..."

"It's not a big deal, *Patatina*."

"Okay. Thank you."

"Anything special? Let me amend; anything other than Mexican?"

Before she could answer, Rocco was out the door, calling, "Just kidding, text me what you are in the mood for – even if it is Mexican."

Chapter 27

Pity Party

Melanie Martinez

Mary carefully packed up her backpack for her day. She didn't need to worry so much about sneaking food out of the house like she did before. These days her mothers were still distracted. First, it was moving to this new house. Now it was fixing things and redecorating. Every day there were workmen and deliveries. Her mom and mum didn't notice much about her these days.

The move was the worst. It was supposed to be the best; it wasn't. It sucked. It sucked big giant balls. The new school was horrible. Something her mom and mum told her would be so much better. Really? How? The kids were mean. The teachers were meaner. The principal was a goober but sort of nice; he at least told her mothers that maybe it would be better if they changed her school. But no. No way. Both her mom and her mum were settled on this school because it was where her mum and her uncles went to school – she was a legacy. That was the reason for moving, too, so they could be in the same neighborhood as the school and her mum's family, her grandma, grandpa, and Uncle Michael.

Her other uncle was in South America. Mary had never met him, but there were pictures of him everywhere at her grandparents' house. He was a priest. All the priests Mary knew were unfortunate-looking guys with hair that grew out of their ears, and that one old priest even had hairs growing out of the top of his nose - gross. Her South American uncle was her mum's twin brother, and he was crazy good-looking, like hot. Movie star hot. To Mary, it made no sense that he was a priest, but she bet he had the pews packed with girls that just wanted to be around to look at him.

Thoughts about her priest uncle always made their way into her head anytime she had to be in church or the church school she now had to attend. Mary wondered what uncle Robert, the priest, would think of her family.

Mary's family wasn't the same kind of family as the kids had in this new school. After the last parent-teacher meeting, when Mom and Mum met with Mrs. Nettles, Mrs. Nettles told her mothers that they were sinning in the eyes of the Lord. That had her mom going ape shit off on Mrs. Nettles, and that was when the war started, and her life ended.

There was one chance to fix this. She, Mary Catherine Slaughter, found out the secret, and she could make the problem of two mothers disappear. She actually had a mother *and* a father. She found the marriage certificate. She found the proof of who her father was and the way out of this mess her mom and her mum had made for her.

It took her some time to figure out who her father was. It was all the little pieces that she finally put together. It was never a secret about the Gagliardi family. Her Grandma had a sister who married a Gagliardi. She had never met those people, so she didn't really think about it...before. But then she overheard her uncle Michael talking to her mum about Rocco Gagliardi. They talked about this Rocco a lot, but they shut up fast if she or her mom was around. She kept that bit of information. That had to be important, and it turned out that it was.

She asked for her own cell phone for her birthday. But no. Her mothers thought they were so smart, keeping her from texting her old friend back at her old school. So, fine, she asked for a laptop for her birthday. Her mothers fell for it when she said it was for school. It could be for school, but it was really for the internet. Now she could stay close with her old friends, and she could find and keep track of her father, Rocco Gagliardi.

A lot of what her mothers talked about wasn't just their crap. It was true. It was true how they met. It was at a 4th of July party over stateside when they were in high school. That part was actual; it really happened. The Gagliardi family had that party every year. There was an article about it in the newspaper a couple of years ago. They interviewed her father, who said the family had celebrated the 4th of July with a party since 1971. There was a picture of the Gagliardi family. Her father, her grandparents, and her great grandparents plus her uncles were in the newspaper picture too. That was the first time she saw her state-side family.

It made her sad that her mothers had lied about it, that they had refused to tell her the truth.

Finding out the truth meant a lot to her. Mostly, it meant she hadn't been a turkey baster baby. That's what a lot of her mothers' friends who had babies that weren't from a regular man-woman way but a turkey baster at a sperm clinic. It was gross thinking about a turkey baster up the coochie to get a baby. It made her feel more normal that she came to be the usual way – that was gross too, but at least it was usual.

When she met Mr. Eastburn that day, she thought announcing that Rocco Gagliardi would scare the guy off. Then she thought she was going to be in trouble. Like her mothers sent him or something. But he had a grudge against her father because her father was dating this girl Mr. Eastburn was crushing on. That wasn't good news for Mary. Not that Mr. Eastburn was crushing on some girl, but that her father was dating someone. Because if Rocco Gagliardi was dating someone, getting him back together with her mom would be more complicated. That was the goal, getting them back together. It wasn't like Mary wanted to break up with her mom and her mum. She just wanted a different story, a mother and father story, so the school wouldn't be so hard, so the kids wouldn't be so mean, and the teacher wouldn't argue with her mom.

Mr. Eastburn had a way to get the girl he was crushing on. That would clear the way for her mother and father to get back together. And that would mean she could also meet her father and the rest of her Gagliardi family.

Mr.Eastburn said the timing had to be perfect, or none of this would work. He also told her to be ready, and that meant getting an outfit for the meeting day. And today was the day they would shop for the right outfit.

Today she would have to nail down her transportation for the meeting that Mr. Eastburn told her was on April the 10th. That meant she had to get the $50.00 US for her ride to Detroit with the Cicconni sisters. That day she wouldn't have to work out a ride back because that day, her father, Rocco Ignatius Gagliardi, would be driving her.

■■■

Caraleigh reluctantly began working for her stepfather this week. It was a nothing job. She knew it, but she snagged a better office, and the job came with a title. She was now Office Supervision for the engineering firm. The thing was, the only office she was supervising was her own. She was bored, but she could deal with boredom.

Her mother was furious with her after Saturday night, the Valentine's Day massacre, and the debacle at Modernesto. The fucking owner knew Richard. He called on Sunday to check to be sure Caraleigh was all right. That set off all the alarm bells. The owner, Dirk Decoursey, said things like stalking, alcohol poisoning, and public spectacle. Those were the only conversation topics for the rest of the weekend. It would have been hilarious if her mother and stepfather hadn't been so insistent that she take a step back from her pursuit of Rocco Gagliardi.

The restaurant owner was Dirk Decoursey. He may have been sort of old guard, but he was still hip enough to be a significant influencer. Her mother practically fainted when she found out whose restaurant Caraleigh got thrown out of. And the situation was made exponentially worse when Dirk Decoursey invited her mother and stepfather out for dinner to chat about the St. Valentine's Day furor Caraleigh had evidently created.

She remembered arriving at the restaurant, asking for the ladies' room, and scoping the place out to search for Rocco and the fucking bimbo. It was suggested to her mother and stepfather that Caraleigh's insinuation into Rocco Gagliardi's life would only bring more social awkwardness for

Caraleigh and land like a pile of shit at their doorstep. They were all ears.

"Decoursey was clear about just who was having dinner in the main dining room when you made your drunken threats to Gaglardi's date. You made yourself look out of control and pathetic. It's not a good look," Richard told her.

Her mother was less kind. "If your father knew you were chasing that Italian, you would find your credit cards suspended and your income from him compromised. This is not a smart move. Richard and I aren't going to finance you."

There was a way out of this that would cost her Rocco Gaglardi, but not her father's support, and that was a move to her father's people in Litchfield, Illinois. Her dad had suggested it before; right now, it didn't seem like the worst idea.

Chapter 28

How Dry I am

Harry James

He slept in your bed, and he never made a move? Marisol's head shake was audible even in the text.

Christina decided to call.

Marisol picked up and said, “Okay, let me repeat, he slept in your bed, and he never made a move?”

“Why would he think about having sex with me under the circumstances?” Christina asked.

"You are so naive. Most men aren't that squeamish. Ever heard of anal sex or period sex? Come on. Why did he say he stayed? Don't answer that. I'll tell you why; he's way into you, girl."

"I think you're right, but I have a new concern. Let me rephrase. A big concern. This morning I got an introduction to little Rocco, and Rocco isn't little. I am freaking out at the prospect of him stabbing me with his blunt instrument. I can't handle him, Marisol. There's no way."

"And this provides more explanation about his popularity." Marisol laughed.

"Not funny," Christina said.

"It's a little funny. Okay, I've had sex with six men. The biggest, by far, was my first. He could have joined a cricket match with that bat of his. That first time, it pinched for a few minutes, and then it would have been wonderful if he wasn't a cheating bastard later. The smallest dick I've ever had actually hurt the most because I wasn't turned on enough to have sex. It was like my pussy had been in the dryer too long, but I allowed it. It was a sophomore mistake. Never ever open your legs if you aren't aroused unless it's for the man to show you a good time with his tongue or you have to have a pelvic exam," Marisol told her.

Marisol was greeted with silence on the other end of the line.

"Christina?' Marisol looked at the phone to be sure the call didn't drop. "Hey, girly? You there?"

"*Yeah*, just thinking about what you said, I guess I never thought about that," Christina mused.

"Thought about what, exactly?" Marisol pressed.

"Nothing. It's nothing. I'll keep an open mind about it... about him."

The light went on for Marisol, and she said, "You've never been turned on when you've done it. Have you."

"I never have," Christina all but whispered.

"This could explain your sexual reticence. Well, good news, I get the sense that you are humid to rainforest since you met the big bad R.I.G."

"I literally have no words, Marisol."

The conversation halted when Christina's cell phone chimed with an unknown number. She squinted, deciding to ignore it when the phone stopped sounding. "I've got to go. Call you later," Christina said, turning her attention to the unknown number. It was the third time the same number came up on her phone but never did the person, or maybe robo caller, leave a message.

She'd do a reverse phone number lookup, but, right now, she had actual work tasks to get done.

Chapter 29

Done

Chris Janson

Rocco's morning wasn't as rushed and crazy as he might have imagined. He had to get home to clean up and dress for the day. That included taking care of the impossible hardon he had from being as close to Christina as he was when he woke up and couldn't act on his attraction. But that was a couple of minutes in the shower. The entire thing was more funny than upsetting, but he was sure he wouldn't be able to really laugh about this with her for a while.

Way back when he and Francine were together, back when Rocco thought about a marriage and a forever, it was in such shallow and completely adolescent terms. There was a page-long list of things he had never experienced with Francine. They had never been completely naked in front of each other, and that was despite having sex for the better part of three years. They had never spent an entire night together. They had never peed in front of each other or farted in each other's presence.

Had they made a life together, all that and more would have happened in time, but his last evening with Christina had been more real and more intimate than Rocco's experience with any other woman. It was crazy. It was insane that Christina stinking up his Escalade, then crapping her brains out, made him feel closer to her than he ever felt with Francine, much less any of his hookups between Francine and now.

It came back to him that one of his gym buddies had shared his experience of being present during the birth of his baby. The guy's wife had natural childbirth, and he was recounting that and answering questions. One of the questions led to the man saying that his wife had pushed so hard and that her effort had been so intense that she broke blood vessels on her forehead and that she had a small BM. None of the men present had any overt reaction beyond commenting that childbirth was better left to women. Rocco ruminated on the revelation and, at the time, thought seeing a body function like that would make any future sex with that woman impossible. Now, after the experience with Christina, he chided his younger self for thinking like a stupid little boy. Had Christina offered her body to him this morning, he would have felt like one lucky bastard to be invited to love her like that.

He threw his head back and laughed, realizing that this was the moment he knew with utter clarity that he was in love with her. He also knew he would never share how he came to this understanding with another living soul.

Chapter 30

Silver Springs

Fleetwood Mac

Tuesday and Wednesday of Christina's week were one minor crisis after another, but no more diarrhea.

Rocco had been by every night with dinner, something she appreciated. She also appreciated his not bringing up Monday's humiliating drama.

It occurred to her that the situation would have been vastly different if it had been Neville instead of Rocco last Monday. Neville was so uptight and hysterical that he would have had a figurative shit fit to accompany her literal shit fit. Why had she ever dated him? Well, yes, she now could admit the why.

Every evening with Rocco made Marisol's interpretation of the situation resonate for Christina. Rocco wasn't overtly sexual, but there was no denying that he was more than ready to be her lover. However, he packed that away. Instead, he was affectionate, and she loved that about him.

After eating dinner, they would end up on the sofa watching TV, talking, or both. Rocco would have her head on his lap or his arm around her. Her vibrator had never had such a workout, and she was going through triple-A batteries like Kleenex.

Christina was wiped out from her days at work preparing for the career fair. This year it would be held at the Novi Expo Showcase on Friday of that week.

By Wednesday, they were prepared, making Thursday simply getting everything ready to be transported that evening. This year they were sending over some of the practice equipment, which meant there would be supervisory staff from Holtzbergs expected to man the area reserved for the company at the hall. Christina made sure the four supervisors, three men and one woman, had jackets in black with the company black and gold logo embroidered on the breast pocket. Christina had crisp white dress shirts and uniform khaki pants for each supervisor. When Christina asked for a budget for this clothing, Danielle, the company accountant, was less than supportive.

That was Danielle's usual reaction. Christina wasn't sure if it was Dean or Doug, but she figured one of them must have gotten the reluctant agreement from the accountant. When the supervisors' jackets were delivered, Doug loved how they turned out and had Christina order the same jacket for any staff who routinely represented the company. That meant that she and the two other ladies from HR had the same outfit. The only negative reaction was from Danielle. Nothing new; Danielle wasn't a Christina fan, and this dislike dated back from the second Christina came to Holtzbergs as a part-time employee.

Back then, there wasn't a specific department that handled Human Resources. It was a side job for the accountant at the time, Vera McMahon. Vera was a capable accountant managing three others staffers for payroll, accounts payable, and accounts receivable. The company in those years was much smaller.

The other sundry HR functions were managed by the supervisors or foremen. Doug decided to look for someone to assist him with hiring. Doug set aside money for an administrative assistant and sent Vera to Oakland University to find him one.

Christina was in her last semester of college. She wasn't sure she'd be able to find the generalist position she wanted. The position at Holtzberg's wasn't ideal. Still, it might give her more opportunities to flesh out her resume than getting pigeonholed with a large company.

Christina started part-time before graduating as an administrative assistant to Doug. She earned a full-time HR director position by her first anniversary with the company. This swift ascent into a director position happened because Christina had figured out where to look for potential service techs. The new hires were vetted with a process Christina came up with; the new hires were head and shoulders better technically than most of the service techs they had prior. Fewer call-back service appointments with the latest techs made the initial service calls more profitable. Christina created a method to monitor the tech's work and created incentives for those who demonstrated superior quality. In six months, the company was more profitable. In a year, the business started growing due to a better reputation for quality.

Doug gave Christina more authority to manage hiring, training, incentives, benefits, discipline, and termination. Payroll was now an HR function.

Vera McMahon retired about a year after Christina was hired, which was the beginning of Danielle's slow-burn that finally descended into a complete hatred of all things Christina.

Danielle was promoted to a supervisory position but not a director. She also did not become part of the company leadership. That wouldn't have been an issue, except Christina was promoted to a director position and recognized as part of the administration's management. It was galling to no one except Danielle.

It seemed to Danielle that Christina made too much money and had too much authority. Any time she had the chance to take a swipe, Danielle took it. The final straw was the hot as fuck Rocco Gagliardi.

Danielle recognized him from the gym and from Hour Magazine. She had a spin class at the same place that Rocco used to work out. She and her friends had been lusting after him forever. One day, one of her classmates mentioned that Rocco was in the latest Hour Magazine for some charitable event. From what Danielle could see, Rocco was with this ugly string bean wearing a designer dress wasted on her. The discussion was that Rocco must like them on the thin side. Well, Danielle was toned with a little more butt than that girl in the picture. Anytime Rocco was at the gym, Danielle made sure to walk by and try to engage him somehow, but that never worked. She hadn't seen him in forever and heard that he had moved. That had to mean he was working out at a new gym – a pity for sure.

Then he showed up at the Holtzberg offices one morning, and she couldn't believe it. She found out that he was coming back the next day. Danielle had the whole thing planned, how she would get an introduction.

It annoyed her no end that Christina was invited to the meeting Rocco was attending. But Christina wasn't there when Rocco was leaving the building.

Danielle decided she'd make her move and approach Dan Holtzberg with a report he had asked for while Rocco was there. It could get her an introduction, at the very least. But when Danielle was ready to make her move, she overheard the discussion between Dan and Rocco. And what was it about? Fucking Christina; fucking plus-size, fat ass Christina, and how Rocco wanted to get to know her.

When that smarmy ex-boyfriend of Christina's called her, Danielle was happy to talk to him. She knew it was petty, and she knew if the Holtzbergs ever found out, they wouldn't be pleased. Still, she was delighted to give that Neville character Christina's news and information. It wasn't really confidential information. So when Neville called to find out when the groundbreaking ceremony would take place, Danielle delightedly offered up the location, date, and time for the charity's event and hoped that it would mess just a little with Christina fucking Pentelino. He wanted an invitation to the event, but that was a hard no. She could only manage if he came as her guest or if she gave her ticket up entirely. She wasn't about to be paired with him, and if she gave up her place to Neville? She wasn't positive, but she thought it might mean looking for a new job.

Rocco's text came to Christina Thursday afternoon. *What would you like for dinner?*

It made Christina smile, which seemed to annoy Danielle, who let out a disgusted breath. The second less than pleased reaction Christina got from Danielle today. The first was when Danielle walked into Christina's office in time to hear Marcy complimenting the flowers that were everywhere. There were red roses in a hatbox, a little arrangement in a soup bowl with a "Hope you are feeling better" printed on a decorative button in a cursive font. The newest addition was a "Best Wishes" for the Career day Christina had tomorrow.

Just listening to that idiot Marcy fawn made Danielle want to gag.

"It has hyacinth in it. That's a good luck flower," Marcy said.

This earned Marcy and Christina a sour look and a huff from the doorway of Christina's office when Danielle strode in.

"I've got yet another invoice from a trash and trinket vendor," Danielle said. "If you expect this to be paid, you need to sign off on it."

Christina scanned the bill, knitting her brows until she recognized the charges, "Sure," she said, found a pen, and signed the document.

"Just so you know, this is going to Dean too," Danielle said, "you might want to get yourself prepared with an explanation,"

Christina was distracted by the text from Rocco at this point. It took her a moment to react, but she lifted her head to face Danielle and said, "I don't know if I have all the information about it, but what I can't explain, Doug can."

"Doug didn't place the order, Christina; this has your name on it," Danielle shot back.

"It does, but I placed the order at Doug's request. Actually, there was an email to Dan, Dean, and Dave about it; Dean already knows, and if not, I've got the email to resend to him."

Danielle flushed, turned, and left.

Marcy waited until the unhappy Danielle was out of earshot. "What is her deal?"

"I'm not sure. I never take it personally. For all we know, she has a terrible home life, or her shoes pinch her toes, whatever; I gave up years ago trying to befriend her. As long as Doug and the sons are happy with her, I'll do my best to be polite and professional and not antagonize her." Christina shrugged.

"I guess." Marcy waved a hand dismissively. "Anyhow, on to the important stuff; I'll be there tomorrow when the doors open to help with the setup."

"Great, they told me we can get in at 7:00. They have coffee, and I'll bring the fruit and pastry trays. Thank you for helping with this. I think it's going to be wonderful," Christina said as she walked Marcy out.

"I think so too. I've got a pick-up at the printer this afternoon. I'll see you in the morning," Marcy said as she left Christina.

Christina turned her attention back to Rocco's text and her return message, which read: *You don't need to pick anything up. Smiley face emoji.*

Rocco got the text and frowned until her next text came through

I'll make dinner. Christina's text said.

Rocco's face relaxed.

"Christina?" Bruno said.

"Yes, Christina," Rocco told him.

"So, just how serious is this?" Bruno asked.

"Pretty fucking serious."

"Moving in together, serious?"

"I don't see that happening. More like wedding serious." Rocco smiled.

"That is fucking serious. When are you going to introduce her to the family?"

"Everyone will be on hand at the groundbreaking, and I'm going to have dinner afterward for the family at Modernesto's. I talked to Dirk. He felt bad that Caraleigh could march her drunken ass into the restaurant. He told me he had a chat with Caraleigh's mother and stepfather; Dirk said the stepfather was royally pissed hearing about Caraleigh and her performance. I think that will be the end of Caraleigh. Dirk will have us in a private dining room. I'm going to let Mom plan the menu." Rocco winked.

"The fam's going to love Christina. She speaks Italian too. Doesn't she."

"It's more that she understands it."

"Nonna is going to lose her mind."

"It's not all clear sailing. Christina is the one, I'm sure about her. Thing is. I want to be sure she feels the same before I try and lock it down. I'd move her in tomorrow if it was up to me, but that's a bridge too far for Nonna and Nonno. I haven't been introduced to Christina's family yet. I don't think they are as old country as our family, but I'm not going to risk anything. And I have one last piece of unfinished business to clean up. Once I get Christina to consider marriage, I'll get the wedding done as fast as Christina will let me."

"I know zero about weddings and any of that, but Italian wedding and fast? I don't know, Rocco."

"I don't either, but if she green lights me, I don't want to be planning a wedding for a year."

"Whatever I can do, you know I will," Bruno said.

Rocco paused, looked at his little brother, and said, "You're the best. You know that? Franco is crying to Dad that you are here with me instead of the east side office. I'd never hold you back if you wanted to go work for Franco, I know it's a pain in the ass with the drive, but I would hate to lose you."

Bruno lowered his eyes and smiled. In his entire life, he never thought he'd be more than the punch line as the Gagliardi family joke. Bruno was given the last thing in the world he thought he might ever have, respect. He had earned it; he understood that. Still, Bruno also understood that Rocco was under no pressure to be the Bruno cheerleader he had been. "Actually, I have been thinking about the drive back and forth from Mom and Dad's," Bruno began.

Rocco would be sorry to see his brother go, but he'd understand. Rocco nodded for Bruno to go on.

Bruno straightened and said, "I think I need to find my own place on this side of town."

Chapter 31

Tell him

Barbara Streisand and Celine Dion

Marisol picked up on the third ring. "I thought you'd be busy with his hotness."

"Not that simple," Christina said.

"I think it would be, but I get it. You have reservations. Or is there something else?"

"Yes, but it's not one or the other. It's both."

On Marisol's end of the line, Christina heard movement, the sounds of covers being thrown off, and a loud snore. “Hey, Marisol, I didn’t know you had company. I’m sorry. This can wait.”

Marisol snort laughed. “Someone could break in and vandalize the apartment, and Garrett would sleep through the entire thing. I was just about to move to the couch anyhow. I’m in the middle of a Sarina Bowen series about alpha hockey players. Even if Garrett provides an excellent example of the sounds a Zamboni makes, it wasn’t really adding to the experience.”

“Does he know you say this stuff about him?” Christina snickered.

“He would hear Zamboni and think it was cool that I know something about hockey. Anyway, I’m all comfy cozy, spill.”

“I just got off the phone with Neville.”

“That’s not the way you want to end an evening. Why did he call? Was the Italian stallion there when S’Neville phoned?”

“No, Rocco left around eight, just when it started to snow, but that’s not why he left. That’s something else I need to talk about, but this first. I’ve been getting this unknown number calling for a couple of days. I’ve let it go to voice mail but no message. I should have ignored it, but I let my curiosity get the better of me; I decided to take the call when the number came up again. And it was

Neville, and it was so unpleasant." Christina let out a breath.

"So... What did Neville Draco Malfoy Eastburn have to say, pray tell?"

Christina groaned, "How did I allow myself to be involved with him?"

"A question Holly and I asked several times in the past year. Quit stalling; what did he say?"

"He basically told me that I have a few things at his place and I should come by tomorrow to collect them. And that he wants to discuss my life choices. He demanded to know if I was so stupid as to buy my condo because it's a seller's market; and the foolish decision to become involved with Rocco Gagliardi."

"What? Why would he know about that?"

"I have no idea." Christina ended that thought with an *Ugh*.

"Right. Being involved with a handsome, classy, smart, successful, and hot AF man is a terrible decision. Not. What the hell? I think the cheap hair gel finally got to S'Neville. So, how did you leave it?"

"I asked him to ship my stuff to me, and I would pay for UPS. He refused. I wouldn't actually care, but I left my grandmother's brooch at his place. I didn't realize that until he reminded me. I thought I just didn't bring it with me when I moved. I hardly ever wear it, but I can't have him throw it out either. I hate myself for spending any time with him."

"I'll go with you if Rocco isn't going."

"If only. Nope, I have a brief window to pick my stuff up. Tomorrow night at seven sharp."

"Did you tell Neville you had plans?

"That's when he told me it was seven tomorrow or never."

"As soon as you and Rocco are done there, it will be over for good," Marisol said.

"I'm not taking Rocco."

"I don't think that's a good idea. Why aren't you?"

"It's embarrassing. Completely embarrassing. And I am feeling so uncomfortable that I gave Rocco crap about Caraleigh. I know exactly how he must have felt. It's like when you dyed your hair blonde. Remember?"

"No, no, no. You promised never to bring that up again."

"I promised never to tell anyone about it. And I never will. At least you didn't have your drunken tonsorial gong show around long enough for anyone but me and my mom to see," Christina laughed, "it really was horrible."

"Thanks so much. No need to remind me. I was there, remember? But back to Rocco. Embarrassed or not, you should have him, or somebody go with you."

"I really think I need to spare myself the humiliation of anyone witnessing my former connection to Neville. If it's just me there, Neville will be less inclined to put on a show for my companion."

"Oh, you are so right about that. If it gets ugly, just get out of there, and we'll figure another way to get the brooch. Hey, is the brooch the cameo from Sorrento?"

"That's the one." Christina sighed.

"Oh fuck no. That's not just an heirloom; that's an expensive piece of jewelry. Shame on you for leaving in the first place."

"I know; I deserve it. I don't have an excuse either. But I'll get it back, and, bonus, I can be done with that part of my life."

"You're moving on. And speaking of...What's the rest of it? You had a moment with Rocco this evening? Was that what you were alluding to?"

Christina groaned. "I have nothing but moments with Rocco. Okay, I never admitted this before, not even to myself, but every time I've ever had sex, I've had to talk myself into it. I have never been swept away and turned on to where the next logical step was into bed."

"Until Rocco."

"Right, until Rocco. I've only had one occasion to second guess. That was when he spent the night with his leaning tower of penis the next morning. Besides that, whenever we start making out, I become ridiculous how willing I would be."

"What stops you then?"

"Rocco. Rocco always puts on the brakes. Tonight though? Tonight, I think he might have, but I think he thinks I'm not ready for him."

"Wait. Is that what he said? Or what you think?"

"It was intense. Actually, lately, it's always intense, but he never does more than hold me and kiss me."

"What? No cheap feels?"

"No. Rocco is... Well, it isn't that he's reserved. He's pretty in your face that he would happily be intimate."

"Jesus, Christina, it's just me. You can say it. He's ready to fuck you."

"No. I mean, yes, but no. It's not like that. I know what you mean. I know what that's like. This is different. Rocco is different."

Marisol was silent on the other end of the phone.

"Marisol?"

Marisol cleared her throat. “Yeah, I know what that’s like.” After a beat, she said, “You do know that all you have to do is talk to him. Tell him.”

“I know, I know you’re right. Hey, not to change the subject, but I’m getting alerts. Are you too?”

“What kind of alerts? “ Marisol asked.

“Weather. We’re supposed to get a snowmageddon. Six inches.”

“There’s a joke in there somewhere. I better get to sleep because tomorrow I’ll probably have to drive Garrett into work.”

“Why?”

“He drove his Corvette over. That thing is lovely in the summer and useless in the winter. Hey, you’ve got your Career Fair tomorrow. You better turn in too, girly.”

Chapter 32

Umbrella

Rihanna

Rocco sat lost in thought, watching the snow begin to fall. His hair was still damp from the shower he took when he got home from Christina's. The evening showers were becoming a nightly occurrence, the location for the necessary jerk-off session. It wasn't his preference, but he could live with it until she was ready for more. And if she was never ready? A small insistent voice whispered.

That voice might have power, except Rocco knew she wasn't unaffected. It was torture to him because the scent of her arousal would be like the green flag at a car race if Christina was the one to wave that flag. Tonight she was ready, more than willing, but he was the one to hit the brakes. The *why* was the subject of Rocco's rumination this evening. The reason was so weird. Still, the more he thought about it, the more he agreed with his decision to wait until he took her to his bed in his house.

After Francine, but before Christina, he never wanted a woman in his home's bedroom or that room's bed. Looking back, he wasn't sorry that he handled it that way.

Now? Now, with Christina, it was different. Now he wanted to claim her and mark her as his. That needed to happen in a particular way. And that wasn't going to happen in Christina's condo or anywhere other than under his roof. It was a totally ridiculous attitude; he knew this. Still, that is the way it would be. Rocco had no idea when that would happen, but this understanding settled the matter for him.

The snow that began to fall a little earlier now fell in earnest. Rocco looked up the weather on his phone. It promised to be a bad one, and Christina was supposed to drive to Novi tomorrow morning in her old car. That was bullshit. He thought a moment and sent her a text that he would drive her to Novi in the morning and pick her up when the event was over. A very cordial thanks, but no thanks came back within seconds. He then told her he'd have a car brought to her. A newer car with all-wheel drive, snow tires, and a better drive train than her car. This, too, was politely refused with a follow-up text from Christina promising a text when she got to the venue. Rocco was a student of negotiation and figured this was the best he might expect. Still, he sent Bruno a text to research the safest car available. After that? After that, this would be entered into his mental list of *to-do* with Christina. A list that he happily added to by the day.

Chapter 33

Bye Bye Bye

N'SYNC

By the next morning, the roads were terrible but passable. Christina left early, got there on time, and was grateful for the snow tires on her elder Oldsmobile.

The weather meant a drop in attendance, but Christina was surprised that the Holtzberg booth was at least as well attended as it had been last year. When it was obvious that the continuous snowfall would make getting home a challenge, the attendees had pretty much cleared out just after lunch. The additional staff members and their equipment demonstrations were the stars of today's show.

Christina sent a text to Neville asking if she might reschedule when the weather was better. Neville had none of it. "*You made it to that Career Day of yours. Yeah, that was mentioned on the radio this morning and that it was sponsored by Holtzberg's. I've always thought it was tawdry that Holtzberg's can't seem to do anything without having the company name stamped all over the place. They're always drawing attention to themselves. If you could drive in for that, you can make it to my place,*" Neville texted her.

She couldn't work herself up to hating him. But resenting him? Oh, yes, she resented the hell out of him, the jerk. And that was her internal rant all the way to his place that evening.

The roads were snow-covered and slick. Christina's old car was doing fine. She just needed to go slowly. Despite leaving an additional hour early, she was pulling up in front of Neville's condo a few minutes late with an unamused Neville standing in the doorway, arms folded across his chest, a surly look on his face, and Christina thought she detected foot tapping.

Well, the sooner she got out of her car and into Neville's condo, the sooner this would be over.

Neville opened the door for her but stood in at the threshold so that Christina had to brush against him to get into the condo. She rolled her eyes and walked past him as quickly as she could.

"Wine? Would you like some wine?" Neville asked.

"Thank you, no. I really need to collect my things and get out of here. The roads are horrible, and it's very slow going," Christina said, standing in the foyer despite Neville's urging her into the living room.

"It wasn't just for your belongings that I invited you over. I think you owe me a conversation at the very least."

'I don't see it like that, Neville. We have talked. You just didn't listen. May I please have my things? I really need to be on my way."

"Twenty minutes. Give me twenty minutes of conversation, and I'll give you your belongings," Neville said.

"Twenty minutes then," Christina said, setting her phone as a timer.

"Won't you sit down and have a glass of wine?" Neville encouraged.

Christina didn't move and only said, "Clocks ticking, Neville."

He gave in with a sigh. "I have been looking at property in White Lake. There's a particular neighborhood that is free from a more urban element. A safer spot than you live now, and I'm told there is a shopping center with a Target and a Walmart close by. I can offer you a very safe, sane life. Yes, there are things you will need to adapt to. I'm not converting to be a Catholic, and I will not have my children raised in any church, but if you insist on that religious voodoo, it will not be Catholic. Also, as my wife, you represent me, and I'm not in favor of you working after we have children. That's a non-starter. Also, I know you think it's some sort of diversity statement you are making with your associates, but it makes it appear that you don't know any quality people. We will not include that loud-mouth Marisol or your little brown friend in our circle. What I can offer is a leg up for you. You'll be breaking into a better class. You'll be marrying up," Neville said with satisfaction.

Christina suppressed her urge to laugh at him. She needed to stay the course, give him his time and the floor, get the brooch and get out. In the mildest tone she could muster, she said. "I appreciate your sincerity, Neville, but I think we are on two completely different paths," she looked at her phone; he still had more time, "was there anything else?"

"That is just it, isn't it? Your path, as you've termed it, is going to lead you right off a cliff. I know you've aligned yourself with another man. And who did you pick? Someone who could make you a better version of yourself. Nope. Not you." He threw his head back and barked out a laugh, "You allow this gumba dago, this Rocco Ignatius Gagliardi, to pull you away from any common sense. It's beyond me why you could want this. And I can say with complete assurance you have no idea who this man is or the embarrassment he will be to you if you continue seeing him. You are a fool, but at least no one knows but me just how big a fool you are. But that knowledge will soon be made public, and when it is, you can be part of it by standing with Gagliardi or away from it by standing with me. Would you like to know who this Gagliardi really is?"

Christina's phone sounded. She held up the phone. "Time's up. I'll take my belongings now."

"So, that's it? No discussion? No questions?" Neville asked.

"You wanted me here. I'm here. You wanted twenty minutes; I gave that to you. Your end of the bargain is to give me my belongings." Christina now noticed the Amazon box on Nevill's dining room table. She strode to the table, and the box had the few things she had left behind. She began to pick the box up but instead looked through the contents to ensure that the cameo was there. It was not. She turned back to Neville. "I'm missing my brooch."

Neville looked away down the hall toward the condo's bedrooms. "That's everything." He lied.

Christina, let out a breath. "Oh no, it is not," She moved past Neville and down the hall to the master bedroom, flipped on the light, and headed for the closet and Neville's valet box.

Neville was moving quickly to stop her, but he was too late.

Christina pulled the Cameo from the box and turned to face him.

"I had that in there to protect it," he said unconvincingly.

"You had my brooch in there because you are a thief," Christina said.

He reached and grasped her arm.

Christina looked at where Neville held her.

Neville let his hand fall away.

Christina headed back to the dining room table to collect the box.

Neville was now on her heels. "You can interpret this any way you want, but we are not finished. I'll be seeing you next week."

She'd think about his parting words later. Now, she needed to get out of here, pray that her old car started and go home. She gathered the Amazon box and got out the door as quickly as possible.

Chapter 34
Adorn
Miguel

The weather had gotten a little dicey since she drove to Neville's condo. The wet snow falling earlier that day was freezing as the temperature dropped.

Her car was still fairly warm inside, and the old girl started right up – a miracle. She was out of Neville's parking lot, down the street, and ready to turn onto Telegraph Road when it happened. First, the Road Commission salt truck whipped by, dousing her car with road salt. She was temporarily blindsided and didn't see the grey Smart Car dead ahead. She swerved, missing the Smart Car but running off the road and into a shallow ditch as the car stalled.

Okay, she was fine. The airbags didn't deploy; she hadn't hit anyone or anything. It would be all right. She just needed to shake it off - catch her breath. It just wasn't happening – and instead of shaking it off, it was she who was shaking. Trembling and a little freaked out.

Rocco was just about home when he noticed the Smart Car in his rearview mirror. The car was behind him, cutting in and out of traffic. He slowed down. Better to have the vehicle in front of him than behind because between the goofball in the Smart Car and the weather, this was an accident waiting to happen. He slowed down to let the Smart Car pass.

Then it did happen. Rocco watched as a beige car that looked like Christina's grandma-mobile pulled out to Telegraph just in time to get sprayed with salt from a salt truck. A few seconds later, the Smart Car dodged the salt truck and headed into the beige car's lane. The beige car took a sharp right off the road into a four-foot snowdrift.

Rocco pulled behind the beige car, put his hazard lights on, and scrambled to see about the driver. He was just at the driver's door when she looked over her shoulder. Rocco's stomach dropped, moving as fast as he could in the snow, getting to the car door just as Christina opened it. He pulled her up into his arms and out of the car in one swift movement. He then turned to close the door with the heel of his boot, carried her to the Escalade, and deposited her in the passenger's seat. He buckled her in and kissed her forehead, grateful she was in one piece. "*Patatina,* hang tight; we are close to my house, like five minutes away, even in this weather. Have you got everything?"

She felt for the cameo in her pocket and then held up her purse and nodded at Rocco.

The SUV slipped a bit as Rocco put it in drive. He righted the Escalade and pulled onto Telegraph.

He did live close, almost uncomfortably close to Neville, but Rocco's neighborhood looked a world away.

They pulled into Rocco's drive, and the sensor house lights went on. Even with the extra lights, it was snowing too hard to see all the house's details. They pulled into a three-car garage where an older Cadillac, a golf cart, and a motorcycle took up residence.

Rocco was out of the SUV and around to her side opening her door, picking her up, and carrying her into his home.

It was a welcome gesture, and Christina sank into him and rested her head on his chest, feeling his warm breath on her forehead as he held her.

Rocco effortlessly brought her to the great room off of his kitchen and carefully placed her on one of the two sofas in the room.

She was still shaken but realized Rocco's state; he looked anxious. “Rocco?”

He threw his head back, “God, Patatina, if I lost you...” he came back to himself, sat down, looked at her, and asked, “are you okay? I should have checked, but when I realized you were in that car, I was a little frantic. I could only think of getting you out of there.”

“I’m fine. It was frightening when that guy cut me off, but fine,” Christina said.

Rocco moved a little closer to her, pulled her onto his lap, placed her head to rest on his shoulder, and wrapped his arms around her.

Christina could feel his heart thundering in his chest; she decided to linger there until Rocco was breathing easier. Not that resting in his arms was a hardship. He was warm, strong, and held her like he’d never let her go.

Rocco was upset at the thought that she could have been hurt, very upset, but even through winter coats, he could feel the swell of her breasts against his chest and her lush bottom on his thighs. His dick was getting hard. As good as it felt to hold her like this, in a second, she was going to get poked in the ass. After that, any words of his gratitude and caring, no matter how sincerely offered, would be cheapened by his wandering cock. There needed to be a slight change in focus. Rocco kissed her cheek, and asked, "Would you like a hot coffee, maybe tea?"

Christina took the hint and got up, "Caffeine right now isn't a great idea for me; if you have something noncaffeinated, that would be wonderful. If that's not possible, I'm fine. Can you point the way to the powder room?"

"It's right around that corner," he pointed as he got up as well and headed to the kitchen.

When she got in front of the powder room mirror, Christina took a good look at herself – it wasn't the best picture: makeup a mess, hair like a wild woman. Her mother would not be pleased, but hey, no help for it. And he had seen her worse, which was not at all comforting. She did what she could to tame her hair and walked back into the kitchen in time to smell the stiff scent of Ponce

Mandarino that Rocco was steaming in the expresso machine. In another circumstance, she would have refused the offer in favor of plain tap water heated in the microwave to warm it. But this was actually soothing, something her mother would serve on a raw night like this.

"I don't have any oranges for a garnish," Rocco said apologetically. He poured two cups and gestured to the great room and the sofa and chairs facing a wall of windows.

"I always thought that was my mother's creation, the orange peel in the drink. It's going to be just wonderful orange peel or no." Christina took a seat, and Rocco placed her drink next to her.

This close, she caught the scent of him. Unlike the Ponce Mandarino, Rocco's scent was more subtle than in your face. It was his soap and the less refined scent of man. She reacted to it. Not overtly, but it made her track him as he set his drink down and then pressed a button that drew the window shades up. He flipped a switch, and the backyard was lit up, illuminated to the shoreline where a gazebo and dock were suspended over the lake, now frozen and snow-covered. It looked like a Thomas Kincade print with soft lines and fuzzy colors.

"This is... beautiful," Christina breathed.

"It's one of my favorite things about this house," Rocco said, eyes out the window as he sat at the other end of the sofa.

They sat sipping the Ponce Mandarino and watching the wind whip the snow. It was several silent moments before Rocco asked, "Why were you out in this weather? "

She drew in a breath. "Neville demanded that I pick up a box he had of my things. I wouldn't have bothered, but my grandmother's cameo was at his place. I don't care about the rest, but that cameo is irreplaceable. He told me I had to pick everything up tonight, or he would pitch it all."

That mother fucker, Rocco said to himself, and his heart that had finally slowed now raced. To Christina, he said, "He made you drive all the way out here? Unbelievable." He wordlessly shot up and stalked to the kitchen.

Later, when he took stock of everything that happened that evening, it felt reflexive, second nature to want to find Neville, pummel the hell out of him, and throw the body of his vanquished enemy at Christina's feet. He understood that he felt particularly protective of her even before tonight. This was more like an instinct, something out of his reptilian brain. He calmed himself and walked back to Christina with more of the Ponce Mandarino to refreshen her cup.

"But this was the last of it, right? Nothing more to pickup. Nothing more to close out?" Rocco bristled.

"As far as I am aware, this is it," Christina said.

"I may not have the right to ask it of you, but if you are going to see him again, I want to be with you when you do."

Christina turned to him; there wasn't an exact word for how Rocco looked at this moment, but it was clear he was less than thrilled about Neville; well, so was she. "I can't think of a reason I'd have to see him. I don't have a problem honoring your request." This didn't eliminate the rumble from the man who stood before her; she was only slightly confident Mount Vesuvius would not blow in the next minute. Still, why the barely suppressed tumult with him? "Rocco, what else is going on? This seems like it's more than being annoyed with Neville."

"I don't have the right words," he said, moving to sit next to her on the sofa and hauling her to him.

Over the past weeks, there had been plenty of necking on her couch. It was enjoyable. More so than other times that Christina had with other men. So it wasn't out of the blue that Rocco put his arms around her and drew her close. And it wasn't the first time he had kissed her. It also wasn't the first time she felt her nipples tighten or her panties dampen. But it was the first time he did all he had ever done before with an insistence that should have left her feeling rushed into something she didn't want.

She should have felt poorly equipped to make the next move. Fortunately, she didn't have to, because Rocco was more than capable.

Rocco pulled her onto his lap moving her legs so that she straddled him.

He felt the heat of her core against him, and in this position, he could smell her arousal. It made him bestial.

He pulled away for a second and pulled her bottom lip down, "Open for me."

Without a thought, she did and felt his tongue against hers; she let out a soft moan. Rocco cupped the back of her head with one hand and her ass with his other.

Rocco was hard. His cock was like a heat-seeking missile only prevented from entering her by the inconvenient jeans they both wore.

Christina would have been mortified had she realized she was grinding her mons against him. Rocco was at a loss himself, only aware that

Christina was as willing as he for the claiming Rocco would have from her.

Rocco braced her against him and stood.

"Where are we going?" she asked.

"Bed," Rocco said with a pant.

"Bed?"

"Yes, bed." Rocco headed to the hall leading to his bedroom.

"Whose bed?" She looked up at him.

"Technically, all the beds in this house are my beds." Rocco kissed the side of her face and met her eyes, "So, to my bed, with me."

"I see," Christina murmured and wrapped her arms a little tighter as Rocco covered the distance down the hall to his bedroom.

There would be time to take in the space later. At that moment, she didn't notice the room that screamed alpha male as much as she was aware of the man carrying her like she weighed nothing and striding to the massive four-poster bed.

With precise efficiency, Rocco stripped her of everything but her bra and panties. He placed her deliberately on his bed before he began divesting himself of his clothes while walking to and from his bathroom, where his condom stash must have been kept. Before pushing his boxer briefs down, he placed a strip of foil-wrapped condoms on the nightstand.

Christina sat up and began shaking her head.

Rocco's cock was so hard it looked like he was ready for a joust, but at the sight of Christina shaking her head and holding her hand out in a universal sign for "Stop." He froze. Still breathing hard, eyes still ablaze with lust. He waited.

"You don't need those." She explained.

Rocco shook his head, not processing the information.

She backed up on the bed and tried again, "We have birth control. I never slept with Neville, and I haven't been with another man for, well, a while. I was tested when I got the implant." In a very small and sheepish voice, she went on. "I got the implant just in case... for you. In case you wanted me."

Rocco sucked in a breath, threw the condoms over his shoulder, and got into bed with her.

Christina was steeling herself. It could never be as bad as it had been because this time, it was Rocco. She just needed to manage her expectations, and it would be fine. Really, the way he had been acting this evening, it was going to be over as soon as it began.

Rocco was nuzzling her neck, kissing her collar bone. That was nice, felt pretty good. He pushed her bra straps out of his way as he continued lavishing kisses over her throat and shoulders. He wasn't taking her bra off. She only gave a little consideration before unfastening it and pulling it away. Rocco noticed; of course, he did. He moved down her body but didn't fondle her as she expected. Instead, he moved down her torso, kissing his way and gently pushing her onto her back. This started to worry her. She thought of hard penises bruising their way inside her. She may be wet, but the remembrance of the times before flooded her mind. As soon as her head touched the mattress, she began to sit up. But Rocco wasn't bearing down on her. He was going down on her.

That wasn't a great idea either. She had never felt very comfortable about that. Men would zero in on her clit like they were either a Hoover vacuum or an angry woodpecker. Both grossly unpleasant. Just as she was about to protest, Rocco began breathing into her panties at her mons. This felt surprisingly good. She moaned, and he growled.

His mouth lingered and became licks along the inside of her thigh. It felt unbelievably good. The best sort of decadently naughty.

Rocco pulled her panties down, but unlike those before, he did this slowly, carefully uncovering her. Kissing and licking his way until he pulled the underwear down her legs.

"You're bare," he said, a little in awe. "I love it that you are bare, *dolce figa.*" Rocco ran his tongue along the seam of her labia just before he repositioned her, opening her legs. That didn't feel as uncomfortable as she might have thought. It felt like the best kind of misbehaving. It made her squirm and want more. Rocco delivered. He gently ran his soft tongue just inside her opening, leaving her wanting. He added a finger, but instead of poking his middle finger into her vagina, he used his fingertips to trace her folds, all the while humming his pleasure. He took his time, and when his tongue finally met up with her clitoris, it felt like she had been waiting for this all her adult life. The sensation was really hot and arousing, and she discovered that she had been holding his head to keep the contact there, where it felt good.

By this time, Rocco was inching his finger up inside her. That too felt good, really good, Different because he wasn't jabbing at her. It felt like he was feeling his way, touching that internal part of her. Christina's heart felt like it would pound out of her chest. She knew that she was holding on to Rocco's head far too hard, but she couldn't make herself stop it. She was throbbing down there. Wet with her muscle contracting, her legs shaking, and her inside clinching so hard she thought she might pass out.

It left her in waves of pleasure, and Rocco stayed with her slowing his movements and drawing the feeling out. Rocco moved up the bed so that he lay next to her. He turned her in his arms and kissed her. She could taste herself, smell herself. It crossed her mind that it wasn't offensive. She'd have to think more about that later. Right now? Right now, she couldn't think.

Rocco now knew his dick to be a foolish absurdity. He wished he had jacked off in the shower to calm himself down. Now the little fucker was so hard it pulsed. If she said no, he'd have to sprint to the bathroom and take care of himself. That was a miserable thought. But the more he touched her and tasted her, he could see that Christina wasn't likely to hit the brakes. *Thank God.*

She was so soft against him. Her tits were perfection. Not overly big and not that water-balloon feel of implants. He could have spent hours just playing with her soft breasts topped with nipples and areolas that could inspire an aria. *Recondita Armonia.* He was smitten with those perfect tits until he moved down her body to find her bare *figa.* Seeing sent a jolt of electricity up and down his spine to his balls, and he could have sung the *Donna non vidi mai*. It was like his grandmother's *Crema Pasticcera*. So sweet. He had a ritual of how he ate that favorite dessert. Slowly, licking the cream out of the shell, savoring it.

Christina's reaction was unexpectedly gratifying, and he knew it would only improve over time. This was just his introduction to her sweet, sweet *figa*.

His skill at cunnilingus was something he had prided himself on when he was with Francine. It was the only sex she enjoyed. He learned this early in their relationship, the summer between their freshmen and sophomore year. Since Francine had reacted so positively to his oral efforts, he made a study of it, of her. Regular penetrative sex was great for him, but he knew Francine never liked it. She would complain about it and him, and she wasn't unhappy that he was quick about it when it happened.

A couple of things changed when Rocco moved on to other lovers after Francine. He had to learn to pace himself. This he did. It wasn't too difficult to do. And after Francine, he never let his mouth venture between a woman's legs. He also never suggested any of his lovers suck him off as an equitable nonexchange. Still, if they were inclined, he wasn't about to fight it.

The first time he caught the scent of Christina's sex, Rocco knew if he ever got her into bed, his face would be in her cunt as fast as he could get there. And that he did, and it was fucking glorious. She was fucking magnificent, a goddess.

Rocco's confidence in his bedroom skills wasn't an overreach. He knew the two assets he had beyond most men were awareness and patience. And he had confidence, too, that Christina would be worth that wait. She was.

Now he needed to take the next step with her. In his head, he knew that this was the bridge to where *he* needed to get with her. She probably would never see it, never really understand it. It was feral, totally animal. Didn't matter. He would claim her the same way men had claimed women for eons. The task wasn't just to put his dick inside her. The task was to be sure she'd want him to put his dick in her the next time, the time after, and the time after that until there was no more time.

"*Patatina,* I want to be inside you, do you understand? I won't go any further tonight if you don't want this."

She moved closer to him, put her arms around him, and said, "I want you too."

Rocco kissed her. His mind went back to the information about the implant. Now he realized for the first time in his adult sex life that getting a woman pregnant wasn't a bad outcome, as long as it was this woman.

She moved beneath him and parted her legs; those simple actions made him want to cry in happiness. "I'll go slow; you tell me if I hurt you." He doubted she would; the tip of his dick was now bathed in her arousal and his saliva. He gently pressed inside. It was a feat of control like he had never exercised before. He literally moved in and not by inches, by millimeters. *Oh fuck, she felt so good.*

Christina wasn't in pain. He knew this by her body's reactions. She was tight, but her pussy wasn't restricting anything. She was firm, wet, and warm; if he didn't get his shit together, he would be coming in seconds. It took him some time, but he was all the way in with his pubic bone hitting her mons and his balls against her ass; he gave it a pause, kissed her, and checked in. "Are you all right?"

"I'm way better than all right; God, Rocco, you feel so, so good."

To this pronouncement, he groaned and began to move slowly, hoping that mentally reciting the Pledge of Allegiance still worked on a hard dick.

He made her feel so full, and he was hitting her still aroused clit. She wasn't sure if he was doing that on purpose or if it was just the perfection of how he fit inside her. Why she would think his cock was too big was crazy town. He was just right. The crown of his cock was catching on something that felt really, really great. It made her wrap her legs around him to pull him against and into her. She loved his hard muscles: his hard chest, shoulders, and back. He was hard everywhere. He sped up a little and began to grind into her, making the contact with her clit more intense. The feeling this time wasn't as spastic as her first orgasm, but it was like free-falling from the high drive. She heard the groaning get louder and realized it was her – she couldn't bring herself to care. When her orgasm hit her, everything convulsed, and Rocco's penis felt twice as big as when it slid into her. It didn't hurt. In fact, it was amazing.

Rocco now began to move with the singular purpose of achieving his climax.

He took her face in his hands and rested his weight on his elbows. Looking into her eyes, he told her, "You are mine. Christina, mine. Say it, Say it." he growled.

"I'm yours," she said breathlessly, "I'm yours."

"Mine," Rocco said as he threw back his head and groaned as he spilled and spent what felt like a year's worth of semen into his woman. The world stopped turning for those moments.

He pushed himself off her, knowing he would land his two hundred and twenty pounds on her if he didn't. He pulled the covers up over them, tucked her head on his chest, and wrapped an arm around her bringing her closer.

When he finally caught his breath, he told her in the language of their fathers, *"ti amo. il mio cuore e solo tuo. Christina, Ti amo cosi tanto."*

Christina looked at him, wide-eyed for a moment, then told him, "*Ti amo, ti amo anch' io.*"

"That makes me even happier than getting to love your body, and just to say, I loved that part an awful lot," he told her.

"You surprised me," she said, settling in, "I didn't just *not* hate that. It was... wonderful."

She could feel his face relax into a smile.

She lay back down, closed her eyes, and replayed how he made her feel. No wonder Marisol likes it so much. And his words. Marisol had told her once that an *I love* you during sex had to be immediately dismissed. But Rocco's I love you was after. It would be totally bad form to leave his bed to look for her phone, so she could text Marisol.

"What are you over there over-thinking, Patatina?" Rocco gave her a nudge.

"Just dumb girl stuff," she said.

"You can tell, you know. You can tell me anything."

"I know I can. It's not you. You had it right; I'm over-thinking. And it's better when I'm not thinking."

"*Patatina*, get some sleep, and when you wake up, I'll give you more not to think about."

"Okay, I'm okay with that," she said, rolling to her side, and Rocco moved in behind her. He was just warm enough. They promptly fell asleep.

Chapter 35

Maps

Maroon 5

The next morning Rocco woke up with his back warm as toast against what had to be Christina. Unfortunately, his front was freezing cold, and his dick, as cold as he was, should have been shriveled up along with his balls and tucked into his groin. Instead, he was morning hard. He turned over to find Christina bundled up in *all* the covers. He chuckled and pried the bedclothes away from her. She moaned in her sleep but didn't fight to hold on to the covers.

Rocco turned her so that she was back to his front. His dick rested in the cleft of her butt, which didn't seem to bother her. The problem was that he was getting harder by the second, and his bladder was full. Not a great situation. He got out of bed to use the bathroom.

Rocco got back to bed; Christina was still sleeping peacefully, so he relaxed into sleep as well. His next conscious moment was Christina pressed up against him, whispering, *"Non vedo l'ora di sentire le tue mani su di me."*

Well, fuck. That had him hard as a rock and raring to go.

He kissed her and did as she asked, putting his hands all over her. He also made sure to employ his mouth and his dick.

When he woke up next, it was in a warm bed, but Christina wasn't in it. He got up, put on some sweat pants, grabbed a hoodie, and rambled out of the bedroom to find her in the kitchen. She was wearing his robe with her hair carelessly pulled up off her neck. She had assembled a plate of cheese, melon, and prosciutto di Parma with buttered toast for him. She understood how to operate the coffee maker, and she placed the coffee before him. It was domestic in the extreme. And he loved it.

He came up behind her, put his arms around her, kissed her neck, and said, "Thank you for this." He nodded to the plate and kissed the back of her neck, "Thank you for this morning," he kissed her cheek, "thank you for last night," he kissed her other cheek.

She turned in his arms, "Thank you." She hummed.

"Like it, did you?"

"Loved it. Particularly the oral."

"I will gladly lick your delicious *figa*," he said, and his shivered dick hardened.

"I probably should have returned the favor this morning," Christina smiled sinfully.

"Not going to lie, I'd have loved a blowjob this morning." He kissed her, smiling happily at his life's fantastic turn of events.

He was enjoying this, her, the breakfast, the morning when the doorbell rang.

Christina looked down at herself. "I need to get into more clothes."

"Not for me, you don't. It's probably the snowplowing service. Who else would be out this morning?"

"Still, I'll be out of the way." As she walked by him, he snagged her, kissed her, and patted her ass before releasing her and walking to the vestibule to get to the door.

Christina heard the front door open, and a woman's voice drifted down the hallway. "Hey, sorry to bother you; this is a big deal. I wouldn't bother you otherwise."

"Vonda? It really isn't a good time."

Vonda rolled her eyes and blew past him into the great room. "Rocco, come on, indulge me. I've done it for you. Think of this as payback for the great blow jobs I've given you over the years." She sniggered.

Rocco looked down the hall, but Christina was out of sight, which meant out of earshot. "Vonda, look, this is not a good time. Can we catch up later?"

"Actually, no." She took off her coat and found her way farther into Rocco's house. "Now, I need coffee. And I wouldn't be on your doorstep if you followed through with the written request I made weeks ago, Rocco."

Vonda wasn't just his former friends with benefits; she was a Lansing attorney representing clients in common. Rocco decided he could get this over quicker if he handled the business question. If he stuck to that, this would be over in a hot minute.

Christina shut the door softly and stood behind it, trying to gather her thoughts. *Blow job over the years?* She knew he had a past. So did she. Of course, hers was the Disney version. That wasn't his fault.

She quietly went about dressing and calming herself. The woman would probably be gone by now. She would ask Rocco about it. She hadn't wanted to think about how many women had been treated to the Rocco I. Gagliardi evening entertainment. No. No, she wasn't going to jump to any conclusion. She and Rocco were in a relationship. It may have been new, but still, this would be resolved with a conversation.

She washed her face, used the mouth wash, and did what she could with her hair before leaving the bedroom to chat with her lover.

Vonda had launched into a recap of the request. Rocco had thought he had taken care of this before. Clearly, Vonda didn't.

"I sent you everything I have on Miller Page and his wife's account. If that didn't include everything you expected, I can't do much about that. I wish I had more to help the Pages," he shrugged, "now, I don't want to be rude, but …."

"Well, you are being rude. I'm offended you never invited me over before. This is nice, Rocco, better than the last place you fucked me. I think we can agree your place has far cleaner floors than the unisex bathroom at the Top of Troy."

Christina was closing in on Rocco and the woman he had shared carnal knowledge with; she heard the woman loud and clear. Christina was just rounding the corner when she watched Rocco's sweat pants drop to the kitchen's flagstone floor, exposing Rocco's firm ass. She let a silent gasp and backed up, stunned.

Rocco reached down to pull his sweatpants up as Vonda began to purr, "Ah, come on, baby, you know you like it."

"Jesus, Vonda, stop it," Rocco said in a low but commanding voice.

"You don't mean that. You have never passed on what I can do for you," Vonda said in a sultry voice reaching for his sweat pants again.

Rocco held tight and moved away from her. "Would you fucking stop." He stepped back out of her reach.

She fell forward before she caught herself, now annoyed. "What the hell, Rocco? Since when are you so skittish? Is your mother here or something?" she now stood.

"My girlfriend is here." Pointing in the general direction of his bedroom.

"What?" Vonda all but screamed. "You never told me you had a girlfriend." She stopped and stilled. "Oh my God, I can smell pussy all over you."

Christina may not have heard all of it, but she heard that. She retraced her steps down the hall ducking into Rocco's home office. She blindly slid to the floor, using the wall to hold herself up. She heard the occasional word like, "when were you going to tell me? Liar, asshole." Then Rocco shushed her to keep her voice down. And finally, the woman said, "Well, maybe if you called me more than once every ten months." There was more indistinct conversation. It was all too much to sort out. Christina sent a text to Holly and forced herself to get up, collect her belongings and get the hell out of there.

Holly's text back was swift; *I'm on my way home from my brother's house. Text me the address.*

Christina shook her head and sent Holly a different message, *I have to get out of here. Meet me at Forest Lake Country Club.*

They were still arguing in the kitchen. The woman was telling Rocco off, and Rocco was trying to get the woman to speak softly. Was he really this obtuse? Boy, she sure knew how to pick em'.

Neither Rocco nor the woman seemed to notice her departure. Shocker. Once Christina was outside, it took her a moment to get her bearings. The morning was crisp, cold, and still icy, but it wasn't snowing. Rocco's service had cleared his drive, and the street was also clear. The trek took her enough time for the adrenaline to burn off. When she was safely in front of the Country Club, she texted Rocco: *I'm no longer in your house. Feel free to get your morning blowjob.*

A white Lexus whizzed by, the same one, Christina was pretty sure, that was parked in Rocco's drive. She couldn't muster up what to think about that. Fortunately, she didn't have to do more than watch for Holly's TweetyBird Yellow truck pulling up beside her.

Holly leaned over to open the passenger door. "I know. You don't want to talk about it. You don't have to. Get in."

Christina gave her friend a grateful nod and climbed into the truck's small cab.

A few moments before, Rocco caught the front door Vonda was trying to slam. "And don't come crying to me when the girlfriend doesn't work out for you, Asshole," Vonda spat.

Rocco took in a breath. He wasn't sure how he managed to dodge the catastrophe that might have been if Christina had heard or seen any of that Vonda shit show. That was a miracle.

There were lessons in all of this. The big one was fucking around was a *past* he was thrilled to have behind him. How had he ever thought it was a good idea to mess around with the likes of Vonda? It wasn't just Vonda; it was any of the other women that made up his sex life before. It was so ridiculously stupid. Comparing one night with Christina to any or all of them, and yes, that included Francine, was a sad waste of his time.

He headed for his bedroom and Christina. She was probably getting dressed, but he could get her out of whatever she had put on. Having her in his robe with that sexy as sin wild hair of hers was about as dressed as she needed to be this morning. He strode into his bedroom, saying, "Sorry about that, *Patatina;* it was a work thing." The room was eerily silent. He walked into the bathroom; it, too, was empty.

He was back out the door and down the hall, looking into every room but not finding Christina. When he returned to the great room, he heard the text message notification from his phone left in the kitchen. He grabbed the phone, still searching the rest of the house for Christina. He finally opened the message, paled, and allowed himself to fall into a seat at the kitchen's island.

The entire trip to Christina's condo had her phone blowing up – Rocco. Rocco's texts and phone calls. On the one hand, it seemed pretty clear to her that he had not invited the woman over and wasn't encouraging her. The comment about ten months since he had called the woman wasn't lost on Christina either, but she wasn't up to it, not right now. She switched the phone off.

She decided to get a few things done at home before tackling Rocco. She was too angry to be making any decisions about anything. And it wasn't like she could easily dismiss and put him aside. They had the Ground Breaking Ceremony this coming week, and damn it all to hell, she may have walked out of his house with most of her dignity intact, but she walked out without her grandmother's cameo brooch.

Christina hadn't started any chores but was finally calmed enough to turn her phone back on to read her texts when her doorbell rang. She looked outside, and yes, Rocco was standing at her door in jeans and a hoodie over his bare chest; he had to be freezing.

She decided to answer the door, but only to tell him she couldn't receive visitors at the moment. She said that to herself in preparation as she went down the steps to answer the door. Christina pulled the door open and steeled herself, telling him, “Rocco, I’m not up for a social call.”

“Patatina, please. Can we talk?”

“I think watching your visitor pull your pants down this morning really said it all. And that was before she yelled at you for not telling her you had a girlfriend. Who knew I was your dirty little secret.”

Rocco began to speak,

“Stop. Just stop,” Christina shook her head, “I’m sure you have a perfectly logical, very reasonable explanation for this morning. But please understand that it will take me a while to get the image of you naked with your booty call ready to perform fellatio. Or hearing that she was the gal who performed that service for years. Years, Rocco. Imagine if you had to be ringside to watch someone from my past do and say all I had to watch and hear. I’m on a sensory overload. Have a good day.” She shut the door, sat down on the bottom step, and began to cry.

Rocco was frozen where he stood. At that moment, he didn’t think he could feel worse until he heard the unmistakable sounds of Christina weeping just inside her door.

None of the scenarios he imagined with Christina involved his causing her a moment's pain or worry.

In his entire life, his self-loathing had been reserved for mistreating Caterina. And that was at the end of her life out of his misplaced loyalty to Francine.

Today? Today it was his cowardice. His unwillingness to set a limit. All he had to do was wedge his foot against his front door and tell Vonda she could either call him at his office or email him, but she wasn't coming in to disrupt his morning with Christina. And if she had made the same ridiculous accusation about not telling her, he had a girlfriend? How was it Vonda's business? She had no claim on him.

He started to knock again on Christina's door when he noticed two women facing him down. Before he could put any of it together, the smaller of the two said to the taller woman, "You see to Christina, and I'll have a little talk with tall, dark, and dimwitted here." Then the very small, very cinnamon-colored woman marched toward him. Her tawny skin was infused with a ruddy color, whether from the cold or her obvious fury, Rocco wasn't sure. He was convinced that the ninety pounds of female's next words would not be *Namaste.*

"I don't know what happened, but it was so bad that Christina couldn't tell me when I picked her up at the side of the road because she couldn't manage to stay in your home after whatever it was you did to her." The small woman got closer and surveyed him in the day's winter light. She knowingly nodded her head. "It's always the same with you guys. You think you can act like a schmuck and make everything fine by dragging out your stupid handsome face and give up a smoldering look, and we all swoon or something." She rapped him in the stomach with the back of her doll-like hand.

It was so unexpected that Rocco let out an *oof* like he had taken a punch.

Holly scoffed and rolled her eyes. "Seriously?" She appraised him. "You think you can have your six-pack and the Adonis belt you probably have, and Christina will melt at your feet. You are delusional."

By this time, Marisol was standing in the open doorway with Christina watching Holly berate, belittle and bust Rocco's balls.

Rocco held up his hands in surrender, "I'm sorry. I know. I handled this morning badly, very badly, and I hurt her. If I could undo it, I would. " Rocco said as he was walking backward as Holly was marching forward.

"So you admit you're a jerk." Holly had now backed him almost to his SUV.

"I have no excuse. It wasn't what it must have looked like to Christina, but it looked horrible. Christina didn't deserve what she had to see and hear," Rocco said, still holding up his hands defensively.

Christina and Marisol watched their friend and Christina's ex-boyfriend. Was he her ex? Maybe not. Christina gave it a moment allowing Rocco to be terrorized by Holly before she was ready to intervene.

Holly was still giving it to him. "You think you can get away with hurting my friend? You think you are somehow more important? That your opinion has any more value? That your actions are somehow beyond any scrutiny? Let me assure you, you aren't good enough to carry her shoes. You are nothing more than a careless, thoughtless oaf."

Rocco wouldn't allow himself any physical contact with this very angry little person. Still, he wasn't about to let Christina go either.

As he stepped back into hitting the side of the SUV, the little woman turned toward Christina and

Marisol. Rocco made his move, striding around Holly's retreating form to put himself in front of Christina.

"*Patatina*, please. I am so sorry. *Tu sei la mia principessa*. I will never let anything like that happen again. *Ti amo*." He picked up her hands and brought them to his lips.

Holly put her hands on her hips, "What did he say anyhow? Something romantic? You are totally going for that, aren't you, Christina?"

The frigid Christina began to melt, but Rocco was freezing.

Christina said, "Rocco, you need to go inside. You're going to be frostbitten."

"I don't care," he said.

"Oh my god," Holly said disgustedly. "Why do you want him? He doesn't know enough to wear a coat or socks in the middle of winter. He's nuts."

"Let's go inside," Christina said, and Marisol stepped out of the way.

Rocco let out a grateful breath. Picked up Christina's hand and headed toward the condo's stairway.

Holly told him, "She's only doing this because Christina is kind-hearted, and she knows you are too stupid to get out of the cold."

Rocco said to her, "Come on, *prepotente,* you can yell at me more inside – I deserve it."

"Don't think I won't," Holly said as they both crossed the small foyer to the front room of the condo.

Rocco held Christina's hand until they were in the middle of the front room. She patted his chest, gave him a weak smile, and said, "I need to use the powder room."

When Christina had left the room, Rocco found himself in the company of Christina's two friends. Marisol looked skeptically at him, but the other one, Holly, still looked like she might twist his balls off.

Holly spoke first, "Look, Casanova, the next time you pull your machismo act on my friend, it will be your last time. The part of today that makes me dislike you is that you made my friend Christina cry. That must make you feel like a big man. You got Christina to cry over you."

Rocco hung his head, "I hate myself for it. I will do whatever I can to never have that happen again," Rocco said.

"I hope for your sake it doesn't." She gave it a beat. She then looked over at Marisol. Marisol nodded. Holly turned to Rocco and said, "We've got things to do and places to be. I'll let you have some time to apologize your stupid muscley tight-butt off. Groveling needs to be included, and lots of it," Holly said.

Christina found them, Holly in a scolding posture, and Rocco hung dog and ready for the next verbal assault. "Are you guys good?" Christina asked.

"We are." Holly cut her large black eyes to Rocco; he flinched. Then to Christina, she said, "Hey, girly, We've got things to do. We'll leave you with pizza brains here, and we'll check on you later."

Marisol hugged Christina, said something the others couldn't hear, nodded to Rocco, and headed downstairs.

Holly took a turn to hug Christina, then she turned to Rocco one last time, widening her eyes and pursing her lips. He got the message.

The door closed after her besties; Christina looked over at Rocco expectantly.

He moved toward her and thought better of it. "Can we talk, please?"

Christina nodded and took a seat.

Rocco got on his knees before her, leaning in to wipe her tears. "Please, Christina."

"Please what? Rocco. Please don't cry. Am I making you uncomfortable?"

“I hate it that I hurt you.”

Christina gave him a watery look. “From your conversation with your friend, your long-time friend, it sounded like what you hated was being discovered. You were more interested in keeping it from me than anything else.”

“I can see how you might view it like that.”

“Oh, please, please tell me the alternate way of viewing it. She practically had your...,” Christina gestured to his crotch. “in her mouth.”

Rocco winced, “I had no idea she would do anything like that."

Christina’s eyes glistened, and her lip trembled.

He thought he couldn’t feel worse. “I’ll admit I wish you didn’t have to have all the details of my past. And, yes, I believe if that remained undiscovered, it would have been better for all concerned.”

Christina blew her nose and gave herself a moment. “I don’t want the details of your past hookups. You’re not wrong about that. But why did you string her along? Ten months or ten minutes, if she was used to swinging by for your preferred morning sex routine and you never bothered to tell her not to, I don’t blame her. And I have to wonder who else, including me, are you stringing along?”

"I never thought about her. I know that sounds cold. It was never an emotional investment. That's as much on her side as mine. Also, I have never had hookups in my house. You are the only woman I've had in my home or bed. I get it. From your perspective, I look like some kind of con artist, a cheat at worst. I'm frustrated with myself because, in your place, I'd draw a similar conclusion. "

Christina watched him, a little fascinated. She didn't think he was lying to her. Still a bit nervous, she said, "I'm in uncharted waters here. So, was the *I love you* just a sex thing or...."

"No," Rocco said in a rush pounding his fist into his thigh. He retook her hand and sat beside her on the couch, bringing her onto his lap. "Okay, Patatina, before I screw one more thing up, I will do what I should have done weeks ago."

Christina furrowed her brow, "What would that be?"

He let out a defeated breath, "I need to clear things up, and I need to tell you all of it."

It didn't take that long, and Christina shook her head when it was all out on the table. "I'm glad you told me, but I understand why you didn't want to bring it up."

She wasn't jumping out of his lap, so he leaned in closer. "Patatina, I can do better. I haven't hit my stride yet."

"Just spare me getting blindsided. I can deal with almost anything, but I'm not a fan of being the last one in the room to know, and you do realize that your past would be coming out one way or another sooner or later."

He got forehead to forehead with her, then told her, "I love you, Christina. You're mine. I don't want anyone else. So, let me make it a little clearer for you. If I had my way, I would move you into my house now. I'd have that car of yours carted off somewhere, anywhere, and you'd be driving the safest car on the market. You'd be deciding where we would go on vacation, how you want to decorate *our* house or if we should buy another one. You'd be telling me what the baby's name would be. There will be a ring and a wedding. I need to tie up a loose end, but you are it for me. The one. If this ends, it's because you end it."

"I'm not going to end it." She let out a breath.

He buried his head in her neck. "Thank you."

They stayed like that for some time before Christina gave her head a slight shake and said, "You really, really got Holly riled up,"

He relaxed a little. "She's a little frightening."

Christina smirked, “You have no idea.”

Chapter 36

Fireman

George Strait

"Okay, what do you think?" Marisol said to Holly just as Holly answered Marisol's phone call.

"He's a smoke show. You were right about that. That guy has put some serious time into that body. He's not a bad guy. He's not at all like Neville. He was just incredibly thoughtless. But... We will have to decide where we will have Christina's bachelorette party. She's as hopeless as he is."

Marisol chortled, "Yup, we will be planning her bachelorette party. I'm not surprised, not really," she then took a more serious tone, "I'm disappointed he was a dick to her, but none of them are perfect. Well, my dad is perfect. But not of the other men of my acquaintance are perfect. So, did you almost kick his ass?" Marisol said.

"I scared him." Holly shrugged.

"Of course, you scared him. You are scary as fuck. Oh, did she say anything more about going to Neville's?"

"Just that he was his usual pinhead self. She got her stuff. But, get this, Neville was trying to keep the brooch. He had it in his bedroom," Holly said.

"That little needle dick. I wanted Rocks-Off Gagliardi to be more than just his leaning-tower-of-penis. Still, whatever he is or isn't, he's far more and a world better than Neville, the sniffler."

"There is that," Holly said,

"Thursday is the groundbreaking, right? I'm not taking the whole day. I figured I leave at noon."

"That's what I planned on. Are Mrs. Pentelino and Cal coming?" Holly asked.

"They are. Hey, Christina's calling me."

"Find out if we still are doing brunch tomorrow. Bye," Holly said.

"Hey you. I just hung up with Holly. Are you okay? Is Mr. Wonderful still wonderful? I take it you finally took it to pound town," Marisol said.

“He’s slightly tarnished. Honestly, I don’t think I would have even noticed if it were anyone but Rocco.”

“What are you talking about? You couldn’t tell when other men were fucking you? That’s not good.”

That got Christina to chuckle. “Okay smart mouth. I mean, I care about him, so it's hurtful when he does something stupid.”

“He’s a little dim for a guy managing billionaires’ money. Got it. So? You got a little busy?”

“If he hadn’t been such a, such a....”

“Tool?”

“Yeah, that. If he hadn’t been that, it would have been perfect. Honest to god, I thought you exaggerated whenever you've talked about sexual congress and other ancillary activity.”

“Oh... My man Rocco is more than a nicely built, good-looking and fills out a well-tailored business suit. Just guessing, but... great orator?” Marisol said.

“Great orator. Extremely dexterous and has quite a spectacular sword. Let me rephrase, he’s got Excalibur, and he’s really good at wielding it. For the first time ever, I’m looking forward to the swordplay, and before this morning wouldn’t mind doing a little sword-swallowing," Christina murmured, "but I'll need to get beyond the Vonda show and tell."

"You aren't obligated, and he's not going to be asking, at least not for a while. Hey, back to the good stuff. It's awesome when you have someone with a particular skill set and the right equipment, isn't it."

"It was a life-changing experience. There's no doubt about that." Christina moaned a little.

"Okay, settle down girl. So, what's next?"

"He wants more time together, and more overnight stays."

"Are you good with that?"

"I am shocked to say this, but I'm fine with it."

"Wow, that's a big corner you turned."

"I know," Christina giggled.

"What's that look like for you?"

"We talked about Rocco staying over at my condo, but... Okay, it's really shallow, I know, but Marisol, his master bath, is amazing. So, I packed a bag, and he's coming back to pick me up. He had my car towed, and the garage fixing it has a loaner I can use until my car is ready."

"So that means brunch is still on for tomorrow?" Marisol asked, "or are Holly and I getting dissed in favor of the Italian Excalibur?"

"I'll be there. I want to figure a couple of things out for the groundbreaking. I need you guys to bounce stuff off of."

Chapter 37

I'll Get Even With You

Foreigner

Christina's Monday was the debrief about the career day last Friday. This was nothing new. She always sat down with Doug and the boys to go over everything. But this year, it was far more intense than usual. That began early in the morning when Christina found Danielle in with Doug just fuming over the list of expenditures Christina had sent over to Fiscal Services when she got into work. It was disheartening to hear all the negativity from Danielle about the event.

Danielle was all wound up and practically unhinged when Christina got to Doug's office.

"I don't know how you justify a $700.00 bill for embroidered polo shirts," Danielle said, staring daggers at Christina as she walked into the room. Dean was on Christina's heels, as was Dan.

"David's just down the hall," Dan said.

"Good, I wanted everyone here to go over this. Christina, boys, have a seat," Doug said as the third Holtzberg son showed up. As he passed Christina, he winked and smiled. This caused Danielle to turn a bright red with her internal fury.

"Before we get started, I wanted to read a message I got from Vincent Clinton, the new head of the community college," Doug Holtzberg said as he picked up his glasses, "*Doug, I wanted to congratulate you on the success of your presence at Career Day. Despite the terrible weather, the event was very well attended. Holtzbergs again provided the kind of leadership my predecessor told me your company is known for. The addition of technical demonstrations was absolute genius. It captured the attention and imagination of the attendees like nothing else did. Holtzbergs was professionally represented, welcoming, and encouraging to the attendees. It was a credit to you and your business. Again, Congratulations; I look forward to our continued partnership.*"

Danielle let out a huff. "That's nice, and I know the company gets good press for that association, but that's not putting any money in the bank," she held up the spreadsheet with the event expenditures, "I've got a full page here that totals almost $5,000.00. Good press doesn't always translate to a bottom line."

Dean held up a hand, "I heard from the Fourtier hotel brass I've been trying to get an appointment with for the past year. They had a booth last Friday. They said Bill Fourtier's assistant visited our area and was uber impressed with the technicians we had there. Long story short, I've got an appointment next week," Dean said.

Doug sat back in his chair. "No kidding? That's great. How many locations this side of the state?"

"Five in the Detroit metro area," Dean said.

"I hate to be Debbie Downer, but that's potential business. I don't mean to disparage it, but that's not a PO," Danielle said.

"That's true, but the Novi Showcase called and renewed their maintenance contract this morning," Dan said.

"I thought they were good with it lapsing?" Doug said.

"Oh, they were. But seems that our Christina had a coffee with the property manager...."

"We didn't talk about their contract," Christina said.

"You may not have, but the property manager mentioned you specifically," Dan said.

Danielle was livid. "Fine, you want me to accompany you guys on your sales calls, and I'll wear something low cut with a short shirt if that's how you want business to be conducted."

Doug cleared his throat and rapped his knuckles on his desk. "Christina, job very well done as always. Thank you, you are an incredible asset to this company. Can you excuse us for a bit? I still need to debrief, but I'll do that later today."

"Of course," Christina said and got up to leave the room.

Dan walked her to the door, smiled, and said, "I can't thank you enough. You always do a great job," he said as he closed the door behind her.

■■■

Christina hadn't planned on going to lunch, but Marcy and Rosemary practically carried her to Rosemary's car. Once inside, Marcy couldn't hold back. "What did she say?"

Christina didn't have to hear the name to know. There was an undercurrent all morning. Christina figured it had to be Danielle and that dumb comment she made to the Holtzbergs. But just to be sure, she asked, "Why? What happened?"

"I could hear her through the wall bitching about you," Marcy said, "I didn't hear the boys or Doug, just Danielle, but she was psycho."

"I didn't hear her, but I know she was ranting like a nut case," Rosemary said.

Marcy was nodding. "Then the boys took over the meeting. And after about ten minutes, Danielle walked out, red as a beet and huffing and puffing. That was this morning, and she wasn't cleaning out her desk, so they didn't fire her, and she didn't quit. Give it up, girl," Marcy directed the comment to Christina, "what happened?"

"Even if I know the conversation, I can't tell you guys; you have to know that," Christina said.

"Did she get disciplined?" Rosemary asked.

"You know I can't tell you that either. But I will say this; the Holtzbergs are not big on discipline or firing. Someone would literally have to steal or do something that would cause physical harm before they would take an action with HR," Christina explained.

Two disappointed groans came from the front and backseat of Rosemary's car.

"I gotta tell ya, I'd rather this high tolerance for iffy employee behavior is a good thing," Christina said.

"How so?" Rosemary said.

"Before I came to Holtzbergs, I had three regular non-babysitting jobs. I've watched the caprice of some supervisors. When someone rubs the boss the wrong way, the classic personality clashes, and the boss either fires them outright or makes work miserable. I was working for a bakery and coffee shop, and the turnover of the wait staff was crazy. The day shift manager was very sensitive. If you appeared to be even a little abrasive, she assumed that this was off-putting to everyone else the world over. It rarely, if ever, was true, but the manager was so self-involved; if she felt that way in her mind, everyone did. Thus a merry-go-round of staff. I worked for my uncle, a guy with a very quick temper. He was a sweet guy, but he would blow up over nothing and did that multiple times a day. The guys in the yard and the drivers weren't around enough or didn't care, but my uncle could not keep office help. My job in college was for the university, and the supervisor was a guy who believed that employees needed to demonstrate their gratitude. If you didn't appear grateful enough, your work-life was short-lived or difficult and short-lived. I needed the job, so I, like the others who needed the job, made sure to appear grateful. It isn't that we weren't happy to be working; we were. It's just that even that level of deception was stressful. The Holzbergs have always held themselves to a higher standard. They aren't perfect, but they are really good men who don't let their feelings have free rein."

Now the groaning was in resignation.

"I suppose, but what makes Danielle so valuable as an employee that we all have to suffer her?" Marcy asked.

"Whatever you think of her, she is good at her job. I don't always like that she's questioning my stuff. But there's a value in not having sycophants and *yes*men. It's important to question things, particularly when it's related to money."

"You seem to have to suffer with her the most," Rosemary said.

■■■

Danielle paced her office so angry she wanted to throw something. She was so fucking sick of that bitch getting patted on the head for the fluff bullshit she came up with. And it was pretty fucking clear Doug, and the sons were never, not ever, going to do anything. They weren't even willing to set a boundary on spending for that lame-ass Career Day. It was ludicrous. Between what the business spent in employee time and resources for that and the other dollar hemorrhages they always had going, it was a miracle the company was doing as well as it was. That fucking moronic playground was another one of little Miss Christina's pet projects. When Danielle thought about it, it was crazy that a Wealth Management Company would get in bed with a project like that. How this was a good idea was a mystery to Danielle. The Parks and Rec built playgrounds, not private companies. But when she said that out loud, it only got her a lecture from Dan and Dean about how this was different, how this would set a new standard. *So fucking what?*

The real rub was that Doug and the sons expected her to go to the ceremony planned for Thursday. Would that be a lot of laughs? Danielle would have to listen to the fucking wonders of Christina. And on top of that, Rocco Gagliardi would be there, probably drooling over Christina. After this morning, having to show up for the groundbreaking and have her nose rubbed into another Christina fest was just too much. Doug probably wouldn't know who was actually there from the company. She really didn't have to go, and why should she? She wouldn't. That decision made her feel better for the first time in a long time. Then she remembered that shithead ex-boyfriend of Chistina's, Neville. Neville Eastburn wanted to know if there was a restriction on who could attend. There was; it was admittance by ticket only. You had to have the QR barcode to get in. It was delivered to her phone. It was delivered to every invitee's phone. But... it could be printed. The instructions said tickets would be accepted digitally or in hard copy. Because they all had a two-ticket option, a primary and a secondary invitee. A second ticket could be printed for the person the primary wanted along; that second person wouldn't have to be with the primary to get in. Did she want to show up with Eastburn? Not really. She didn't want to show up at all. But there was a need for a second ticket; Eastburn mentioned two tickets; he needed two. Well, she had them.

It took her a good fifteen minutes to find Eastburn's number. He answered and seemed pleased to have the opportunity. They arranged a meeting place, and she would hand over tickets tonight after work. She debated what she'd do to steer clear of Christina and the Holtzbergs for the rest of the week. It wasn't that difficult. They were all preoccupied with high-fiving each other over Career Day – gag me - and getting ready for the groundbreaking.

■■■

The parcel of land looked like any construction site. There was a mobile office trailer off to the side with some of the larger pieces of equipment already on site.

But that was where the look of the conventional site ended. Two trailer restrooms were positioned near a mammoth white tent with a small tent off to its side. After getting checked in, the invited guests were guided to the tent down a temporary walkway that had been set up so that no one had to walk through the mud and residual snow.

Rocco was just inside the tent waiting for Christina to arrive when he spotted a familiar figure. "Michael? You came?" Rocco embraced his cousin, kissing each cheek.

"Well," Michael looked a little sheepish. "Of course, I wanted to come, but extenuating circumstances made this a *must* for me."

"Your mother? You had to bring your mom and dad?" Rocco said.

"No. If they had a problem driving over, I would have brought them, but Dad drove. They are looking forward to the dinner afterward and seeing the family; it's been a while," Michael said.

"Then what's the extenuating circumstance?" Rocco asked.

"Two things actually; I got some paperwork and a little note, a nice one, from Roberta and Francine for you," Michael withdrew the paperwork from his pocket, "and I heard you are good with members of the press attending, so I ...." Michael began as a woman in a grey pants suit approached. She was attractive, blonde with a serious look on her face and barreling toward Rocco and his cousin. She thrust out her hand to Rocco.

"Hi, I'm Joy Devry; I'm a friend of Michael," she said.

Michael circled her waist and drew her close, giving her a kiss at her temple. "Rocco, Joy is a reporter with the Windsor Star."

Rocco shook Joy's hand with the professional decorum called for. "We are very pleased to have you cover this. Thank you."

Michael looked relieved.

"Michael wasn't sure this was a good idea. I'm happy he had that wrong," Joy said.

"He did. We are proud of this project and want to share it with everyone interested. There will be a press conference after the event, but if you like, I'll make time for an interview," said Rocco.

"That is very nice of you. Thank you." Joy beamed at Michael.

Rocco's phone was vibrating. "Joy, Michael, I'm being summoned. Very nice meeting you, Joy. Let me know about the interview," Rocco said as he began to walk toward the front of the large tent that would shelter the invitees and committee members.

Rocco marveled at the setup. Christina had made the arrangements. A huge tent large enough to hold over one hundred people with a podium, chairs at the front, and heaters stationed as needed. When the speakers all took their turns making remarks, the front of the tent would be opened to reveal the mound of dirt and the twelve shovels for the groundbreaking and the photo opt it was staged for. The invitees would be served punch and cake while the committee members would adjourn to a smaller tent outside the large one for the press conference. It seemed to Rocco she had thought of everything.

His grandparents, parents, and brother Franco were just being dropped off by the car service

Christina had arranged. The Foundation, Beaumont group, and Holtzberg family, were accorded the same courtesy.

Bruno passed Rocco and said, "I'll take charge of the family; Christina will be here any minute now; you wait for her."

"Thanks, bro. I'll bring her over as soon as she gets here," Rocco said.

Bruno stopped, "You good?"

Rocco caught sight of Christina and said, "I'm great."

Bruno intercepted the Gagliardi family and guided them to their reserved section.

"I saw Michael," Theresa Gagliardi said. "Where is he sitting?"

"I've got Aunt Mary and Uncle Joe with Michael and his girl near the press tent. Mike's girl is a reporter. They'll be near the front but behind the committee section."

"Where are the Mayor and the city people?" Antonio Gagliardi asked.

"They are behind the Holtzbergs but before the Holtzberg employees," Bruno said.

"Where are the Gagliardi employees?" Nonno asked.

Bruno smiled and gestured. "They are behind Michael's row, back here."

"Well, you kids have thought of everything. This is comfortable for a Michigan winter," Antonio said.

"That would be Christina's doing," Bruno said.

Nonna turned. "That's Rocco's girl?"

"That's Rocco's girl, Nonna," Bruno leaned in, "I think you will be very happy; she understands Italian like a *compatriota*."

Christina entered the tent and looked around.

Bruno motioned to his family. "There she is now." And they all began walking toward Christina, who was leading her party. Rocco made his way over to her.

When everyone was within a few feet of her, they watched as Rocco intercepted Christina and leaned down to kiss her. Rocco turned to begin his introductions when a decidedly hostile voice interrupted them.

"You are such a gullible little idiot," Neville said.

Christina stiffened and looked over to see Neville standing off to the side with a young girl.

"You'll never guess who I have here, Christina." Neville goaded.

Michael and his parents looked over to where Rocco and the Gagliardis stood. Michael let out a disbelieving, "What the hell?" and moved quickly to where his young niece stood.

Neville had an audience; *it couldn't be working out better*, he thought. He'd let Rocco Gagliardi stew for a few more moments. He'd let him try to deny it, try to explain. This would be too much fun. Now Neville caught sight of Mrs. Pentelino and that reprobate Cal Pentelino. Neville turned to Rocco and gestured to the girl. "Quite a family resemblance. Don't you think?"

Only Rocco was silent. It was Christina who spoke. "Neville, what are you doing here? How did you get a ticket?"

Neville scoffed. "That is not the question of the day, Christina; the real question is, why didn't Mafioso here tell you about his wife and daughter?"

Christina rolled her eyes. "That's your play, Neville?"

"Not my play, Christina; this is Rocco Gaglardi's daughter," Neville said.

"Mary Elizabeth Slaughter. What are you doing here?" a woman's voice made the young girl startle.

"Grandma?" the girl said as the woman approached.

"Do your mothers know you are here?" Mary Gagliardi stood in front of her granddaughter.

Joe Gagliardi stepped in front of Neville, "Who the hell are you?"

"He's helping me, grandpa," Mary Elizabeth said.

Michael approached the girl, "Helping you do what, Mary-Contrary?"

"Get my Dad and Mom back together." The girl pointed to Rocco.

Christina looked at Rocco, who looked utterly mystified.

Mary Elizabeth began to cry.

Michael bent down to catch her eyes, "Honey, he's not," he said softly, "but why did you think he was?"

Mary looked up at her uncle. "I found a marriage license for him," she pointed at Rocco, "and mommy Francine."

"Oh my god," Theresa Gagliardi said and took the nearest chair.

Christina looked at Rocco, who no longer looked mystified.

At that moment, Doug Holtzberg clasped Rocco on his shoulder and said, " Come on, my boy, they are ready to start, " he said as Dean, Dan, and Dave all came over to get everyone to their places.

Bruno caught Christina by her wrist. "Before you have any kinds of thoughts about this, hear my brother out. There is something way off about this."

Christina nodded, "Will you get my family and my friends seated?"

"Of course, I will," Bruno said.

Michael, Mary, and Joe Gagliardi led a crying Mary Elizabeth out of the tent. "We'll call your moms so they can explain everything to you, honey," Michael said.

Joy Devry came up beside Neville. "That's a very interesting announcement. Do you have anything to back it up?"

"Of course, I do," Neville said petulantly.

"I'm with the *Windsor Star*. I'd love to hear what you have." She nodded to the mobile office. That's open and private. Are you interested?"

"The Star. That's not a big paper," Neville said dismissively.

"The Star is owned by Postmedia, headquartered in Toronto. An American firm owns Postmedia. If I have a big enough story, it will be on the news service wire, and it will be picked up by whatever outlet is interested. Now, do you have a story for me or not?" Joy said.

"Okay, let's go." Neville jerked his chin toward the tent entrance.

They made their way into the trailer. It was minimal, but it was heated and had a desk and chairs.

Joy took the seat behind the desk and pulled a legal pad, pen, and recorder out of her cross-body bag. "Do you have any objection?" she asked.

"I suppose that's par for this sort of thing," Neville sniffed.

"Indeed it is," Joy said, taking her coat off and getting comfortable. "Now, why don't you begin from the beginning."

The interview went on past the actual groundbreaking that Joy could see from the trailer window. She knew this meant she would miss the press conference, but this story was the one she needed to nab. So she conducted the interview like the professional she was. After Neville went through it once, she made him go through it again. Joy made notes, particularly reviewing the dates and times he had met up with Mary Elizabeth. Finally, she felt she had enough to work with. "Can you show me the documents you've collected?"

Neville delightedly produced the file he had assembled.

Joy picked each up and examined them, "Where did you get these documents?"

"The bastard child," Neville said dismissively.

"I see. This Rocco Gagliardi is a very wealthy man from a wealthy, influential family. This would be quite a stain on not just his reputation but the family's as well. It might even impact the family's business," Joy mused.

"I don't think those people are strangers to the seamier side of life. They are obviously of the lower class dressed up in custom-made suits. But the grease isn't so easy to hide, is it?

"Back to Rocco Gagliardi, his girlfriend is Christina Pentelino? Do I have that right? She was there as one of Holtzberg's representatives. Isn't she one of Crain's 30 under 30?"

Neville gave Joy a self-satisfied look and said, "I know Christina very well. She and I used to date, but her lack of breeding made anything more than casual with her impossible. I tried to be sensitive; she's very young, but kid gloves weren't working," Neville said confidentially, "it doesn't really surprise me that she is in so thick with Gagliardi. She's also very unconcerned with the people she gets close to. One of her best friends is from Bombay," he made air quotes, "very third world and practices that form of Medicine Man Voodoo they cling to even after they land in our country. I had more than one conversation with Christina when I knew about her poor life choices and the people she aligns herself with. But she's the one that hires and promotes people from *Detroit,* if you get my drift."

Chapter 38

Glass

Thompson Square

Rocco had answered his parent's questions about his relationship to Francine and Roberta's daughter. They were still more than a little mystified by the whole Neville Eastburn drama, but it was clear that his aunt and uncle were now watching over the child who was their granddaughter and not Theresa and Antonio Gagliardi's.

Still, Rocco couldn't concentrate on the event, not like he thought he should. His parents never really understood the relationship between

Roberta and Francine. Before Rocco confirmed, they probably thought it just might be possible that the little girl might actually be his child because, even though Neville might have every other thing wrong, he was dead nuts about who that kid looked like.

Rocco had to own up to his stupidity here and the fact that he was the asshole who demanded that Roberta and Francine stay away. *Fuck.* It would look like he did that because he hid them like a dirty little secret. God, that was petty. And now, now when he had everything put right, this was all coming back to bite him in the ass. He looked through the tent's plastic window; he saw that fucker, Neville, through the windows in the mobile office trailer with Michael's girlfriend. They looked deep in conversation. What the hell was that about? The applause from inside the tent brought him out of his stupor.

The tent wall was now rolled aside; Rocco got up with the others to take their place near the mound of dirt staged for the event. They each took a hard hat and shovel as they filed toward the mound of dirt. Rocco was next to his parents. Theresa and Antonio were flanked by Rocco and Bruno on one side and Franco on the other. Christina was sandwiched between Doug and Dean Holtzberg. Why wasn't Christina next to him? It took Rocco a moment to remember everyone's place in the line was planned before today. She wasn't avoiding him.

The Gagliardi and Holtzberg families, Christina, the representatives from Beaumont, and the Reynolds Foundation principals took their places in the press conference tent. Again Christina was with the Holtzberg as predetermined. It just felt like she was keeping her distance.

As soon as the press conference was over, Bruno hustled Christina out the door before Rocco could intercept her. Michael grabbed Rocco and led him out the door before he could put his thoughts together enough to complain.

When they reached the parking lot, a service car pulled up, and Michael all but pushed Rocco inside. Michael slammed the door and knocked on the roof as the car took off. Rocco tried to find the control to lower the privacy panel to talk to the driver. He needed to get the driver to stop and go back for Christina. It was then Rocco heard someone clear her throat.

Rocco turned to look at her; she seemed very upset, "I am so sorry about Neville. Rocco, I feel horrible about all of this, bringing this mess to your doorstep. That poor little girl. And your parents.

They don't know the whole story, do they? My heavens, I thought your mother was going to faint. I feel sick about it."

He gathered her in his arms, "Patatina, none of that was your doing. I may not be good enough for you, but Neville Eastburn never deserved your time. Right now, I wish I could make him pay for the pain he's caused, particularly for the pain he's caused Roberta and Francine's daughter. I couldn't really have the talk I need to with my family, not in that setting," Rocco nodded back to where the tent was located. "but they know I'm not that child's father. That's all that they needed for the moment."

He pulled the paperwork out of his breast pocket. "Michael gave this to me before all the drama. I didn't have a chance to look at everything yet, but..." he handed the envelope to Christina, "this should be the notice Francine got,'" Rocco said.

Christina read the name on the envelope, "Rocco, this is for you; I don't need to see it," Christina said.

"But you do, Christina. It wasn't my halfway comment about getting married. That is my intention." He held the paperwork for Christina to read.

"Archdiocese of Detroit? An annulment? I thought you and Francine were divorced?"

Rocco took her free hand in his. "We were divorced, but... As soon as I realized I wanted my future with you, I knew the wedding I wanted would be at the Church's center altar with both of our families and all of our friends. That could not happen without this," he pointed to the document.

Christina unfolded the annulment paperwork, and a small envelope fell to her lap.

"Open it, please," Rocco said.

Christina opened it to find a *thank you* note card signed by both Roberta and Francine. There was a handwritten message from Francine. Which read, *Rocco, a million thanks for putting yourself out when you didn't have to and when I was being particularly cruel – less women's studies and more Zoloft have mellowed me out. I've always wished I could have a do-over. You deserved so much better from me. Just know my father had a very good end of life and peaceful death, thanks to you. All the best, Francine.*

"You really need to rethink the ban you imposed on them," Christina said quietly.

"You are right. You've been right about so many things. Sitting there today after Neville showed up, I thought about what would have happened if I hadn't told you the entire Francine story last Saturday."

"It's in the past," Christina thought a moment. "frankly, it's very upsetting that Neville had that child with him. That poor kid. That needs a much deeper dive. I can't believe that her mother or mothers knew about this. How in the heck did Neville have her with him?" Christina said.

"I saw Michael and my aunt and uncle take the little girl with them. I know she was okay, but you're right. How did Neville have her show up with him?"

■■■

Moderneasto was prepared for the Gagliardi party of thirty-one. Theresa Gagliardi called to ask for three more to be included. She also asked Dirk to please make a place for the Windsor Gagliardi family before everyone arrived. Theresa's sister Mary and her husband Joe from Windsor, Canada, would be there shortly with their granddaughter. Then they would be joined by Roberta Gagliardi and her partner.

Dirk was there to let the Windsor group in and get them settled in his office to have some privacy. The granddaughter was very upset. So Dirk got her a cup of hot cocoa and left his two West Highland Terriers, Connie, and Conrad, to keep the little girl company. It worked because, by the time Dirk delivered the second hot cocoa and a hearty Tuscan red wine for Grandma and Grandpa, the girl was on the floor playing with Dirk's Westies. Those dogs were zen. And Dirk got a hug from Mary in thanks. The girl's mothers showed up an hour later. Dirk wasn't clear what transpired, but from the red eyes around the room, he figured they would need more wine and a tissue box; he got both.

The first of the Gagliardi party arrived at the door just after five, pretty much when Dirk expected them. Whatever Dirk could do to make this a wonderful evening, he would.

Francine was the first out of the back office. She went to find Rocco. The years hadn't been unkind to her. She still had that careless beauty of her youth, but it had been many years since Rocco had been in her company. And when she approached Rocco and Christina, Rocco was at a loss.

"Oh my god. You can't say hi to me," Francine's signature voice literally was her calling card.

"Francine?" he said dumbly.

"Of course, Francine," Francine looked over at Christina, "you have to be the girlfriend. I'm Mary Elizabeth's mother."

Christina extended her hand and smiled warmly. "Hello, Francine. I'm Christina Pentelino."

Francine caught the civility, took Christina's hand, and smiled back. "God, you are... well, a beauty." Then turning to Rocco, she said, "She suits you." She dropped Christina's hand, looked down for a second, and said, "I'm sorry about Mary Elizabeth. She's been going through a few things. We moved, and she's in a new school that's not totally accepting of Roberta and my lifestyle," she air quoted, "she found some old paperwork, the marriage license, and built a fairy tale that she liked more than our life. That's a little hurtful," she looked over at Christina, "I mean, you think you're doing everything to make a happy, well-adjusted daughter, and it all falls short," she took in a breath, "anyhow, sorry for the drama." Francine turned to Rocco. "And and I know this is a violation of the terms. Please know it wasn't intentional."

Rocco took Christina's hand; it wasn't as much to claim her as it was to keep her with him. "About that. I wasn't in the headspace I should have been when I came up with the prohibition for you and Roberta. I'm sorry about that. I don't know if it would have helped Mary Elizabeth, but it was petty on my part. Please don't stay away because of it in the future. Please tell Roberta, or I can."

Francine's face softened. "That's good of you. It will mean the world to Roberta," Francine smirked, "you can't know the silly excuses Roberta has come up with to explain why we don't come over for the 4th of July barbeque at your grandparents' house," she rolled her eyes and said, "thank you."

"You're welcome," Rocco said.

Roberta walked out of the office with Mary Elizabeth and the two Westies on tricked-out leashes. Dirk was in danger of losing his dogs if the girl's face was any indication.

Mary Elizabeth walked up to Rocco, head down and solemn. "I'm very sorry, Mr. Gaglidari, that I interrupted your groundbreaking ceremony."

Rocco bent down to look the kid in the eyes. "Thank you. No harm done, Mary Elizabeth," he offered a hand and said, "we're cousins, you know."

"I know, my mom told me. I'm sorry you aren't my dad," Mary Elizabeth said as Roberta and Francine gasped and then groaned.

"That's a nice compliment. Thank you, but you've got two pretty special moms," Rocco said as he stood up.

"Oh, I know. I love my moms, but you are muscley like the Star-Lord in Guardian of the Galaxy," Mary Elizabeth said shyly.

"Star-Lord? Who is Star-Lord?" Roberta asked, not comprehending.

Dirk came around the corner and answered, "He's a superhero stud, that's who. Very, *very* muscley." Then clapping his hands. "Okay, boys and girls, I need my puppies back. Sorry Mary Elizbeth, but they have to stay in my office, and you need to come and eat."

"We really need to get home," Roberta looked at Francine.

"We aren't dressed," Francine added.

"You guys look just fine," Dirk said.

Christina stepped forward and nodded toward the dining room. "This dinner is my introduction to the family; you three are family. Please?" Christina asked.

■■■

Chapter 39

Gives You Hell

All American Rejects

The reporter said she would send the story to her editors and contact him when the piece was to run. Neville was thrilled at the success of his exposing Rocco Gagliardi. He got the email last night. He made plans to pick up the newspaper in Windsor. He suggested that Nigel meet him for lunch at the Treehouse Bar and Grill on Quelleet in downtown Windsor right across from the Windsor Star offices.

Neville could have read the online paper from the privacy of his home office, but this would be so much more delicious. He was delighted with the prospect. Neville decided to bring the woman he was now dating along. That way, he could kill several birds with one single stone. He would revel in the success of bringing down the house of Rocco fucking Gagliardi. He would introduce Tiffany to his brother, and Neville knew Nigel would pick up the check; the whole thing would cost him the price of the paper, the tunnel toll, and the gas for the trip.

Tiffany was so much more compliant than Christina had been. Neville had to admit Nigel had been right on that score. In fact, it was Nigel who reviewed Tiffany's dating bio and suggested that Neville contact her.

Tiffany didn't have the baggage of an off-putting nationality or religion to deal with. She was a college graduate from Ohio State, no less. She was a bookkeeper for a small accounting firm. If the relationship worked out, Tiffany's ring size was the same as Neville's engagement set for Christina. He found this out very early on, just in case. He wouldn't have to trouble about getting anything resized. So many pluses with this girl.

Neville was very familiar with Windsor these days. He had been over several times to meet the girl, the bastard child.

Neville and Tiffany had ordered cocktails and settled in when Nigel arrived.

Nigel decided he'd give this one hour max and get back for his Saturday date delivering dinners to Abby and all the others. That was a far more appealing prospect than this. The girl Neville had with him looked a little rougher than her online photo but not fifty pounds heavier and a decade older. So that was something.

Neville made the formal introduction and waived over the server.

"I see you have the paper. I don't know if this is really anything to celebrate Neville. It won't be just Rocco Gagliardi who could be a casualty here," Nigel said.

"I think it's like Neville says, one bad seed and all." Tiffany sniffed.

Nigel said nothing, just nodded for Neville to read the article.

"Well, it starts out with the headline about the groundbreaking." Neville read a very well-written summary of the project and the contributors. The article mentioned both Rocco and Christina by name, with the most ink devoted to accessible playgrounds. "This can't be right," Neville took out his phone to pull up the email. "Ah! This isn't her only article. She says the one about me is in the Life section. Here, here it is," Neville's face went purple.

"What?" Nigel asked.

"That bitch. That fucking bitch." Neville held the paper up for Nigel to see. The section headline read. *Don't be this guy* with a subtitle that read, *Break-up Don'ts.*

"She did a fucking hatchet job on me," Neville wailed.

Nigel took the paper from his brother and read. After a few moments, he squinted and said. "So, let me get this straight, Neville. You conned an eleven-year-old girl into showing up and telling people Rocco Gagliardi is her father? The interviewer obviously did more research than you did because the girl's biological father is absolutely not Rocco. Or, what does the paper call him?" Nigel scanned the article once more, "Jean Valjean to your Inspector Javert. Perfect. Another guy almost done in by obsessive pursuit." Nigel gave his brother a dismayed side-eye. "And Rocco is absolutely not married to the girl's mother."

Neville's face now paled. "What do you mean? Of course, he is her father."

"Where did you get your information about that?" Nigel asked.

"From the kid," Neville said.

"From an eleven-year-old child? Seriously. Well, buddy, your biggest problem isn't that you look like a fool."

"What do you mean?" Neville said, annoyed.

Nigel looked disgustedly at his brother. "You will probably have to explain why you were in the company of an eleven-year-old girl without her parent's permission or even their knowledge. The article doesn't paint you as a pedophile, but you might need to explain yourself to the authorities if you did what this says. Thank God the reporter didn't mention the Gagliardis by name. This could be so much worse."

"Let me see that." Neville took the paper from Nigel and began reading it. "She took this all out of context."

"Oh, so you didn't drive an eleven-year-old to the groundbreaking ceremony? You didn't pick the kid up to take her shopping for an outfit to wear, especially for the day, which would make her look more, and I'm quoting the reporter quoting you, *like a schoolgirl*. Fuck, Neville, you really boxed yourself in this time. I think the only thing you've got going for you is it's a Canadian paper, and the police haven't come knocking at your door."

Neville was gasping for air and throwing back the vodka cocktail he had been sipping only a few moments before.

After reading some of the article over Neville's shoulder, Tiffany came to life. "You mean to tell me you did this because you wanted to get back at your girlfriend?"

"Not my girlfriend. She's an ex," Neville hissed.

Tiffany took on a face of disbelief. "Ex or not. You didn't tell me that. You said this Rocco person was a threat to the community. You said he was with the Mafia."

Nigel shook his head, "Neville, what is wrong with you?"

Tiffany stepped back, "We aren't going to be seeing each other again, Neville."

Neville just looked indignant.

Tiffany's face flushed, and tears threatened.

Nigel held up a hand, "Tiffany, take my car." He fished a business card out of his wallet and got his car keys out of his pocket. "Here's my number. Text me the address where you leave the car, and I'll come and get it. It's the grey Tesla parked on the street outside."

"That's very decent of you," Tiffany said as she pocketed the card and took the keys.

Neville followed her out of the bar with his eyes.

Nigel cleared his throat to bring his brother back to the present. “Neville, I know this isn’t the outcome you wanted or strived for, but it’s time you faced the facts and prepared for the potential fallout.”

Neville turned back to his brother, not at all chastened. “I’ll be calling Jeffery Figer first thing tomorrow morning. The Windsor Star will be forever sorry about their fake news.”

Nigel just looked down and shook his head. “It is doubtful you’ll get an attorney to take your case. But, you absolutely need to call a lawyer.”

Epilog

White Walls

Macklemore & Ryan Lewis ft. Schoolboy Q & Hollis

When Christina held out her left hand with the 4 carats, Asscher cut engagement ring and asked her to be one of the two Maids of Honor; Marisol thought it would be a year, maybe two, to book the church and the reception hall and organize everything. Christina told them that Rocco said whatever Christina wanted as long as it was as soon as possible.

"I think maybe I can get a reception venue in the offseason. Rocco's mother has invited my mother and us," she pointed to Holly and Marisol, "for a day of dress shopping in Toronto. Mrs. Gagliardi is confident we can get the dresses quicker there. She has a relative that owns a bridal shop. I'm not sure about booking the church. I know we'll have to take classes. All my cousins had to. I'm confident we can marry by the year's end."

The next time they got together was just before their trip to Toronto. Christina had the wedding date, a June wedding date.

"But how? That's not even two months away." Marisol looked at Christina skeptically.

Christina giggled softly. "He's a groom in a hurry. The wedding will be at the Gagliardi's home parish. We met with the priest. We do have to have classes, but that's been arranged. Rocco worked it out with Father Denofreo. I think there may have been a contribution to the church's altar society fund. It will be every Monday at Nonno and Nonna Gagliardi's, where we will first have a family dinner. My mother and brother are included. Rocco's grandparents will be hosting the reception at their home. The grounds are four acres on Lake Saint Clair. I was told I have no limit on the number of guests I want to invite," Christina shrugged, "they said if they need to, they will get a bigger tent."

Thus, hundreds of family and friends, some local and some from several time zones east, filled the church that perfect June day.

Marisol and Holly would be riding in style as members of the wedding party. A line of beautifully restored classic cars lined the approach to the church. A classic black 1961 Lincoln Continental with suicide doors, followed by a 1957 cherry red Ford Thunderbird, champagne color Studebaker Gran Turismo Hawk, a Turquoise Oldsmobile Toronado. Rocco's 1967 Eldorado Coupe with the hound's tooth interior was the last in the line.

The wedding party was a small one for the number of guests. Christina knew the protocol; a bridesmaid for every fifty invitees. She knew the ratio, but Christina's choices centered on her connection versus rounding up ten female relatives based on how they would look in the bridesmaid's dress she'd pick out. Therefore, the bridal party consisted of two maids of honor, Holly and Marisol, one best man, Michael, and three groomsmen, Bruno, Franco, and Christina's brother, Cal.

Bruno distractedly walked up, looking at the various cars. "Okay, ladies, we get the T-bird with Cal.

Marisol squealed.

Holly let out a *booyah,* then dug through her clutch bag, pulling a Kennedy half-dollar out. "Call it," she said to Marisol.

"Heads," Marisol answered as Holly tossed the coin, caught it deftly, slapped it down on the back of her tiny hand, and slowly uncovered it to reveal JFK's profile.

Marisol turned to Bruno and held her hand out expectantly.

"I think I'm supposed to chauffer you over to Nonna's house unless Cal is supposed to do it," Bruno said, a little mystified that it was even a question.

"Nope," Holly said, plucking the keys out of Bruno's fingers and handing them to Marisol. "Cal is driving Mrs. Pentelino. You didn't get a coin ready or call it. Sorry, not sorry, Marisol is the driver today. You sit in the back."

"What? I can't at least sit in the front?" Bruno asked

"You didn't call shotgun," Holly explained as she opened the passenger door and pulled the seat back to allow Bruno access to the coupe's backseat.

Bruno got into the car, chuckling, realizing there could be no winning with these two.

The rest of the wedding party took their car assignments. Michael watched as Rocco helped his bride into his Eldorado.

Roberta left Francine and Mary Elizabeth chatting with Dirk Decoursey and sidled up next to Michael, "I wonder," Roberta said.

Michael turned to his sister, "Seriously? You wonder why he married her?"

"No. Goofball," Roberta crossed her arms in a stance of contemplation and nodded toward Rocco's El Dog, "I wonder if I can ever talk Rocco into selling me that car."

The End

ABOUT THE AUTHOR

"I love stories, and I love characters. I like to tell stories in a series of books because some of these characters are so special to me that one story doesn't give us enough time to get to know them fully. All my stories are set in places I know personally. The characters may start off somewhere else or visit the world, but they live in southeastern Michigan, just like I do."

Every book by J. Ellen Daniels has a companion musical playlist. Visit JEllenStories.com for more information.

BOOKS IN THIS SERIES

BESTIES

Who's going to get the ice cream and box of wine when the new guy you've been dating is ghosting you? Who's going to tell you not to buy the smaller size bathing suit just because it's on sale? Who will help you throw the gender reveal party your mother insists you host for your cousin who never returns the clothes you lend her? Your bestie, that's who.

This series is about the besties Christina, Marisol, and Holly. Twenty-somethings that know when life hands you lemons, there is a bottle of Lemoncello at Christina's, a whiskey sour or three at Marisol's, and Holly knows a bartender who makes lemon-drop martinis by the gallon.

Approach with Care

Besties Book 1

It wasn't love at first sight, but the night Rocco first saw her left an impression. The second time he saw her, she got him thinking. The third time made him want to meet her. But how? For the many times he's seen her, he still knew nothing about her, not even her name.

Christina's life was one success after another, except for her love life. She learned early how to steer clear of intimate connections and avoid the failure that was sure to follow. She must never, under any circumstances, allow the hot guy with the smothering look into her personal space.

Romance Revenant

Besties Book 2

For Adam, Marisol was the one that got away. It may have been high school, but it wasn't a crush or puppy love. It was the real deal; she was the real deal. As the years passed, Adam tried to move on. It never worked. His love life departed the night Marisol's sister murdered Adam and Marisol's relationship.

Marisol's love life wasn't dormant. It was dead. Three serious relationships, and all three had been with faithless partners. The last disappointment would be the final chapter, the end. The absence of a boyfriend was better than the death of a relationship.

Badass

Besties Book 3

Viggo thought he was a badass, a tough guy. The one to call when the situation needed brawn as well as brains. He was confident in his abilities to be the hero. He was, after all, a little better than two hundred pounds of fine-tuned and regularly tested muscle. It wasn't only the weight room but weekly Krav Maga training with a former Navy Seal that created and maintained this manifestation of male badassery. And then he watched Holly vanquish a monster.

She may be just tall enough to ride the rollercoaster, and her weight never tops out beyond double digits, but Holly Jain has mad skills in martial arts. But that's not the only way she can bring a man to his knees. Just ask Viggo Van Vargot.

BOOKS BY THIS AUTHOR

Second and Other Chances

Second and Other Chances Book 1

Connie Fausse's marriage wasn't a happy one; understandable when your husband reminds you as often as possible that you are physically repulsive to him. When Victor died almost two years before, it meant more questions than answers for Connie. It did nothing to erase her negative feelings about herself. Mike is a man with a man's needs and tastes, but that never distracted him from being the kind of single father he wanted for his son. Over the years, Mike had his rendezvous with the female of the moment. Still, he never allowed himself anything more permanent. That all changed when son Liam moved into his first home next door to Connie Fausse. This might make for a happy ever after, but how do you believe in yourself after years of day after day of negative narrative? How do you commit to a woman after a lifetime of keeping them at arm's length?

Beginnings

Second and Other Chances Book 2

Roslyn is a beauty, but she spent her teens and twenties getting an excellent education and working hard to have a career. Men? It isn't that they were around; she just never had time for them. Then she met Liam - great but now what? Liam's had his heartbreak, then the sky cleared, and the sun shone when he met Roslyn. Now, if he can only step up to the grown-up table and take this to the next level.

Connie and Mike are taking their first steps into newly married life. Liam and Roslyn are finding their way in a new relationship. Falling in love was the simple part; now, the realities of day-to-day life begin.

For Connie, it's getting used to a man in the house. It isn't that Mike is lazy or inconsiderate, he's just being who he really is, and sometimes that can make a woman a little crazy. For Mike, it isn't that he doesn't love Connie; he does. She is the love of his life, but that can be a bit annoying.

<u>Ditching the Bitch</u>

Second and Other Chances Book 3

Kelly Fausse had it all figured out. Right. She is the only one that misses completely what a shamble her life is and always has been. And now it's a life spinning out of control. Bad personal choices, bad men, bad career moves - Kelly's life has been one misstep and wrong turn after another, all of it cascading over the cliff and into an epic wreck. For the girl who is most likely the smartest person in the room based on her actions, the generous description of Kelly is that she is mildly stupid. Climbing out of the hole she's so carefully dug for herself takes time and patience. The big question is whether she has either and if she does, will there be anyone left at the surface, or has she succeeded in distancing anyone who ever cared for her?

Who's Your Daddy?

Paternity Book 1

Who is Ben's father? Was it Victor Fausse, the man who sired him? Was it Granddad Arch Logan, the man who pushed and hugged Ben until Arch's untimely death? Could it be Dirk Decoursey and his partner Ed Jura, the couple whose strength taught Ben the difference between gentle and weak? The optimistic Ben wanted his granddad Arch's genetic gifts to trump Victor Fausse's heftier contribution. Ben's same hopeful attitude wanted the nurture from Granddad Logan, Dirk, and Ed could fix Victor's nature. But that positivity could easily dim most days. Now, in his early thirties, Ben works in a field he loves, lives in paradise, and what he might lack in personal charm is made up for by a face and body that attracts all the women he could want - he just doesn't want them too close or for too long. Could the arm's length posture and short attention span be the result of daddy issues?

Bachelor Father

Paternity Book 2

The world lost one woman, and in the grand scheme of things, that's no big deal; it's just one person, right? But when the world lost Claudia, Ben lost his entire world. And what did Ben get for his loss? His mother-in-law, Sybil. From the moment Ben met Claudia's mother, Sybil, he did his best to tolerate her. It was a monumental struggle, and he wasn't always successful, but he did it for the sake of his beloved wife. Just hearing Sybil's voice set Ben's teeth on edge. Having to listen to Sybil's opinions and pronouncements, mainly when the subject happened to be Claudia, was torture. Added to that, Sibyl had worked tirelessly to have Claudia pair up with Derrick, a coworker of Sybil's and the guy that Sybil ended up marrying. How's that for a Jerry Stringer episode? When Claudia suddenly and tragically died, the last thing on his mind was what would be done with Sybil? Ben thought that no other event could bring him to his knees the way that Claudia's death did. Until he realized that Claudia's mother would be living with him and his children - forever. Can Ben's next version of forever include opening his heart to the beautiful veterinarian who bonds with Sybil and his children?

Married with Children and Dogs

Paternity Book 3

One year of wedded bliss, and it looks like clear sailing ahead for Ben and Julia. They have settled into a very comfortable family routine, enjoying their relationship, children, and all the dogs. Together, they've built a new house big enough for everyone and moved in just in time for the wedding reenactment Sybil spent the last year planning. This promised family event would be the celebration of their new home as well as their first anniversary. That isn't the only thing to throw a party over; Julia's childhood friend, Cecilia, finally shed her loser husband, Alec Vogel, and is working on rebuilding her life. However, something in the air blows foul. The dogs know it and are trying their best to get the people they live with to know it too

The Straits of Detroit: Nations Within

The Straits of Detroit Book 1

Edek Casimire Jura is a Detroit cop with dark secrets. Chief among them are his parentage and his lifestyle. Ed joined the force in 1962 and cut his law enforcement chops on Detroit's east side. 1960s Detroit was a place of contradictions. Motown bands were celebrated around the world, but even in Detroit, not welcomed into all-white neighborhoods. Even after the legislation that mandated fair housing and did away with Jim Crow laws, that reality hadn't caught up. Black Detroiters had to move carefully and quietly if they were to survive and thrive. Racial discrimination wasn't the only kind of intolerance alive and well. An apparent LGBT community was decades away, but that didn't mean one didn't exist.

Counterfeit Life

The Straits of Detroit Book 2

Some unfortunate souls fall into bad situations through no fault of their own. Such was the case with Mitchell and his mother. Victor Fausse's nephew Mitchell suffered a closed head injury in the same car accident that killed his father and condemned his mother, Victor's sister Marci, to live out her life in physical and emotional pain. Then there are the people who throw their promise away with both hands. Victor Fausse might have had it all. He was handsome, loaded with talent with a promising future, but he turned his back on his own dreams and pushed away from whom he might have been to run toward perdition. As the 1970s drew to a close, Victor wasn't the only casualty in his chase to ruin himself; he took down anyone close to him. Victor's wife, daughter, and son were all casualties of his decisions, but it was Michell's innocence that was the fatality.

Finding Fidel

The Straits of Detroit Book 3

At the dawn of the 1980s, JoAnne is the local party girl. She's a foxy redhead that has men following after just to see if maybe, just maybe, she will put out; she never disappoints. Rose is the Morrison family matriarch. Now a widow in her seventies, Rose is an integral part of her children and grandchildren's daily lives. To the world, Rose's life seems full, maybe even a bit hectic. No one might imagine there would be room for romance, and that's the way Rose intends to keep it. Mrs. Pauline Roland is a proud member of her church community, attending services throughout the week as well as on Sunday. Her adult son Eddie used to be an active member as well, but his head has been turned – by a woman. Mrs. Roland will use every resource a mother has to put this right. Doris Schmidt was no more than a teenager when she lost her young husband, the father of her three sons, all under the age of four. Just as she entered her twenties, life gave Doris a second chance at love and another son. That chance meant change, more change than Doris was willing to accept. Now, Doris' decisions have left her alone, maybe for the rest of her life

Made in the USA
Columbia, SC
21 February 2023

12697048R00259